Peace, Love and You

A Spiritual Inspirational Self-Help Book about Self-Love, Spirituality, Self-Esteem and Meditation - Self Help books and Spiritual books on Meditation, Self Love, Self Esteem

A spiritual self-help guidebook to sooth the soul...

Nerissa Marie

Title Imprint Self Help Books an imprint of The Quantum Centre, Australia
Published by Happiness Bliss Press an imprint of The Quantum Centre, Australia

ISBN: 978-1-925647-49-5

Happiness Bliss Press books are available at special quantity discounts for bulk purchase for sales promotions, premiums, fund-raising, and educational needs. For details contact books@happinessbliss.com

National Library of Australia Cataloguing-in-Publication entry
Creator: Marie, Nerissa, author.
Title: Peace, Love and You (A Spiritual Inspirational Self-Help Book about Self-Love, Spirituality, Self-Esteem and Meditation - Self Help books and Spiritual books on Meditation, Self Love, Self Esteem) / Nerissa Marie (author)
ISBN: 9781925647495 (paperback)
Target Audience: Adult.
Subjects: Mindfulness (Psychology); Meditation – Buddhism;
Self help techniques; Self-perception;
Crystals -- Therapeutic use.
Mind and body; Healing.
BODY, MIND & SPIRIT / Crystals.
BODY, MIND & SPIRIT / Healing / Energy (Chi Kung, Reiki, Polarity)
HEALTH & FITNESS / Alternative Therapies.

FIRST EDITION

The intention of this book is to serve the will of the divine, and recognise love and light, as the foundation of reality. To embrace love consciousness. This book is here to give you a hug, recognising the beauty that is you.

Disclaimer

The author of this book does not dispense medical advice or prescribe the use of any technique as a form of treatment for physical, emotional, or medical problems without the advice of a physician, either directly or indirectly. There is no guarantee you'll achieve any result through use of the techniques and ideas provided in this book. No information provided within the book is construed to constitute medical, psychological, financial or accounting, legal or other professional advice. Please consult an appropriate licensed professional if you seek any such advice.

The author's intent is only to offer information of a general nature to help you in your quest for emotional and spiritual well-being. In the event you use any of the information in this book for yourself, the author and the publisher assume no responsibility for your actions. The author is not responsible if information made available in this book is not accurate, true, complete, or current. Any reliance on the material in this book is at your own risk.

For Joao De Deus
Who showed me light.

And Mark...
Who opened me to love.

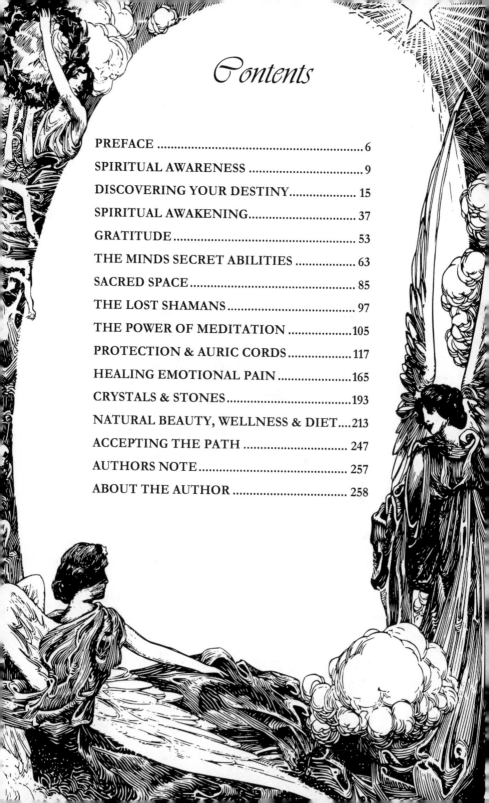

Contents

Preface

Throughout this book words such as Divine Love, God, Spirit, Light, Universal Consciousness, Universal Awareness, Oneness, Mother Nature, Creation, Divine Presence, and Source Energy, are used. These words are presented in direct correlation to reflect the oneness and connection of creation with everything. We are one; we are manifestations of divine love, and we are beings of the light.

I used to be afraid of the word God. I thought of a man who was going to tell me off, and quite possibly put me in hell. Through direct experience, I learnt this was not truth. This was a possibility that could manifest from fear thoughts, a creation of my imagination. I then heard the simple truth, *God loves you.*

Letting go I realised only one thing is at the source of our creation, the source of our being here, the source of our physical being, Divine Love. In essence, God is love.

I hope this book awakens you to the light of your heart. The core of my soul knows we are beings of light filled with infinite potential. Our physical reality feels like a slow dream which when awakened with love, creates ricochets of divinity throughout the universe.

We are divine beings. Our existence is simple, our purpose is simple, connect to love and dissolve the walls that delude us to feeling trapped. It's connecting to the divine grace that made you manifest, your true nature. We are all beings of light.

When I surrender to the love in my heart and tune into source energy, I feel peaceful and connected to all creation. Fear dissolves into the reality of infinite being.

It's my wish to live from the awareness of truth, love, and light, which filters through our consciousness like a bright sun. Everything is connected, we are one. We all deserve, peace, love and respect.

Navigating through the physical world can sometimes make us feel small, disconnected, and alone. When we connect to the source of our divine spiritual nature, we live in love. *Your heart centre is pure, even if you don't feel it.* You are already perfect, whole, and complete. You are love itself.

Your true nature, the core of your beingness is light and love. The ancients show this truth through the Sanskrit word Satchitananda - meaning *existence, consciousness, bliss.*

This book delves between worlds, between states of consciousness, between realisations and truths. Nothing is fact, everything is an expression of what I was guided to write. This does not make it a truth. I slip between duality and love, ego and peace. Please take what you will, and discard the rest, for the truth of your being, no words can describe.

Let there be peace and love, amongst all beings of the universe.

Peace. Peace. Peace.

Om Shanti Shanti Shanti Om.

You are beauty beyond belief.

Be Bliss. Be Light. Be You

CHAPTER ONE

Spiritual Awareness

The truth of our existence is love. There is no greater, more finite truth. Life is magic. We are living in a dream. When you go within your own heart and become the witness, you realise you are whole and complete. Your cup is filled. You are the essence of the universe. Everything that you're looking for, you are already that. We are all beings of love and light.

Truth is an illusion. Seeking truth is one of the most complex journeys you'll ever embark upon. Freedom is our birthright. Everything is a dream and we are but boats floating on the waves of illusion.

Your divine purpose is not to be rich, famous, successful, educated, well-bred, or polite! It's to embrace the essence of love pulsating through your entire body. To really *know* divine love, to know the self.

You're here on Earth, for a reason. Life is powerful. Galaxies explode beyond galaxies. It's infinite and tangible. When you feel lost or depressed it's an indication from source that you're choosing to feel disconnected from love. It's also an indication that you are ready to wake to the truth of your nature. Even if it's an unconscious decision.

Divine Love is your purpose. Divine Love, is the truth of your nature. Love is the purpose of every single person on the planet. The way we express love may be different. The way we use it to channel great strength into our life may be different. Love is the purpose of creation.

There is a difference between divine love, and other expressions of love. When I talk of divine love, I'm not referring to that shared between a man and woman, mother and child, or an adored pet. I am talking about love which centres in the heart and permeates all beings. A love which encompasses all, and lets us know we are worthy of existence, at the core of our being.

Love is all pervading, beyond the abyss of bliss; made from infinite rays of sparkling light. You can experience this love, if you let go of thought, and surrender into your heart. In the fraction of a moment, you discover the heart of your being.

We all have spiritual guides who are constantly attempting to put us on the path of love. Guiding us to recognise our oneness with creation. Whether you listen to your guides, or your intuition, is free will. Source doesn't care if you're happy, broke, healthy, or victimised. It only cares that you align with love. We are being guided to heal the wounds, which we perceive as ours alone. In reality, there is nothing but love.

Any obstacle or boulder, that may come into your path or appears to stunt your growth, is source giving you a wakeup call. Trying to teach you kindness, compassion and most of all forgiveness. Forgiveness of ourselves, and for the anger and disillusion we've project onto others.

When we forgive, we align with love. When we are kind, we align with love. When we have compassion, we align with love. If our guardian angels have to shake things up to connect us back to love (as we emerge from love), they will.

It's important to understand you are not being judged. Source does not judge. We are being divinely guided to search within, seeking the truth of our existence. This is evolution. Once you realise that your purpose is love, to simply be you embracing your true nature, it becomes easier to accept what has happened to you, in your life.

Discovering where love isn't flowing in your life, helps manifest smoother pathways. Whom are you judging? Who are you angry with? Who do you blame? When you fill these spaces with love, and non-reaction, you set yourself free.

The interesting thing is, when you align with love the sea of destruction, laying out on the path ahead dissipates. You are left with a clear channel where you can walk through life with ease. We attract good things into our lives. Sometimes it can take walking down a windy road filled with roadblocks as we clear our consciousness, to allow our being to feel worthy of divine love. To feel worthy of experiencing the beauty of your essence. As we love others more, they reflect love to us, and our life can take flight.

It's one thing to understand these spiritual concepts. It's another to *know* them to be true. We have led many lives before this one so everyone is at a different point of evolution, connecting to source, divine love and realising the truth of their nature. Yet we are all equal manifestations of the divine. All that exists is a dream. No one is witnessing life through your eyes. So who is the witness?

Where do you go when you die? Where were you before you were born? Are the concepts of who you are, who loves you, and what you possess, even real? Or, will they disappear into the abyss, like dreams at dawn, when you awaken to truth?

We are all journeying together to discover the truth of our being. To remove the veils that keep us trapped in the mindset of him, her, you, me. Travelling beyond form, experience, and conscious perception. The world is a reflection of joy, grace, gratitude, fear, lack, and loneliness. It is a dualistic plane of existence where both positive and seemingly negative emotions are felt. When we look to our hearts, we discover that the essence of peace, grace, and harmony is found beyond our everyday perception.

Caught in a yo-yo of emotions and beliefs we try to control perception. Literally masking the fact in our daily life, that nothing in our reality is permanent. Wisdom comes when we seek the essence beyond our reality. When we give ourselves permission to witness the unchangeable true nature of our body, soul and breath.

You are love. Love is your essence. No one is ever truly disconnected from source. You are one with creation. You are a good person; divine love is the heart of your true nature.

You are love, loved and lovable because you exist.

In bliss,
we realise nothings amiss
There is nothing to fear
Love is already here
We are the light
that shines so bright
The one we seek
Take a step back
look for a crack
Nothing is real, it's all surreal
The air; I'll let you in on a secret, nothing is there
It's all a dream
Shift the screen,
you are the abyss
The place you miss
illuminated bliss

- *Bliss*

CHAPTER TWO

Discovering Your Destiny

Everyone's highest purpose is enlightenment, to know the self as satchitananda: truth, consciousness, bliss - to merge with source consciousness, divine love. Connect to source and realise you are one with creation.

Your higher path is simply to discover the truth of who you really are love, bliss, and consciousness. Along the way to finding this road you may encounter pathways that lead to both positive and negative feeling experiences. All pathways are guiding you home. To find the most comfortable pathways home, in your career, daily encounters, relationships, etc. listen to your heart. Meditate in silence and learn to trust spirit. You are always being guided; it's up to us to listen.

If you don't hear or feel any pathways that feel good, you are most likely paralysed by inner fear. This is fine! We all experience fear. Acknowledge your fears and create a safe space to heal; emptiness, hollowness, lack of inspiration are all signposts leading you on a path inward. Through connecting to the soul in silence and meditation you allow love to permeate your being, creating its own pathways of love and joy.

You don't have to 'be perfect' in order to succeed in finding your hearts higher truths, career paths, lovers etc. You simply need to accept yourself in the now. Accept your perceived flaws; the illness, failure, depression, numbness, and blankness whatever they are. In every moment, we are given the opportunity to love the Self deeper. Ignore the critics, your ego, and the silent voices of others that haunt your mind and simply witness. From this space, you give your soul permission to heal. You create space for love.

Stop running from your fears, let them be there. Through presence, you invite grace into your life. We don't need to heal our relationships, our failures, our bodies, or our pain; we simply need to accept their hold upon our being. No matter how angry or fearful this leaves us feeling. Anger, pain, and suffering are simply guiding us inwards, when we try to bury them for fear of the disconnection and sense of failure we feel internally, we simply feel more discontentment. Accepted they become our greatest healers and teachers.

You are a blessing to this world right where you're at; you are already living your perfect destiny. You are already home. It's just a matter of awakening to this awareness. Give yourself time to breathe, if you've been running on the treadmill of, 'I'll never be good enough'. You'll need to catch your breath and give yourself permission to realise that in this moment you already are a divine being of love and light.

We came to Earth to learn particular lessons that ultimately guide us to love consciousness. To partake in sacred contracts with loved ones and those that surround us. These contracts were declared and agreed to, by you, before you even arrived. People who rub you the wrong way are often beings who care deeply for you and made sacred agreements with you before you arrived on this planet. So they can intermingle with your karma and guide you towards forgiveness consciousness.

We break the bonds of karma by practising forgiveness, and unconditional love, and if need be by letting go of those that cause us pain. We step into a path of light and love as we free the other person's energetic bonds to us. As we release the need to react and instead move towards a pathway of healing and forgiveness.

Think of it like a metal chain that links everyone together. People chain themselves to one another no matter how destructive. As these are invisible chains, many people don't realise how bound they are indeed. Even in conscious thought, we can be haunted by memories. This can be broken and healed through practises of meditation, compassion, positive affirmations, and a willingness to surrender. When we let go, we break the chains, and the locks that bind. Freeing ourselves and those involved.

Sometimes knowing we've chosen to be on Earth at a particular time to learn from karmic relations with others and to clear our own past karma; can help with the forgiveness process. Knowing that people who hurt us are linked to us inexplicably and the only way to release the pain is with love, in replacement of fear, can make life feel easier. This helps us connect to source and guides the process of forgiveness.

Life is about experiencing the feeling of free will, set on backdrop of the ultimate goal, enlightenment. Merging with source consciousness and discovering the true meaning of the self. I am that. Source only wants us to connect back, realign, and remember our true nature. Source is love.

You can never truly pull away as you are one with source, even if you don't acknowledge it. When we try to disconnect we remove ourselves from the path of our higher destiny. Spirit wants us to be successful, to sense love in every fibre of our being. Spirit will attempt to put us back on the road to our higher path. Even if this wakeup call comes through the path of adversity, pain, betrayal, sickness, anger, hurt, poverty etc.

When we overcome these obstacles driven by fear, we step into a life lit by infinite love. An empowered life where we accept ourselves, experiences and our destiny. We glow and we embrace our true nature. When we walk in love, we are freedom itself. That's why it's important to release hurts, forgive and to step into a pathway that guides us home to source, divine love.

You can manipulate your will and imprint into the consciousness of the universe what you want for your destiny, and how you will achieve it. This is similar to practising black magic; it goes against universal laws of love and compassion for the self. Ignoring the truth that you are perfect, whole, and complete in this moment. It's one thing to gently open ourselves with affirmations to smoother planes of awareness, it's another to judge, deny and try to force into the universe who we think we should be. When we stamp our definition of what we should be into the path of our life, we ignore the divinity of our being. We are refusing to accept that we're already complete. We are nothing but love.

The tricky part can be loving yourself unconditionally where you are at, versus judging and bullying yourself. Know first that your purpose is to connect to the infinity of your being then surrender all to Spirit, and take instructions from universal consciousness. When you live a life of magic and love, you align yourself with a higher path of love.

Stand outside under the night sky, spread your arms wide and declare, "*I am open to all good, joy, peace and abundance. And so it is.*" You are literally opening yourself up to all the wonderful joyous moments available to you in the universe. You are declaring, *I'm ready to experience all goodness.*

Declaring to yourself and to spirit that you want to step into the path of light, commands your higher self to bring forth your true destiny. Connect to spirit and source in the best way you know how and you will be rewarded. A good indicator to know when you're aligned with your higher purpose is that it makes you feel good, you feel loved and safe. Whatever aligns with love, joy and bliss shows you are connecting with your higher purpose.

Yes, at times fears may arise even when you are walking the most soul-aligned paths. This is okay as well and can be seen as running anxiety. Fear also can arise as we face karmic blockages. Reassure yourself, *all is well, and everything is aligning with my highest good.* At the core of your being, you will feel a presence of peace. This peace is where we want to reside.

Sometimes we look around and we see others living spectacularly wonderful lives. This often happen when watching television, viewing social media, reading magazines, or admiring the neighbour's new car. We may try to pull the exact essence of their life towards us. We are overridden with the subconscious desire to be *just like them.* The first step is to connect within and discover what you truly want, and who you are. Meditation helps this process; it helps us to connect to our inner being. To listen to the silence within, from this space, this gap, all answers emerge.

Here's example of ignoring your inner calling and trying to live a life that seems wonderful, but doesn't align with your soul calling. We'll take two women, Violet and Charlotte, as examples. Both are models, both are happy-go-lucky, both are charismatic.

Violet has intense spiritual beliefs, practises a vegan lifestyle, and reads widely on spirituality. Charlotte is obsessed with makeup up, looking good, and marrying up, these things make her feel safe and happy. It's important to remember this isn't a bad thing. We are not here to judge - release judgement and love will flow.

Now if Charlotte, chose to marry a successful man, and continues to pursue a career in modelling and being glamorous, her life will flow with ease (there will only be shake-ups due to karmic and spiritual realignment – otherwise the path should feel easy and positive). It's aligned with her sacred contract. Her path feels joy filled and exciting. Sacred contracts lead you to finding the heart of your inner wellbeing and guide you to the truth of existence.

If Violet ignores her spiritual yearnings, emulates Charlotte, and in this process denies her inner truth, her will life won't be as fluid as Charlotte's. Violet thinks there is something wrong with her soul's urgings and denies her inner truth. This leaves her feeling hollow and empty. As she is rejecting her inner yearnings, the core lessons she is here to learn on Earth, in this moment.

However, if Violet connects to her spirituality, honours this yearning and continues to model - if it makes her happy - her life will flow with ease. This will allow money, success, and other positive things to flow into her existence. It's about honouring your soul calling, and accepting where you are at. Living your dreams, whilst accepting sacred inner heart truths.

No matter what is happening in your life, you are at the perfect place to realise your divine nature, to accept peace, love, and compassion into your being. Sometimes when we want something desperately to show up in our lives, we scare it away. We need to pull back and allow things to unfold naturally. Forcing something is destructive to our soul. Just as it's important for a baby to develop in the womb for nine months, our angels are allowing our destiny to brew. As we strengthen ourselves for the power of our path.

Feeling hollow and empty is a guiding force, hoping to redirect us inwards and onto a path of unconditional self-love. If you ever feel this way, thank the Divine for showing you that there are new directions in life waiting to be explored by you. Sometimes this new direction can be as simple as learning to love and accept yourself and your choices despite the pain and internal strife flooding your body.

Make peace with all that's present in your life. It's okay, if it doesn't look fabulous from the outside or if you believe you've failed or made mistakes. Internal peace helps us to grow and develop so we can step into our true power. Everything is as it's supposed to be in this moment. Your failures and successes are all part of the divine plan. We need to learn to have faith in the Divine. You have the perfect platform to learn, heal, grow, and discover self-acceptance. You are in the perfect place to learn and grow.

If you have a vision of your life you wish to manifest, and it's just not happening step back. If something isn't in alignment with your soul journey, you will unconsciously push it away. Essentially gifting yourself the opportunity to grow and expand. Look at where you are pushing; meditate to see where you're forcing something instead of allowing it to unfold in divine timing. Allow yourself to be guided.

Important Truths:

1.   You always have been, and always will be enough.

2.   In the eyes of God, Spirit, or Source you are Love.

3.   Life loves you, just the way you are.

You can deny your core essence and try to fit the image you perceive society has created for you or you can live your truth. Even when we are scared to live our truth, it's important that we simply watch this fear, allow it to be there and watch it through loving eyes.

Take for example a man who is a billionaire. If he is calling money to him with the strength of a king, and denying fears, which lurk under the surface of his skin, blocking love, or trying to forget memories from his past, he may become sick, which could lead an early death. Departure from this life happens when our spirit has a new plane of consciousness it needs to experience in order to grow and become closer to recognising the self. Material and financial success are irrelevant, unless we feel peace; we possess nothing of eternal value. Spiritual forces are guiding him to a new karmic cycle of birth and death. He refused to clear pain and allow love, whilst also stepping into abundance and prosperity. Thus a new loving pathway was created to bring him closer to alignment with the heart's truths.

You want to create a ripple effect of vibrational frequency in harmony with joy, light, and love. This attracts abundance, health, wealth, and happiness into your life.

Often we're told that it's fear that holds us back. Where we do not allow love, we create resistance. Fear suppresses things, but love is the greatest conqueror. Love is all, and fear is a reflection of human emotion.

Shifting the arrow of our perception helps align us with abundance and inner harmony. The nature of abundance is spread through the wings of creation. We attract through arrows of love aimed at our desires. Masking our hidden fears and need for acceptance leads to internal and visible destruction. When we love ourselves enough to step onto our higher path we call in our divine guardians and the universe cocoons us in love.

All it takes is to ask and genuinely wish to be brought into alignment with our true nature. To surrender our life to spirit, to trust in the hands that created us. Our true nature is divine love. The wish to live in alignment with divine love creates this as an inevitable outcome. *Where love consciousness is present, harmony flows.*

Simple exercises for aligning to your higher purpose:

☆ Meditate daily. Allow a space between you and your fears, and desires to surface and for love consciousness to fill the void.

☆ Learn to notice signs that help to guide you in the right direction. Signs can be as simple as a butterfly crossing your path - you're left feeling good. Or a bee stinging you - you're left in pain. When something like this happens, think immediately of what you were thinking of and tune into love to guide you to what is your higher purpose.

The universe is always speaking to us; we simply need to relearn how to converse in its language. Listen to your intuition. Listen to your heart.

☆ Learn to read the tarot, runes, I-Ching or study mediumship. This can aid communication with your guides.

☆ Give yourself permission to tap into the ancient knowledge that hovers within your aura. You can pull the power of this knowledge to you, you only need ask. Take your own advice. Listen to yourself, and your intuition.

☆ Call upon your ancestors, guides, Gods and Goddesses, loved ones, enlightened beings, and fairy friends for help whenever needed. Call upon anyone that makes you feel safe, supported, and loved.

☆ Study the stars, using astrology to gain a sense of the spiritual truths you're being confronted with and progressing through at this moment.

☆ Practise positive affirmations. Such as, *I love and approve of myself as I am now.*

☆ When we love ourselves, just the way we are, only then can we love and forgive others. Forgive yourself, for not being your own definition of perfection, and know true perfection is divine love. You are already that.

☆ Connect with nature. Take a walk in a forest, along a beach or watch the sunset. Be still, be present. *I am safe and all is well.*

☆ Accept your current circumstances; it's hard to move forward in peace when we refuse to accept the traumas of our past. Even if you feel you're responsible for the perceived failures in your life be gentle on yourself. You are in the perfect place to learn acceptance, unconditional love and to move forwards with grace and peace.

We are not particles swirling lost in the universe, we are powerful, we are magnetic. When we think there is something wrong with us, or that we've made unforgivable mistakes, this is only a thought. It is a perception in the dream of life. It isn't truth. A thought can be changed. Your perception can change.

In the arms of the divine, you are perfection itself. We try to ignore this, and bully ourselves into feeling less than. Becoming consumed with life, with reality when really reality is ever changing and we are all preparing, day by day, to die, to leave this planet and continue the journey onwards elsewhere. The arms of creation made you manifest and it is through this grace that you discover your real nature. Love, consciousness, bliss.

Just being willing to jump on the train and take the journey to live your truth allows for good to unfold. Sometimes fear can create such dark shadows and spells of paralysis it's hard to see the light. If you were on board a train, it may pass through dark tunnels, but you will come through into the light. Light is the core essence of your being. However bleak, bad or destructive the path of your life looks it can only get brighter as you learn to surrender.

Spirit doesn't seek to control us. We always have a choice. There are choices that align with our higher path. Choices that may be right for others may not align with our soul path. Allow yourself to be the full expression of who you are.

Release judgement of others and replace it with compassion and understanding. Witness through eyes of unconditional love. You have the choice to feel terrible, or to open to the possibility of living the path of light and freedom.

Fear of the oppression placed upon us from others, often stops us from pursuing our dreams. What would your friends, family, and neighbours think if you suddenly appeared to have it all? If you were a little different from the rest? What would you feel if those closest around you stepped into alignment with success and happiness?

It's important we learn to have compassion for others in this moment, as well as ourselves. We live in a society that likes to bully, believing it keeps us well behaved. Learn to forgive and feel empathy, no matter what. This is so powerful as it sets you free and creates bravery rather than suppression in the group consciousness. It's up to you to claim the right to be powerful.

Often that which we are afraid of others inflicting on us, we inflict on them. The first step is to remove jealousy, and resentment from our being. Many people enjoy holding onto negative beliefs such as - *I don't deserve success. God favours them. Life is so unfair. Everyone else has all the luck. I am worthless etc.* Do any of these beliefs ring true for you?

If so, good, that means you've been an excellent learner and have embraced all the negative beliefs placed upon your subconscious mind by society. Through absorption of the information shared with you by your parents, media outlets, marketing teams, and the people who raised you. As you are such an avid learner, and so blessed, you'll be able to remove these blocks. The conscious choice to let go of past beliefs allows a flow of divine light to stream through your being and create shifts.

Remember not to pressure yourself when learning to release and create a positive mindset. Surrender negativity into the consciousness of all that is. Accept the darkness, or fears that reside within your soul rather than trying to suppress it and run away.

As much as you may perceive yourself as 'bad' or 'not good enough' this is an illusion created by belief. You are a physically manifested expression of the divine and no matter your past or future, you always will be enough. You are a blessing to this world. Suffering occurs when we refuse to see the light of love burning within. Self-hatred, fear, rejection, and denial, all suffocate our light. You are purity, love, light, and infinite grace. You are a sacred being and I honour your soul on every level of my being.

If you started to learn a new language, you wouldn't expect to know everything in a day. Change can take time, *be patient with yourself*, this is an excellent, fear relieving practise. Bless with love all negative thoughts held within your aura, including negative experiences that seem to have scarred your soul, and then embrace a path of positive change. Bless everyone you're jealous of, who's bullied you, betrayed you or you just dislike. Imagine three good things happening to each of these individuals. This helps to bring a love consciousness shift.

We don't have to surround ourselves with people or media that instils fear. Oftentimes on a subconscious or conscious level, we feel obligated to be peacekeepers. Taking care of yourself first, is the greatest gift you can bring to this world. When you learn to love yourself, it's like turning the light on. You may before have been shrouded in darkness but when your light goes on you become peace itself. The blessing of you is the greatest gift you could ever give to the world.

Your greater destiny is a safe place. We think we're protecting ourselves by withholding our inner truth. Sometimes we believe when we suppress our light from shining and radiating out into the world like a shooting star, we will be safe. This is not true; this is a false perception of reality. Have you ever wished upon a star you couldn't see?

Allow yourself to be the light. If we suppress ourselves with fears that others will berate us, we stay trapped. How can we clear this? We must learn to see the bigger picture. To be able to accept ourselves fully in the present.

When you release the need to depend on others for approval, you give yourself the gift of ultimate freedom. Where do you want to live? If you have children, how do you want to raise them? How would you like to feed yourself? What quests would you like to embark upon? You can tip the scales and allow your fear mind to become aware that good awaits, as you allow yourself to open like a flower to sunlight.

Your past is in the past, and a magical future awaits you. If it feels selfish to honour your soul remember that the divine created you. The divinity of the universe has brought you to life. To experience this moment. All of creation conspired to bring you into fruition. In the eyes of the divine you always have been and always will be worthy of experiencing all of life's joys.

Don't worry if anyone berates you when they see you stepping into the path of your life purpose. It means you are opening to a new way of living. You're changing your current perception of the world. Eventually they may come to ask; "How did you do it?!"

Sometimes our ego likes to send us fear reminders of 'see I told you, you are worthless'. Your mind is not your friend, learn to accept the negativity and fear energy that lives within your being. Shelter yourself when you feel you need to. Retract, give yourself time to heal. When you feel safe enough step forwards into love and living your truth again. Tiptoe if need be. Be gentle on yourself. The more you learn to trust yourself, and have faith in the universe the easier life flows.

Life is a journey, finding your inner truth and learning to walk with your head held tall is a process. For some the journey may appear easier. These people may have been clearing negative beliefs and karma over many lifetimes. You have a higher purpose. Your presence on this Earth at this moment is intrinsic and definite. You are meant to be here. Otherwise you would never have been born. You are valuable and worthy.

You're here because a part of you chose to come; even if you don't remember. Your time on Earth, no matter how you spend it or what you do with it, is important. It is a gift. The fact you've discovered this text and are reading it right now means you are a Blessed Being of Light.

If the mind wasn't present, you'd experience your essence. In presence, the truth of our being reveals itself. Our thoughts make us feel. If you stop the mind, you'll discover the truth. You are love. You are peace. You are source. The mind unwinds until we discover our true nature. You are the light behind the mind.

All are loved by God/Source/Spirit. There's no exclusion. God is Love. You are love. It's important to see that no matter who we've been we are lovable because we exist. You don't cease to exist when you die. We are all divinely important.

Many people have been raised by false and fearful beliefs perpetuated by spiritual organisations. These beliefs, even if your family does not attend spiritual institutions, have been passed down through generations. When we realise that everyone and everything is an extension of ourselves and we truly, truly, truly love ourselves, we do not hurt others. That's why the most important form of discipline on this planet is to learn our true nature. Love. Love is a guiding light, and it protects all.

When we align to love, we attract love. Suffering is a reflection of a lack of divine love awareness rippling across the surface of humanity. The more we allow ourselves to remember our true nature the more we're able to forgive and surrender. As you step into love, your consciousness affects the whole universe, galaxies upon galaxies. Your bright light allows others to move into a place where love is at the core of their existence, *and they know it*. This is how everlasting peace is created.

We cannot blame our parents, or caregivers for our life, be it good or bad. They did the best they could with the knowledge they had. When we leave one life and move to the next, all we take with us is our conscious awareness.

If in your past life you were a poor, depressed suicidal monk, you may take these beliefs with you into the next, if you haven't cleared them. Different past lives come through at different junctions in our life to be cleared, released and forgiven.

You may have had a past life as a beggar, and you may hold anger and resentment in this life. This energy will come through until it's released. Conversely, you may have lived as wealthy merchant in a previous incarnation and be wonderful in this life at trading goods.

Once you release past life lessons relevant to your current evolution, you'll clear unresolved issues and step into your life as a proficient, happy, divine being. Good that comes to us in this life, be it expected or unexpected is from positive past action. This is why you don't need to feel guilty for any of your good fortune. Thank it and allow more!

You'll know when you've released a past life as the issues that once affected you will dissolve into the nothingness of all that is. Alternatively, they will crystallise into a vortex of positive light. You'll be guided to step up to the path that will lead to discovering the truth of who you are. The path to the knowledge that we are light and love and are positive manifestations of source consciousness.

The only negativity we encounter is formed from a resistance to loving the self. We live in a conscious, expanding universe and people act as mirrors and mere reflections of the way we feel about ourselves and or others. Our parents are sometimes the voices in our head. Be them positive or negative. The good thing is you can override these voices with positive thoughts, and by honouring your pain and letting it flow through you, as you step into your true nature.

How does your life reflect that of your childhood guardians? By witnessing the discord reflected from their life and into your own and noticing the cyclic and reflective nature of life, you create space for change.

The five people you hold closest to in your life are mirrors of your current life perceptions. If you're not happy with your life circumstance, look around you and connect to a tribe that enlightens, uplifts and protects. As we change our own consciousness those close to us evolve or evaporate from our life. Those that are negative towards us either move away, or we walk away from them and no longer seek approval or anything else from the relationship. Alternatively, they begin to support us and enrich our sense of inner peace.

If you are practising meditation, positive affirmations, and choosing to think clear thoughts of light and love and still find negative forces grasping at your soul, look at your self-esteem. People with healthy self-esteem don't allow themselves to be brought down to someone with low self-esteems level. It is okay to walk away.

Empaths or psychic intuitives absorb the positive and negative energy of the people who surround them. When their aura is open, they intuitively pick up on the emotions, pain, suffering, and joy of others. This can be overwhelming. Especially when a large amount of negativity is absorbed and one is unable to discern between their and another's emotions or sensations.

This intuitiveness can lead to a breakdown of the immune system causing autoimmune disease and other health disorders. Many mystics spend long periods in isolation. Being away from others means they aren't influenced by interfering entities, dark possessive thoughts, and mass fear consciousness.

It's advisable for people suffering from fear consciousness and ill health to wear protective crystals, practise sage smudging, to use Feng Shui in their homes and to remove clutter (especially items which may be older and have negative energy imprinted onto them). Use gem and flower essences and play musical spiritual mantras. The power of positive prayer can call in angelic guardians to protect and heal. Embracing love helps to release these concerns.

Often we become frustrated at what 'they' did to us. Blaming others for our internal pain. The good that comes from being annoyed at someone is that you begin to recognise your internal anger, shame, and fears. We need to go beyond 'them' and look at how we really feel about ourselves. The anger, fear, and frustration you project or reject from others is always reflected internally. We need to accept our inner demons, and be willing to look them in the eye before we can move forwards into a path of grace and inner peace.

Having a spiritual relationship with yourself isn't always about feeling happy-go-lucky with every situation in your life. Or always being your own upbeat cheer squad. It's about honouring your darker aspects, accepting your taunting fears and being willing to forgive yourself and others. Until we release the need to block out shame, blame, terror, emptiness and lack we create a wall where it's hard to see where we want to go, what truly makes us happy, and the smoothest pathway to peace.

When we feel disillusioned, empty, hollow, and lacking motivation these are pathways of murky stagnant fear energy being cleared from our body. Sometimes we need to step back and allow spirit to guide our life. Wanting to control every aspect of our destiny is crazy. It's like trying to push the sun above the horizon each morning. Not only is this physically impossible but you'd get burnt to a cinder just trying it. We need to trust the process of life. To trust in the energy that helps the sun to rise.

Until you can truly see the reason why things happen it's terribly stressful to try and control every situation, or to spend hours wishing you were different or that things happened differently. Trust that no matter what, you are being taken care of. Bow with compassion to your negative thoughts, judgements, experiences, and feelings.

You are not responsible for the actions of other. You are also not to blame for anything that you've done that feels inharmonious. Be gentle on your being. This is aligning to love. The physical world isn't as all-pervading as we think it is. There are others realms of consciousness and planes of existence that you can experience. When we truly align with divinity we step out of the need to harm ourselves or others. We step into forgiveness, acceptance, and compassion. Each action is a pathway to greater peace for everyone.

Speaking your truth is another part of stepping into alignment with your higher purpose. If you find it difficult to share new habits you've been embracing in your life with friends or family, your guides may be encouraging you *not* to tell these people. It's not that they are necessarily malicious or vindictive. They just aren't living in synchronicity with their own higher truth and watching you take the centre stage of your own life, whilst moving through turbulent and joyous emotions, may bring up uncomfortable feelings for them. This isn't your problem. Dealing with projections from others can hold your evolution back. If you haven't claimed your power, and if you're learning to love yourself they may rock your blissful boat, and absorb your illuminated energy.

You are a ship floating across the ocean, no longer drowning in longing or desires. The ocean is calm, cool, collected, beautiful blue ripples caress the surface. You are in a wooden boat floating across the top, the path ahead is clear. When it's time to speak your truth, people will come with genuine sincerity. Give them tools that have helped you and resources to brighten their lives.

Light is the essence of your being. When you light a dark room, everyone in the vicinity can see. Light the path to inner wisdom and allow others to illuminate your spirit. You are enough. You are whole, complete, and perfect. You are the light.

Trust in the dream that spirit has woven into the tapestry of your life. The hands that created you are here to protect and guide you. No matter what happens or what you experience when you surrender to spirit, you are guided by infinite love and light. You are in the perfect place right now to live a life of peace and grace.

Connect to the light of your being and fear will dissolve from the body. Connect to your uniqueness. Uncomfortable experiences are there to guide you inwards and help you to become compassionate towards others and yourself. To learn acceptance.

The number one way, to step into alignment with your higher purpose, is to learn to love yourself in this moment. You are more than enough. If you can see yourself as the mirror image of source; pure unconditional love, the art of sliding into your purpose will manifest.

Your desires and sense of purpose will naturally align with your being and your life will flow in a positive direction. The purpose of life itself is love. *You are divine light; you illuminate the Earth by allowing yourself to step into this truth.* By simply being you. When you claim our power, as an energetic being of light, the force of the universe flows through your every move. You can live a life beyond your greatest dreams.

In the morning flowers open to embrace sunlight. Salute the sun. Salute the light within, and watch just as the trees reach their branches and leaves towards the light. When you embody light, when you embody the truth that you are a perfect, beautiful manifestation of spirit the universe brings your desires forth in a positive and healthy way.

You don't have to chase after goals and dreams. Step into divine love and surrender. Spirit will present to you a mastery of miracles.

Life isn't all it seems
A jumble of dreams
The ego, leaves us hollow
So we don't know where to turn, or who to follow
Trying to prove, we are better than the rest
we get into the groove, of putting our mind to the test
Take it slow
There is nowhere to go
You are the creator
not a dominator
We try to dictate
Attempt to create
A life of achievement
a universal dent
You are already complete
There is no need to compete
The wires in your brain have crossed
it's why you feel so lost
Release control
the effort to be an independent soul
All hearts are connected,
infinitely protected
We are one with all
can never fall
We think we need to BE
cannot see
We are everything and nothing
Travel the road home
Return to the twilight zone
Stop, even for a moment, and you will see
when you sit and just be
you dissolve reality
The 'I' merges with the divine
there is no mine
only the infinite sublime
Surrender all
You hear the call

of the place within
dive in, swim
Let the current take you
No one can make you
Forget who you are
Discover you're a star
Peace and love doesn't come from above
it's in your heart
the true place to start
Rise anew released from the glue
You're not the mind
Unwind
You've reached the peak
You are what you seek
Love consciousness and bliss
the light of the abyss

-    *Life Seams*

CHAPTER THREE

Spiritual Awakening

An awakened being is one who feels and knows their divine connection to all that exists in the universe. The knowing that everything reflects us, comes through us and is us. We are all awakened, we just don't know it. Our spiritual core knows this truth for we come into being from this essence. It's only from an illusion of the mind that one does not perceive the awareness that they are a creation, and manifestation of pure, divine love.

We awaken when we allow stillness in mind, body, and spirit. Light pervades through time and space and courses through our body. The light brightens and illuminates our conscious awareness. The gap between reality and illusion. Heart consciousness, one love. Mind-blowing bliss swirling through the universe pulses the awareness that we are one, the light.

Everything emerges from source energy, spirit, oneness. All is love, satchitananda. Bliss, completeness of the soul, divine love, comes from the same source as pain, suffering, greed, anger, anguish, and lack. In knowing this truth, we learn we are cared for, loved, and divinely guided.

A spiritual awakening is the flicking of a switch as the hands of peace encapsulate our awareness in the knowledge that we are divine manifestations of source itself. Everything comes forth from divine love and this love can clear the mind and connect us to silence.

We are always being guided back to the truth of our eternal beingness. Towards the stillness of love, no matter how much hurt floods our body. For source energy is compassion, and we are compassionate beings. Through universal peace, we connect to our soul's purpose. Love.

During the human experience things happen which reflect that we are awakening and merging once more with truth. It need not be a slow journey, awakening to the truth can happen in an instant. Acknowledge the silent breath of your soul and see source love reflected throughout your being.

There are different levels of spiritual awakening. Enlightenment is when one answers the call of love and their mind turns to pure light energy, the 'I' or individual ego disappears and the self alone exists. Merging with source and discovering the divine truth of creation. No words can aptly describe the aware merging of mind, body, and spirit with the divine. We see the interconnectedness of life, the one heart from which we all breathe.

We become more spiritually conscious as our soul progresses to higher energetic plateaus of existence. As people wake up, they become aware of former lives, lives lived on higher dimensional realms where we lived to the song of unity, divinity, and love. We may remember lives in Atlantis or Lemuria. On this planet or on others.

Glimpsing into these states of awareness helps to shake the formal foundation our ego has created to imprison our mind through our existence. Life on Earth is short. But it feels so real, so tangible. But is it real?

The physical body is not a permanent structure. From a seed, great trees form. This is magic we see every day. What is the unseen power that guides the tree's growth? When we nourish our heart we can soar to magical heights. We are one with the entire universe. An unseen, magical, vibratory thread links us with all creation.

You are the light. Creating a ripple across the whole of reality from the love that radiates through your being. Tuning into love, and love as the eternal, guiding light of our being helps us lift the veil of how we perceive the world. When we see this and can feel it always, we are freedom itself. Through setting ourselves free, we give others the power and permission to do so.

Here are ways in which the soul begins the awakening process. These may reflect truths within you, everybody's truth is different and yet the same.

☆ Spiritual Awakening ☆

☆ To awaken is to acknowledge the silence. To witness the light of consciousness. Stilling the mind, comes through acceptance of the now. When we're consumed by thoughts we are living in a mind based reality. When we discover the watcher behind thought, love becomes all pervading.

☆ Depression can be the result of our soul realising what is projecting around us, is not us. We may feel separated and isolated, and as though we are unworthy of existence. This is a guiding light, a bridge leading us to heart consciousness. Guiding us back home to our soul's palace - the infinity of creation.

Where were you before you were born? Where are *you* when you're dead? Depression is waking up to the fact that nothing surrounding us is reality. It is a path home.

When we view depression from this perspective, it can allow the burden of suffering to weaken. For when the weight of our life presses upon us, we realise we are being guided back to love. It's like being shaken in bed, after a peaceful night's rest, and being forced to enter the day. But where does the dream end and reality arise?

☆ When you allow yourself to feel the pain that burdens your soul, you create an awakening. By giving yourself the time to embrace pain, which transmutes to disconnection from divine love awareness, you encounter a space where you can shift boulders of suffering.

Sometimes we're so hard on ourselves. Trying to support everyone, we forget to tune in and feel what is hiding in the depths of our heart. This disconnection, even if we are layering it with positive affirmations and thoughts, becomes a hidden key to our happiness.

It's like having a splinter in your foot. You can still walk and smile, but you're in pain. When we're brave enough to face our internal suffering (or forced by destiny), we create room for deep healing. Once the splinter is removed, what is vital for comfort fills the void. We need not know how we're healed; we need only create a space for it to happen.

One of the greatest gifts we experience as we transform through an awakening is acceptance. Through this knowledge, we see that no experience is here to punish. It's here as a step on our path to merging with divine unconditional love, with source. We are divine beings of the light and everything is in perfect order. We accept we are in the perfect place, for our own spiritual evolution. The frustration occurring when things aren't the way we've envisioned, is created by the idea that we are separate and unworthy. The idea that something is wrong. Trust in life. Acceptance speeds up the manifestation process. True acceptance leads to bliss and inner joy.

☆ When you are awakening, you naturally gravitate towards people and places, reflecting the peace and love you feel in your heart. When confronted in environments filled with masses of fluctuating points of conscious awareness one may become very disturbed. Such places can include shopping malls, schools, busy cities, parties, pubs and nightclubs or large groups of people who dwell in negative mind arenas.

When you succumb to low vibrations, it can be very depressing and disturbing. People and places that may have always held lower energies become uncomfortably present in your awareness. Until you feel the divine light and love of source energy at all times these energies can distract from your internal healing and affect your inner peace. As you become centred in your new vibration of peace, feelings of disharmony drift away naturally.

At one stage, your consciousness matched these awareness levels, places and people. Anything that brings in fear can be physically repelled by the body. Causing internal pain and mental discomfort.

Find places of respite where you feel free to attune to love and light. Go out in nature, walk barefoot on the beach or in grassy fields. Discern where people are on their own spiritual path, and before becoming intertwined with their being make sure you're in spiritual alignment.

Associating with positive places and people helps us to accept the psychological changes occurring as we develop. You may feel most comfortable spending time with yourself. What an honouring, opening, and accepting experience it is to be your own best friend!

When you take care of your own needs, you become more open to helping others. Honouring your soul, honours your associates. Choose where you want to stand and how you want to grow.

We are like trees, and with love, water, and care we can develop into wise old beings whose knowledge is shared through the whispering of the wind.

☆ Experiencing a spiritual awakening can lead to an opening of psychic channels. We may feel vulnerable as we learn to tune in. As we have never tangibly experienced such intimate connections with neighbours, family, friends and people. Attending events or walking through shopping malls can be intense. We're open to receiving all aspects of life and we pick up and collect the thoughts of others, positive or negative, happy or sad, optimistic or doubtful.

When confronted with such situations try to stay in the heart space. When you feel from the heart, you connect to peace. It's like beginning a romantic relationship. As you let your barriers down, you allow more of the other person to enter your life and energy field.

When we open our hearts, we experience unconditional love. Opening our hearts to the universe can be overwhelming and frightening especially when we recognise the pain of our own being, reflected in others. You can step beyond this and into the realms of source energy. Seeing all through love, and viewing world as a divine manifestation of grace.

☆ Food choices may change for awakening beings, as a deep connection to nature is formed. Respect for each creature's evolutionary process creates the desire to abstain from interfering with another being's karmic journey and experience on the Earth plane.

As we become spiritually awakened or activated, certain foods become indigestible to the body as our higher self refuses to consume low vibrational foods.

Organic food becomes desirable and fruits and vegetables become sustenance. We can react to food sources overnight. What was once considered suitable food, now feels toxic, even if addiction remains. We override this when we learn and acknowledge everything manifests from source. A clean diet helps us to float on the spiritual path with grace, comfort, and good health.

There is wealth that comes from living and eating through conscious love. As we connect to love based awareness and our vibration rises we perform best on high vibrational food sources. High vibrational natural and organic foods support the awakening journey.

☆ Severe debilitating illness can be created as the spirit attempts to awaken. Whilst the body still governed by the ego resists the light, deep pain is caused through the refusal to acknowledge the truth of our essence, love.

Believing we are a separate being, living only within our body, creates a robotic malfunction. Our energetic wires connecting us to the power source of light and love, blow an abundance of fuses. Through our refusal to absorb the universal power which surrounds us, we cave and fold as our circuits cross wires.

Illness is the body's way of saying, Wake up! We are forced to notice the fragility of life and the control we are exerting to stay solid in this world, in our beliefs and on our current conscious platform.

Life supports us to the extent that when we become a danger to ourselves and refuse to heal our hearts, disease forms in the body. This is spirits attempt to wake us from our slumber. For we are worthy of love, no matter our past or future. For love is all.

☆ Sometimes illness will come through high vibrational beings who have incarnated on planet Earth to raise the consciousness of the Earth's field. This illness may act as a safety net. As when these beings become caught in the dualistic nature of this planet they succumb to the reincarnation cycle of the Earth plane.

When illness hits, it's a safety net. Pulling them away from the circle of life, so they don't drop their awareness and become trapped in the illusionary web of the Earth's creative, cyclic cycle. It is an automatic safety combustion switch that's been pre-programmed. Activating when they drop their awareness, becoming caught in the illusion. We all need to rediscover the light.

This is one reason many blissful, wonderful, kind, generous and beautiful beings consider suicide. They know deep down they are being caught in the, 'I'm not good enough trap', and that this will keep them locked in a karmic cycle. They want to return to their home planets and realms overflowing with peace. Suicide may however trap them in the belief, that they're not good enough. Though there is always healing and love available wherever they are.

☆ Our body is flooded with inner life, inner light. As we awaken we can still hold onto old addictions. Enlightened beings have gone beyond all vāsanās - mental tendencies - awakening beings are still called back and forth between ego and dualistic natures and habits. This is fine; it's the journey to understanding spiritual truth, our personal truth.

☆ Awakening can bring forth turbulent emotions. Floating between total bliss, safety, and love, we can then fall into anxiety and depression. Once waves of love flood our body, we're aware of a higher truth. We know we're more than our physical being. A spiritual awakening can come in an instant. A surge of energy blowing through the ego, illuminating the third eye, awakening the heart and opening us up to infinite potential.

The wish to live in this state of love is palpable. We may crave this light constantly. We know it's the path for us as our hearts fill with love. Falling back into old habitual patterns may be scary. But we have been gifted with the truth of love, so we can progress towards living in this state of peace. Don't worry if you fall back and forth, as your heart is always guiding you towards truth. Spirit's guidance will lead you home to love.

☆ After a spiritual shift, you may disconnect from things you've been attached to prior. Friendships change, when we change. We may no longer resonate with people whom we used to enjoy associating with. Relationships evolve as your internal compass guides you in new direction. When you make conscious shifts such as changing your diet, lifestyle, drinking habits etc. you naturally align with people who encourage your positive life changes. When your consciousness shifts people either change with you, or find someone else to join their experience of reality. This doesn't mean that we are judging others. We learn to accept all, and respect our heart enough to associate with people who help us feel safe to surrender and immerse our being in love.

Cutting relationship ties may leave us feeling lonely. See beyond the 'I', and accept we are all one. In this way, we allow for those beings who can guide and inspire us to step forth and enter our lives.

We're connected to every being on this planet, physical and non-physical. As our thoughts change, our experiences change. Awakening to our spiritual truth allows wisdom to pervade our stratosphere. People in your life may turn over quickly as you awaken. This may sound harsh but we need to give others permission to enter our lives and leave with grace when the time is right. We don't need to become hung up on changing others. Accept people as they are without the need for interference and release them with love as life takes you on your own unique journey. Respecting the process and trusting life.

☆ During an awakening, you may feel the need to extricate yourself from close friends and family. Feeling the need to shelter your sensitive nature. The truth is your heart will guide you to do what is right for your personal development. When you pull away, people may reflect why they need an external point of validation for the love they are expressing and repressing in their own heart centre.

Surround yourself with people who support your awakening. Stay heart centred and allow the process to unfold naturally. Learn to step back and witness rather than give yourself over to the tug of separation so easily instilled by individuals collectively believing you are you. You, as the ego embodiment of someone on planet Earth, rather than a peaceful entity who experiences encompassing love for all and is one with all.

☆ You are divinely guided as you align. As you open your consciousness, it's important to pay attention to gentle nudges from spirit, divine love. Signs show up everywhere. If you have a wonderful idea, this is a gift from creation of something to pursue which can bring excitement, abundance, and peace into your life.

☆ Signs can come in the form of sequential numbers, things that remind you of loved ones, saying they are watching over you. Feathers, butterflies, number plates, actual signs - with messages pertaining to your innermost questions - beautiful clouds, rainbows, double rainbows, images on t-shirts, feelings of love emerging from the heart, animals, crystals found in interesting places, healing messages from strangers etc.

Anything that holds some symbolic message to you, be it small or large is your guides' way of talking to you. Saying we're right here, holding your hand. You are not alone and we are doing our best from the astral heaven realms to show you that you are loved, supported, and divinely guided.

☆ The search for a guru or guide often pre-emanates a spiritual awakening. Yes, we are one with source and we are all enlightened beings. But some beings *know* this, *they live from this awareness*. Their ego has effectively blown up and their light and presence of a living embodiment of realised divine grace raises the consciousness of the entire planet. Being in the vicinity of these beings helps to rotate the structure of our own mind and facilitates in the conscious connection to truth, love and spirit.

Some examples of these beings throughout history include, Buddha, Quan Yin, Jesus Christ, Ramana Maharshi, H. W. L. Poonja (Papaji), Robert Adams, Sathya Sai Baba, Shirdi Sai Baba, Mata Amritanandamayi (Amma), Mahavatar Babaji, Lahiri Mahasaya, Paramahansa Yogananda, Nisargadatta Maharaj, and Kabir, to name a beautiful and blessed handful.

☆ Contact with these guides, or spiritual masters can increase the pace in which our ascension or awakening process takes place. They can dissolve karma and illusion. Helping to awaken you to the truth of self.

The guru is like a hot stove. Our unconscious negativity would normally stay level and cool in the pan, but it boils up in the presence of great sages. Our resistance to change is transcended through their presence. Their gift of peace and bountiful love is palpable in our body. Through the blessing of their divine connection to all, our awareness opens.

☆ Awakening can be a gradual building of energy, a discomfort felt in the body. Forcing us to reach for higher vibrational thoughts, conversations, texts, and foods. Things that guide us towards the light. We realise tools such as crystals are living beings that can help assist us on our spiritual path. We feel connected to all that is and we allow love to guide our pathway.

☆ If spirit has a predetermined destiny in store for us, no matter how much we try to resist we'll need to adapt and dedicate ourselves to our destiny. It can be frustrating when we want to stay in our comfort zone. When our whole being is screaming *Wake up!* And we refuse to hear its cries. Life becomes akin to banging your head on a brick wall and asking it to open. A painful, depressing and stubborn task.

Surrender to your destiny and fate as you have already chosen particular lessons, before you arrived on Earth. Allow your life to lift you to the light. This does not mean to remain stuck in negative situations that cause you to experience hate and retaliate with suppressed emotions, of resentment and anger. Trust the process of life. Accept the completeness of your existence. You are a divine, magical being. A gift to the world.

☆ Awareness floods the body and we question all we once perceived as real. As we transcend time, we discover the heart centre holds the key to undiscovered truths. We look outside ourselves only to turn inwards to the silence that illuminates the truth.

☆ The ego is part of source consciousness. Nothing is good or bad, it's a manifestation of source energy. The ego allows us to experience the feeling of separation from source. It creates the 'I'. Who am I?

See the ego as a bubble surrounding your being, distorting perception. Creating a mirage, an illusion of separation. If you pop the bubble, you realise it was keeping you stuck. When the bubble bursts, you discover you are one with everything. That you reflect source energy and everything is a reflection of you. This brings tremendous peace.

Allow yourself to go beyond words and feel the divinity and peace of your own nature.

It's okay to forget our truth and to dive back and forth between bliss and suffering as we open, like a lotus flower, to the light. Be present with all of your emotions; be them positive or negative, painful or joyful. Know hidden deep in the depths of your being there's more than the conscious mind can contemplate. You are one with everything. You don't have to know this as fact, but as you begin to believe it, help will come, guiding you back to the heart.

Open your heart, you are an angel sent by the divine,
to experience what it's like to live amongst mankind
A kingdom of angels who've forgotten the way
to heaven's gates, which are open today
Stop for a moment, listen, breathe
Let the mind be still
and discover the secret of free will
There is nothing to gain,
desire brings suffering and pain
Be as slow as a snail, to remove the veil
The light beyond
the distant shore
that is our front door
Love, light and bliss
nothing's amiss
We think it so
until we know
we're beings of love,
of ether and fairy dust
We are the light,
consciousness itself
The ocean of love is our true home
We're already there
The thread is unravelling
and we are travelling
to a place so close
it's a wonder we haven't noticed before
we are already at heaven's door

- *Eternal Angel*

CHAPTER FOUR

Gratitude

We are beings of light, pure reflections of source energy, the spirit of the universe. Divine manifestations of pure love consciousness. This realisation dissolves karma and allows the progress of the soul into a state of infinite truth. We step into the awareness that we are reflections of God's light, source light.

We are infinite love, joy, and bliss. Most of the time, we don't live from this stream of conscious awareness. Creating the illusion of separation, we appear to pull ourselves - through our ego - away from the source of our existence.

Free will manifests through our ability to disconnect our awareness from our inherent connection to all that is. As well as being liberating it masks us with the delusion that we're not enough. Deep down, we know we are the light. It is so simple.

Through acceptance we learn to acknowledge and take responsibility for all that is. Often the word 'responsibility' can pressure us into doing what we perceive others see as acceptable behaviour. Which can lead us to please others and ignore our hearts inner callings.

When we hate something or someone, we're not accepting. Instead, we're ignoring the divinity that permeates our being, choosing fear. Leaving no room for gratitude. Gratitude comes from a place of allowing and acknowledging the divine within.

Everything we focus upon expands. We are all expanding manifestations of living light. Therefore, when you shine your light on something, more of it comes into view, into focus, and into your reality. Accepting creates pivotal points of light from which your soul experience orbits.

When we acknowledge the truth, that we're divine beings living in the physical realms of divine manifestation, we connect to the light of spirit. To the purpose of our existence. The need to *be* something else other than ourselves dissolves into the nothingness from whence it came. This light filtering through our body assists in opening the consciousness of those who are trapped in illusion, and the experiential process of free will.

Connecting to light, helps us to live purposeful, abundant, lives. We see bliss in all beings and our actions unfold in such a way they direct the harmonious energy of source awareness into our daily life. We are complete beings who need not suffer through our ego's blindness to the truth of our source.

Light, love, and source energy is constantly trying to awaken within us. People who are depressed are often close to uncovering the light within their hearts as they are waking up to the illusion of duality. Suffering is a vehicle pushing us towards releasing the shell of who we think we are, so we can step into the light of who we are, divine love.

Why use gratitude? Gratitude is a wonderful tool for awakening our hearts. It creates cracks in the mental framework that has enclosed our minds with darkness. Guiding us as a precursor to experiencing love. When we experience love, at its core, fear dissolves as the illusion crumbles. Thus creating clear pathways in life. For when we create through love consciousness, we do so ethically, intelligently and peacefully. We remove the need for shadows of pain and our life becomes a joyous game.

When we act from integrity to serve through love, the suffering of trying and striving to be something dissipates. Through service to a higher purpose of light, we are guided. Things become less personal. The knocks, bumps, and fears of shame, humiliation, or failure, less relevant. Through acting as a conscious guide; through service, we surrender our ego that would otherwise hold us back with fear.

We realise no matter what suffering or embarrassment may befall us; it reflects where our consciousness is blocked to the light of love. We forgive the parts of ourselves that desired to experience this energy and connect with our higher purpose and awareness of simply being. We are already enough and we are being guided to realise this in every moment; regardless how painful the moment may appear.

Gratitude helps us become present and thankful for all that already is, for all our ego's eye can see. This helps us to awaken and project peace consciousness. Through gradual practise, gratitude opens you to the awareness that in the fullness of our being, *you are good enough right now.*

The light projected through gratitude - a high vibrational experience - awakens your consciousness to accept more good. It's like turning the lights on in a dark room, you suddenly realise it's full of interesting things. Feelings of lack become a visible illusion, so you allow more positive experiences and joy to show up in your life.

Surrender to source. Surrender to God. Surrender to life. Even when you feel scared to do so. In fact, this is the best time! As it can help transcend painful thoughts and experiences. When we're trying to push ourselves into something, or some way of being we don't allow for life to come towards us. Unfolding pleasures and great happiness which we couldn't otherwise imagine. When we respond with gratitude and blessings, we float through life as though going downstream in a river.

If something isn't manifesting or materialising in the way you want it too, let go. Be open and receptive to seeing how and where you can flow in a new direction. Look for signs from your Guardian Angels. Be grateful for the experience of life and know you're part of a bigger picture.

This isn't giving up on your dreams, its allowing the awareness of your desires to be present. Sometimes we need to heal our hearts before our dreams take flight. Trust that source energy has guided you to Earth, to be manifest in human form, to bring your awareness into alignment with love. We are not here to become engulfed on the path to riches, we are here to realise the self. Acceptance of your journey brings inner peace. This is the biggest form of grace any one of us could ask for.

From the depths of despair and darkness, love emerges. Life flows like waves on the ocean. Storms pass, seasons change and yet love remains the constant haven for all who seek her shores. You are a magical blessing. Your life is a blessing. Your existence is a blessing.

Know spirit is ready to pick you up and submerge your being in the essence of love. You only need wish, and a way will be made. You are a child of creation and you deserve to know love from the inside out. Creation will take care of everything created. Everything is okay just as it is. All is well. Trust in the hands of creation.

Often we become obsessed with feeling better, and we believe that more 'things' will permeate the experience of completion. You are already complete. A billionaire and a beggar has just as much connection to source. When we seek the place from where we arise, we truly seek inner peace, compassion, and bliss. We seek an awakening from the human experience and we step into the truth of existence. That goes beyond our individual 'I' and is the permanent, loving, joyous substratum of reality.

We are pre-programmed to look for perfection. We expect people to be good, to live in a manner we perceive as worthy. We don't allow room for mistakes and this can lead to us being incredibly hard on ourselves and others. It decreases our ability to spread our own light and love throughout the universe.

Perfection is a major issue in society. We all want to be loved, loved by our source of religious comfort, loved by others, and loved by life itself. It's only until we realise *we are beings of divine love* and know this as fact that we surrender to the process of life. We are all on Earth to experience the truth of our being, to have fun, to experience feelings of separation.

Compassion allows you to be gentle on others and yourself. When we only allow perfection, we become unforgiving of mistakes. Thus neglecting the human experience as being just that, an experience. It's not the defining source of our being.

It's fine to have desires, and to want for things to be different. This is simply an indication that you are open to change. It's more than okay to feel angry that things haven't worked out the way we envisioned. That we do not meet our perception or society's standards of perfection or success. There comes a time though when you need to practise non-reactance. To accept the flow of your life and understand that whatever has happened to you is the perfect platform for you to forgive, surrender and accept. To let down your walls of judgement and just be. Creating peace with the shame, terror, and fears haunting the present moment.

Through acceptance, you invite peace, and compassion. The dull thud of self-hatred weakens. The tinted glasses of perceived reality become blurred and we realise our limited vision is not necessarily a reflection of divine truth. *You always have been and always will be good enough. You are a good person. You are a living manifestation of the divine. As are all of the Earth's inhabitants.*

I used to hear the word gratitude and recoil. In my childhood, gratitude was unconsciously used as a replacement for guilt. Being grateful for your possessions meant; 'Feel bad that you have something that others don't!' It took me a long time to make peace with feeling grateful and understanding the soul nature of gratitude. There's a difference between guilt and gratitude.

Trying to be yourself all the time can be a struggle as we naturally create faces and personas for different people. Until we know the truth of our essence, the love in the heart of our being, we keep searching for completion outside ourselves. Authenticity stems from self-love. When we have gratitude, for the way things are, for where we are on our spiritual journey, we allow peace and an abundance of compassion. This emotion is a light guiding us towards serenity.

The push for being authentic versions of ourselves stems from the need to love our every action. To be accepting of our thoughts and behavioural patterns. Most of the time we are not allowing the divinity of our true nature to express through our being with conscious awareness. This feeling of inauthenticity keeps us searching for truth in illusion, we are love, and we are both inauthenticity and authenticity.

Comparison is a tool that annihilates gratitude. It makes you want to hammer the nails on your own coffin - which is a terribly depressing feeling. The first step is to remove comparison triggers from your life. The second is to reframe your mind when these triggers are activated. Bless the success of others. No matter how low you feel, or how much you're justifying that you will never be good enough.

When you put positivity on the success of others, you also raise your own emotions to more harmonious levels. This helps to heal your inner child that feels neglected, left out, forgotten, and unworthy. It aligns you to a path of wellbeing.

Limit the amount of time that you devote to comparing yourself to others. When you get the urge to look up that old friend online who's doing fabulously, or compare your body or wealth to celebrities and the world's rich list, find something self-enriching and positive to give your attention to instead. The high you get after doing a quick compare does not last when you crash into the, 'I knew I wasn't good enough' spiral. It doesn't matter if you occasional succumb to the comparison lure, you don't want to beat yourself up as you release old habits; be gentle on yourself. Nevertheless, aim to cut it out as a habit totally.

Everyone's thoughts swirl, and dip and dive. It's only when we calm the mind, reach for the silence within and on the rare occasion catch a glimmer of stillness we find peace. Find compassion for yourself in the moment. Be real, by loving your perceived flaws. This is divine gratitude.

Gratitude consumes our bodies when we realise just how magical we are. Fear can taunt and haunt, but if we keep guiding our mind to our heart centre, we can live in harmony with creation. We're like caterpillars in cocoons, as our heart unfolds we are given wings to fly, as we merge with the living consciousness of love.

Gratitude can help bring material desires to fruition and it can help you to accept where you are, on this divine spiritual journey. It opens you to the awareness that holds the key of the truth of your being. Gratitude manifests from the heart, and it's in this space your greatest treasures are hidden. The most obvious space to bury life's greatest secret is within our hearts. We've been given wings; we simply need to practice how to fly.

You can bring a constant conscious presence of gratitude into your daily life. When you bring presence to the objects you use and the way in which you interact with the world you are practising gratitude.

Start your day with gratitude. Thank your bed for a good night sleep before opening your eyes as you awaken. Bless your teacup, the chair you sit on; thank your letterbox, your computer and telephone. Bringing love and thanks to the items you use daily spreads goodwill and creates friendship with these things instead of fear or resistance. In addition, having a good relationship with the objects that surround can help you to feel more comfortable when you're in an emotional place, which is often shadowed by resistance and fear.

Simplicity in our spiritual practise can often have the greatest affect. Gratitude helps us accept the now. When we become present, we release the need for judgement. We tune into higher destinies and are much more accepting of things that at one time, we'd have rather ignored.

To practise gratitude, take a diary and each evening write a list of ten positive things that happened during the day. It can be as simple (or profound!) as being grateful for opening your eyes in the morning. Awareness of the good in your life allows the flow of positivity to increase.

When something happens in a way that you're left feeling pain, anger, or disdain, allow the negative emotions to arise, breathe into the feelings. Allow the body to experience the crippling anguish of the desire for things to be different. Know life is trying to teach you to release pain and connect you to love. Negative experiences reflect where you're energetically blocked. Pave the way for gratitude, by changing your attitude, and outlook.

Think of ten things you're grateful for in this moment. This inner reflection of good changes your life's compass direction. Guiding you away from fear and resentment, towards the manifestation of your dreams, be them physical or centred in your heart.

Another wonderful way to create gratitude in your life following ancient Feng Shui wisdom, is to empower your helpful people sector in your home or residence, in the North West. Write a list of people who inspire you and help you and place this list into a silver bowl (the NW sector is enhanced by metal). In Feng Shui when clutter is removed and positive energy is placed here, the planets and Earth energies can help to bring about changes.

Positive resolutions can be manifested, through your intent to create a harmonious outcome. You can even write gratitude notes for things you wish to bring into fruition.

Using the technique of blessing everything that's a part of your life, you make way for positive changes. For light to express through your heart and become physically tangible in your life.

Instead of forcing that which we desire into being. We can have gratitude for the present blessings in our life. When we take the time to smell the roses, life becomes a whole lot sweeter. We realise everything unfolds in divine time.

Gratitude allows your heart to open and appreciate the life before you. It welcomes love consciousness with open arms. Allowing the light of love to shine upon you.

A simple change in attitude can spark great changes
Encouraging us to rewrite life's pages
A spark, in the dark, lets your light shine bright...
even in the blackest night
Follow your heart, your dreams will unfold
Experience magical stories as yet untold
Where the mind goes,
physical experience will expose
the divine manifestation of creation
Until this game is up,
that which we allow the ego to focus upon will create
Let your mind lead you to a place that pleases you
Trust your heart
Gratitude is an art

–   Gratitude

CHAPTER FIVE

The Minds Secret Abilities

Recently, I had a dream where spiritual beings new to the Earth plane explained manifestation. Why individuals can feel blockages and have difficulty manifesting what they desire, and completing their soul objectives on Earth. The reason is simple; we're now living in a physical reality. Deities live on higher planes of reality that are non-physical. Hence, when we place faith in these beings they assist the manifestation of miracles.

As we're living on the Earth plane, we are governed, to a certain extent by physical laws. *Please note: The law of physical reaction is not higher than the law of belief.* For example, when we touch a hot plate, we believe it will burn our fingers. It's a physical reaction to heat. However, if we believed we wouldn't burn our fingers, we wouldn't. The physical response to the heat we have creates a belief and confuses us to think we burn because the hot plate's hot. This makes us start to believe in physical laws. These can protect us and cause havoc with our sense of personal power and ability to have control over our thoughts - the ultimate cause of manifestation.

We believe we need to eat, or our physical body will die. Yet some people practise breatharian lifestyles, living off air. They've overcome this physical barrier. Another simpler example is the belief junk food makes you fat. This common physical belief is reflected in the majority of society who gain weight from consumption of junk food. Contrary, to this mainstream belief some people eat loads of junk and stay thin and lean. Why is this? It's because they believe, and it becomes a truth for them - no matter what they eat they remain slim. Even a fast metabolism can be a product of the mind. This is also reflected in the belief smoking causes cancer; the majority of people believe this to be true. Yet there are others who have put up a wall to this 'fact', smoke daily and live long healthy lives.

Our beliefs are so strong that it would be insane to jump off a building thinking if we believe we'll fly, or walk in front of a car believing we are divinely protected. If we didn't believe in this experience we'd seen as insane, yet we really don't understand the full extent of our reality. We believe what, we see, hear, taste and touch, yet there is a world beyond our perception which creates space for miracles and magic.

If we surrender to the physical experience on Earth, we'll be governed by physical laws. We're living in a physical reality that reflects physical reaction, *it doesn't demand this*. As seen in examples of people who walk on hot coals, or eat flames. The Shaolin monks are wonderful at showing how chi can be focused to create *mind-blowing* abilities.

It's easy to get confused and mislead whilst living in a physical reality. We start to believe physical law as fact, cutting off our receptivity to miracles, God, angels, spiritual guides, deceased loved-ones, conscious creation and universal power. We are powerful creators. That which surrounds us is a direct reflection of our thoughts, the outside world is reflecting our inside world. In essence, they're the same.

We're living in a dream of our creation. Just like in a dream sometimes we create things we wish to happen, other times, our dreams become nightmares and we're desperate to escape. When we awaken we know what we saw wasn't real. We have died in dreams; escaped, fought back and sometimes we've been paralysed by fear. Life is the same.

People hurt us in dreams and when we awaken, we realise it never really happened. If this individual exists in our daily life, we forgive them with ease. Forgiveness is a part of letting go of the illusion we've created. When we cross over, leaving this physical form behind we wake up, and it's much easier to forgive. If you can learn to apply this knowledge to your current state of reality, it can be an invaluable tool for letting go.

Sometimes we're constrained by past lives. Earlier dreams that have pushed ideologies into our ego and consciousness systems. These affect our comfort and discomfort in this moment.

We may find, as we believe in physical laws, we deeply believe the truth of the words spoken by the ones who taught us the effects of physical reaction. This is a physical universe; thus physical beliefs are easily reflected as true. We assume the majority 'facts' we've absorbed into our learning experience are truth, as we develop from babies to adults.

Our primary caregivers become encyclopaedias on life. We trust their assertions as their physical truths taught to us manifest as truth. Thus we're lulled in to a waking sleep, where we believe the non-physical truths they tell us are real. These beliefs can range from, 'you're so beautiful', a lovely belief to experience too, 'you're so ugly', which can be a depressing experience that cuts into your self-esteem. We take on beliefs projected through mass-conscious exposure.

Our soul is non-physical. We continue to exist even after death. You cannot weigh, or measure the soul. As we learn and grow we realise we're one with creation itself, with all planes of existence, and that anything is possible.

Our brains are powerful tools. If we didn't have a brain, we wouldn't be able to think. Which is a ponderous thought indeed! How would we brush our teeth, go to the toilet, take a bath, jump on a plane, or go on holidays? When we step back beyond menial things, the mind has several main negative programs and patterns.

Many people's thoughts run in negative loops:

☆ I don't have enough.

☆ I'm not smart.

☆ My mother/father doesn't love me.

☆ I'm unsupported by life.

☆ God (Source) doesn't love me.

☆ I'm not good enough.

☆ I hate myself.

☆ I wish I lived in a better house.

☆ I don't do enough.

☆ I don't deserve.

☆ I'm ashamed of myself.

☆ I feel guilty.

☆ I'm so jealous of - friend, family member, neighbour etc.

☆ They betrayed me.

☆ I'm afraid of…

What if these fears and concerns playing like broken records are untruths? What if they are stories we've picked up from the media, our parents, our day-care and or schooling years, and the people who shaped our reality when we were little?

Just because you think something, it doesn't make the thought a truth. It is just a thought, and a thought can be changed. There is nothing wrong with you, that's just a thought. You are a divine being of love and light.

Truth comes from source, it comes from within, it resonates in your heart. Your higher purpose always feels good. When we experience a negative emotion, we're coming from a state of fear, and are out of alignment with our true nature. What is your true nature? Your true nature is bliss, love and light – it is beauty beyond words. When you know you're part of a conscious whole you step out of fear because it's not the truth of your being or nature.

Thoughts become things. You can use the pull of the moon, the pungency of herbs, the vibrations of stones that align with love, abundance, peace, protection, healing, depending on what you desire to help draw these feelings and experiences towards you. The key ingredient is always your thoughts. Organisations have tried to disempower the people by hiding this knowledge. Burning witches and suppressing spiritual truths. That which we avoid, or shame symbolises what we're afraid of. When you claim your power, you shift the balance of light on the conscious playing field of life.

As we're one with the universe, one with all that is we have the ability to call into our consciousness that which we desire to experience. Align with love, and use mantras of love, to connect to source, which allows vibrations you desire, to pull forth into your reality. Choose not to react to internal pain and suffering. Instead of letting these uncomfortable, anguish filled emotions control you, let them be with love and grace.

It's not the way you demand things to come to you. It's the allowing that helps them manifest into fruition. The surrender and release is where the magic is present.

When we live from a love-based awareness, and bring acceptance to all the perceived good and bad in our lives we draw positive things into our consciousness and into our reality. Our mind is a magnet; it draws to us that which we focus upon.

If you constantly listen to negative mind thoughts, you'll never be satisfied and will always feel afraid. Negative thoughts are in no way as powerful as loving, compassionate thoughts. Even though they sometimes feel like they dominate our reality. Being aware of our fears is healthy; we all need to accept that which we are afraid of and to acknowledge past traumas. Through acceptance and love, pathways to inner peace are manifested.

Thoughts hold vibrations. We are vibrational beings. When we wish to attract something into our life, we need to become a vibrational match. Allowing ourselves to tune into the vibration of love is the single most powerful tool for releasing vibrations of lack, neglect, abandonment, and low self-esteem.

It's important that we identify our negative mind messages and replace them with positive ones. Negative thoughts halt our evolution in health, wealth, and joy. They keep us from expressing and experiencing our true potential. They can keep us stuck, even when we wish to move out of our current circumstances. Trapping us in the illusion of duality, hiding the truth that we're divine expressions of source consciousness, love.

They pull us into a downward spiral when we are experiencing a complete lack of love awareness. When we express love, it has the power to dissolve obstacles. When we acknowledge we are divine beings, and are therefore worthy, we step into infinite potential. Love as our guide helps to release the fears that have held us back. We can overcome our challenges and obstacles from a state of positive consciousness and illuminate our soul with the infinite light that creates our beingness.

♥ Exercise: Play with Love ♥

Light a candle. Focus on the flame and see what arises. Write your negative thoughts, the people you hate, the jealousy, resentments, bitterness, hurts, failures and hardships that stay with you even in a black room lit by a candle. Ask the candle to help you forgive yourself for the roadblocks that pierce your mind. Surrender. Let go.

Once you have your list, create positive affirming sentences to counter your negative beliefs. *I don't have enough;* may become, *I now experience an abundance of wealth. So, and so ruined my life;* may become, *I forgive and let go with ease. Goodness always comes to me.*

Practise your new affirmations in the mirror daily. A beautiful daily affirmation is, *I love and accept myself just as I am right now.*

Take a stopwatch and set an hourly timer, each hour have the alarm chime and practise a particular affirmation. If this is too intense, try to practise your affirmations morning and evening for ten minutes in front of a mirror. You can even use sacred prayer beads. Flick a bead over your fingertips each time you affirm your new, positive mindset. Each cycle being repeated 108 times.

☆ Jealousy ☆

Desire emerges from the perception that we're less than, and incomplete. We believe we need things to make ourselves feel better about our present lives. Often when we see people's lives going well, especially those we love, we fall prey to the jealousy trap. This is no coincidence. We are pre-programmed jealousy and comparison machines. You need only turn on the television to instil seed desires. We're superb at making ourselves feel the physical pain of jealousy, lack and embracing the universal untruth that we don't measure up.

Getting something because we see someone else with it, creates vicious cycles. This is because the thing we desire, be it a home, car, business, holiday destination, career, success, item of clothing, jewellery etc. may not stem from our own inner yearnings, our inner truth. Rather a need to collect things that sparkle in the moonlight; in the hope we too will learn to shine. When the sun comes out, we realise what we wanted isn't sparkling as bright as we thought it did and we go in search of more treasures.

Everybody wants fulfilment and inner peace. Often we trick ourselves; denying we're worthy of this state of being. Life becomes incredibly busy when we're trying to keep up with our friends, fulfil the needs of loved ones *and* acquire all the things we feel will fulfil the empty void inside.

We have become addicted to the need to be more than our inner state. Alternatively, it may be we believe we're not enough, and in the quest to prove otherwise we compete. This state of living is reflected across all levels of wealth.

It's a wonderful and powerful thing to desire to be the best version of yourself. What if I was to tell you, "You're already the best you can be?"

You might say, "But I need more money", or "When I make it at this career my life will be complete", or "I need to lose weight", or "When I find the perfect partner who accepts me just as I am I'll know I am lovable", even "Try telling my parents that!" As you may feel like you need your family's approval.

The invisible, evasive truth is *life loves you*. You are perfect and complete just as you are. You are in the perfect place to grow and bloom. Tuning into this awareness is like changing the radio station; the music is playing somewhere you just need to tune your consciousness to experience the rhythm. The music of self-acceptance plays deep within the Self.

When you tune in and realise everything is perfect and in divine order as it's supposed to be, it's easier to let go of judgements projected from and about others. To tune into the signals of the universe that are always guiding you to this higher state of awareness. When you tune in your heart turns on, creating a safe zone where you can express your true soul desires. (Please note: All soul desires stem from the heart and are pure, loving and compassionate to all beings.)

You can choose the path in life that best supports your spiritual evolution. When you walk this path, it's much easier to attract what you desire, because you're at peace and allowing the universe to take care of you. It makes room to meet your soulmate, or attract the perfect career. We learn to live in love, not jealousy.

This being, this body, may or may not yet own things that are a part of the world upon which you've chosen to incarnate. Everything expresses around you, as bubbles of love. Our light flickers from awareness of the interconnectedness of all life to the fear that we are separate. However, through remembering we are one, the need to begrudge another dissolves for we are *that*.

Surrender into source consciousness, Divine Love. Know you're a tiny light, being guided by source energy to oneness with creation. Therefore, you may merge with the light of creation. Life loves you, and is here to support you. Let the light of love guide you, taking you home to love. Where you lack nothing and are everything. *Where you are safe.*

When we open ourselves to source. We take intuitive steps to surrender the pain and suffering hidden deep within our hearts. We're carried upon angel wings to divine presence.

Lack is an illusion; the feeling of not being whole haunts our being. Allow yourself to find peace through feeling separate from source. Allow the pain of *not enough*, to flood your body. Then pray for the *love in your heart* to guide you towards *true peace*. Be willing to surrender to the realisation that your ego doesn't always know what's best. There is a divine presence waiting for you to merge with peace. It's guiding you in this moment towards a loving space. Love transmutes suffering and when you surrender to a higher power, you kneel before the altar of love.

Jealousy creates major roadblocks when creating the lifestyle we desire. We can fall prey to patterns of jealousy when we don't guard the gates of our mind. If you lament on lost lovers on social media, grit your teeth over another's good fortunes, or constantly push your chest out boasting about the good things you possess - to make others feel inferior, or respect and admire you - you're succumbing to the allure of jealousy and its trappings.

Jealousy is a mind virus. It makes us feel powerful, vulnerable, and weak depending on the lessons we need to learn. However, this power is an elusive and illusionary force. It marks hidden emotions of lack of self-worth, self-hatred, and guilt at not having achieved our hearts desires. At its core, we feel we are struggling with the belief (not truth) that we are failing life, as a human being.

Methods to release jealousy:

☆ Beat a pillow and release your anger. This may need to be repeated several times. Allow yourself to *feel* the jealousy and resentment on every level of your being.

☆ Stop bitching, get off the phone, and stop conversations with those who allow you to indulge in jealous and spiteful comments. Instead, focus on good things when you chat, things that made you happy today. Focus your attention on happiness and joy. Yes, it's healthy to verbally release feelings of jealousy and our insecurities but we don't have to live there. When you do need to verbally purge your sticky, negative emotions do it with someone who is non-judgemental, doesn't feed off of the energy and is there to help you release and then come full circle into acceptance. A friend or family member who is connected and healing through their presence and nature.

☆ Don't criticise yourself. Often we're jealous because we don't give ourselves permission to feel good about ourselves.

☆ Know you're in the right place, at the right time. You've done the best with the knowledge you have and nothing is permanent. Surrender to source, to the will of the beat that's pressing upon your heart. You're alive through the grace of universal love. This moment is perfect for guiding your being to the heart space of silence.

☆ Sometimes jealousy makes us feel we are inferior, hopeless, or worthless. Know you don't have to be peaceful all the time. Allow yourself to witness your pain, fear, anger, and emotions. You cannot hide from the tears inside, but you can learn to love them. Love awareness is taken from one life to the next. Life isn't permanent. Suffering isn't permanent.

☆ The Divine loves you. Let go of the need to control every thought and release the need for your thoughts to control you. For you are perfect and complete, with all you feel you have, and all you feel you don't have. Spirit loves you, *for you are made from stardust, light, and love.*

☆ Your spirit is love. I love you and accept you right where you're at.

☆ Learn to meditate. Close your eyes. Watch your breath, inhale, exhale, let go of your thoughts. Ask yourself, Who am I? Follow this thought back to its source.

☆ Bless with love your feelings of jealousy. Look at what you're jealous of and say, "That's for me, I allow myself to prosper, have the new house, take the holiday, develop meaningful relationships etc." Then let it go.

☆ If you're watching shows on television that make you feel envious cut your cords for a while. When you understand what you really want, you stop putting feelers onto things that aren't so important to your life. After clearing your mind and discovering what you want bless with love your desires and the good fortune of others. This helps allow good to show up in your life.

☆ Cut your cords to anything that sparks flames of jealousy be it aforementioned television shows, video channels, news programs, celebrity feeds, books, magazines and social media. These external triggers can be removed with a little dedication and willpower. Instead, tune into that which soothes your soul and inspires.

☆ Bless your mother, father, and/or childhood caretakers with love. Forgive them for gifting you the belief that you do not deserve. Release it into consciousness and let it go.

☆ Obtain a photograph of whomever you're jealous of; look at it and in front of the mirror and practise EFT, Emotional Freedom Technique - find demonstrations on YouTube. Practise letting go of jealousy, feeling resentment, and feeling not good enough.

♥ Connecting to Love ♥

Love is the strongest force in the entire universe. We are placed on Earth through God's love, source love. The fact you're here, means you are fulfilling your divine purpose. No matter how stagnant, lost, unworthy, or scared you feel at times.

Divine love allows channels of angelic light to flood through your body. When you learn to reside in your heart, you open the gates to acceptance and balance. Learning to let go of who you believe you should be; allows ripples of white light to emanate from your being manifesting the experience of Peace on Earth.

Often times our consciousness is not functioning from a state of love awareness. We act out of fear, resentment, jealousy, and judgement. These emotions are powerful pullers. Have you ever noticed when you see something you hate, judge or dislike it starts showing up all around? Judgements are seeds that can attract weird and funky things into our lives.

Everyone lives in his or her own state of awareness. The universe revolves around our consciousness. You can create your own world. This can be your hell or it can be heaven.

To slip into states of love and open yourself to receive good fortune you need to halt five things:

☆ Feeling guilt and shame.

☆ Being critical of others and yourself.

☆ Being caught up in times other than the now.

☆ Consuming fear.

☆ Listening to the mind's chatter.

It's true that people in our past may have hurt us. They reflect the hurt and separation we feel in our own soul. We need to forgive and release them from our lives and/or consciousness. Sometimes when we forgive people they change, but there comes a time when we need to give up on changing others and discover the peace, love, and acceptance that we were always searching for and demanding from life, and people; that has always and will always live within us. The core of our essence is divine love. You are a gift to the world.

We can be incredibly harsh and judgemental of ourselves. You're not worthless, nothing of the sort. The divine created you, you are the divine. You are here on Earth for a reason, even if that path and reason is not yet clear. Let no one tell you, you're not good enough. Simply don't react to their negativity, don't buy into the game. Be at peace, present within your own heart, this is where the power of self-love, deservability and love-consciousness resides. It may be true for their reality; it doesn't have to be for yours. When you connect to your inner divinity, fears dissolve.

You deserve to be here as much as the next billionaire, and as much as the next beggar. Everyone is equal. Everyone. We come from love and we all return to love.

Regret is another painful trigger that can make us feel like peace is an impossible destination. Learn to accept yourself with the regret. It doesn't matter if you've made mistakes or haven't lived the 'perfect' life. Choosing to stay in regret is choosing to stay stuck in fear consciousness. You are lovable with all your perceived flaws, despite any mistakes.

Use regret as a signpost that you are slipping into deep fear energy that most probably has haunted your family for generations. Instead of focusing on regret switch your attention to all the good you can do. To the good that you are in this moment. When you switch your channel of perception, you start to move in new directions. Out of the past and into the now.

Regret can show us ways we would like to help the world and create positive change. Create a vision board, filled with images of how you would like to be of service in the world. Service helps to align our awareness with infinite peace. Remember when you serve another to remind yourself of the divinity within this being. To see spirit reflected in all. Act as an instrument of universal conscious love for all beings. Respecting others allows you to respect and forgive yourself. When you see love reflected in another being this opens your heart.

Humans are an interconnected race. The whole universe is connected, created through oneness. Separation is only a mind concept. Often we get caught in other people's energy fields if they've hurt us, or if we're fascinated by them and become obsessed with their lives. We are so enchanted by the dream of life that we forget nothing is permanent, that the seasons change and our time on this planet is limited, if it is real at all. When we are consumed with the lives of others, their future, our future, their pasts, our pasts; we forget to simply be. We need to call our power back to the present moment.

Be abundance, be joy, be peace, be compassion. Fill your body with love and live in the now, the present moment.

Fear consumption can have devastating effects on the entire planet. What is one of the easiest ways to sell to consumers? Fear. Fear paralyses us in life. If you scare a human long enough, you can tell it what to do, and it will do your bidding.

Consume love instead of fear. Here's how:

☆ Read positive, uplifting books.

☆ Practise positive affirmations in front of a mirror. For example, *I love, respect and accept myself.*

☆ Listen to positive affirmations constantly. A great way to start this practise is to leave affirmations playing in your home on a loop, even whilst you sleep. Your home will absorb the positive energy. Alternatively, listen to them on your phone with headphones, when you can. Play them in your car etc.

☆ Acknowledge your pain, anger, and self-hatred, let it be there, let it rest. Accept your suffering with grace and love rather than simply burying your pain deeper.

☆ Only watch TV Shows that uplift you and don't scare you.

☆ Stop watching the news, advertisements, reading the paper, and admiring celebrities, or the 'beautiful rich people', on the internet.

☆ Find people promoting positive messages that uplift your soul and choose to focus you attention there. You are worth it!

☆ Eat healthy foods. Anything that can be grown! Indulge in delicious fruits and vegetables.

✯ Carry rose quartz, a transformational crystal filled with love vibrations.

✯ Use natural skin care and essential oils as perfumes.

✯ Drink purified fluoride free water. Place words such as love, peace, joy, and abundance on your water bottles, to infuse them with positive vibrations.

✯ Meditate daily. Twice a day for half an hour or more is a lovely habit, sunrise and sunset

Every time you pass a mirror say, "I love you darling. *I really, really love you!*" Be your own mother, praise yourself in the way you wish to be praised by your childhood guardians.

✯ Garden! Gardening is so healthy and creative. It connects us to the fairies, and the earth has such wondrous healing powers! You can create a garden anywhere. You could even design a fairy garden!

✯ Paint, practise pottery, learn a new language, dance, find fun and uplifting hobbies.

✯ The Fear of Death ✯

Nature is ever changing. We are cyclic beings. To escape death, is to know thyself. There are only a few masters who truly know this and we refer to them as avatars. There's no difference between an avatar, billionaire and beggar. We're all the same; beings of bliss. The only perceivable difference is the avatar *knows* they are one with source. Once we realise a state of peace and enlightenment, desire vanishes. For how can you desire something you already are? Thus, the seeker becomes the seer.

For us living on the mortal planes of existence, death can be a very frightening thought. Most people don't like to discuss death. We're so busy running to and fro with tasks, we forget life is not permanent in this physical form. Consciousness is permanent. You take your consciousness with you, through many journeys in this world and into the next.

Don't you find it strange that the grieving process of life to death is rarely shown in movies and on television? Yes, we can watch people being mindlessly terminated, but we rarely watch the emotions of someone leaving their family permanently to embark on the next adventure. In most movies when a main character dies, they instantly come back to life. We also rarely see the beginning of human life. When have you ever seen a baby being genuinely born? Coming through the birth canal and emerging into the world? Why are we hiding from birth and death? Sacred passages upon which we all embark?

When you sleep at night, then begin to rise from a dream, do you want to come back to the now? Most often, if experiencing a pleasant dream, you want to hold onto the moment. A lover's kiss, a beautiful home, an exciting holiday, meetings with fairies... then you *wake up* and you think this moment is real. Your lover, mother, brother and sisters, etc. are real. We forget the dream and dive into this world thinking it is a truer form of reality. But is it?

If everything dissolves when we die, what makes us so connected and grounded in this experience? It's perfectly okay to be deeply rooted in the Earth experience. To have compassion for the suffering of others and ourselves. However, at some point we need to realise that life is an experience. It is not the one defining definition of who you are or the true source of your reality. If we cannot hold onto the reality of dreams, why do we believe we have such a strong grip in this moment?

We believe someone can watch us whilst we sleep, therefore we must be real. How do you know life is real? What if this world manifests the moment we open our eyes, and the people who surround us are reflections of our consciousness? Life is like an extended dream and we need to wake up. *Live with love and compassion for yourself and others in each moment, real or unreal, love is the path to take to reach inner freedom.* I believe in the goodness of the human spirit, of the divine love that empowers the existence of all. The real fear is a dream that can turn into a nightmare. If we surrender to the higher process taking place, and become of aware of the consciousness that witnesses the illusion that arises before us, the illusion dissolves.

This world and all that exists is an illusion. Until we're fully realised to this, other energies can influence our reality. Gods, goddesses, angels, demons, entities, planets, Mother Nature, fairies etc., it's important we delve into conscious perceptions and use tools to help raise our vibration from fear and into divine love. Letting go of your mental tendencies and desires, to become consciously aware of your divine presence here and now.

Capital punishment is a crime against humanity because it perpetuates the belief of fear. If you don't understand the suffering you are inflicting it becomes irrelevant. It creates negative karmic vibrations for everyone involved, which needs to be cleared. Fear of death, is used by higher powers to keep their minions under control. But what is death? The vibration of murder holds in the perpetrators aura. This needs to be forgiven and released so we can step into a path of light.

Most people are so afraid of death; they avoid the thought at all cost. Know you're one with creation. We're on such a small journey here, a blip in the consciousness of our existence. We're a single water droplet amidst an ocean. However, you are here, and everything here has been created for you. Allow yourself to know this. Take a breath. You are source. Love beats your heart.

Your abundance is as vast as leaves on a tree, all the blades of grass, every breath of air, and the water in the oceans. You're put here on Earth to have a spiritual experience. The experience is a quest to direct you to love. To the discovery of your true nature; bliss, peace, light, and oneness.

On a major journey, it's easy to get lost, and find ourselves stuck in uncomfortable situations. If we remember that divine love is our goal destination, we need only use our inner compass, that's connected to our heart chakra, and we will be divinely guided in the right direction. Even when you feel like you've made a wrong turn and have been on the wrong path for years you are still travelling the most healing journey for your soul's ideal pathway back home to your true nature. There are no mistakes, it's only research.

Return to your essence and dissolve into bliss.

You are being divinely guided. No one and nothing is separate from you. You are everything and nothing. Connect back to your higher source. Death is a gift, like birth. Take the pain, the pleasure, and transform it into love; and miracles will abound in your life.

In the palm of your hand
lies a distant land
Hidden from view, created by you
You've become a player, in this world of maya
Trapped in the net
we all forget
the distant shore,
isn't real at all
the place beyond
where you've forgotten you originate from
Life feels so real
Everyone thinks it's a big deal
If we evaporate when we die
maybe everything is a lie
Search for freedom,
that's your kingdom
We were right about something
life isn't; for nothing
Through the shadows let stillness peep
into your heart, embrace it deep
Rise from the sleep
Go back home
Remember you're never alone
You create the world
It's one swirl
Created with dust
Formed by lust
Desire and greed are not what you need
Discover the seed
watch it breathe

-     *Distant Worlds*

CHAPTER SIX

Sacred Space

Allow only those beings into your mind and heart who promote a space of peace, unity, and love. Images of death, destruction, shame, and war can break the soul's connection to infinite peace; unless we are aware our true form is spirit, one with love. These premonitions and the promotion of fear drops our energy levels so it becomes more difficult to merge with love conscious awareness. Watching suffering does not create peace, peace is found in the heart. When we live in a fear based mindset it becomes much more difficult to help ourselves and others.

Our outer world reflects our inner world. We have the power to choose what we read, what we watch, who we focus upon. Whom we *allow* into the horizon of our life. *What do you place on your horizon?*

Dreams and television shows are premonitions. Foretelling what may come to play in our future, simultaneous realities manifesting into the physical realm. They are virtual dreams to which we can become addicted. We can let negativity flow through our hands like small grains of sand or it can weigh upon our spirit, like the weight of a rock.

Positivity always outweighs negativity. You don't have to be positive all the time. We need to allow ourselves the freedom to move through our negativity.

Advertising works. If it didn't huge corporations wouldn't spend billions of dollars a day to sell us their stuff. When we switch off to destructive messages promoted through the television, internet, radio, pop songs, newspapers, books, magazines etc. we allow space for positivity. The average person spends at least four hours per day watching television. Be picky with what you watch, choose shows that uplift, inspire, and are not filled with advertisements, traumatic drama, material obsession, murder, rape, illness and war i.e. fear inducing shows.

Many television shows and advertisements promote fear and shame to manipulate us to buy products. They're made by wonderful psychologists who encourage us to believe to experience love we must step into the path of *their* grace. Be it through the purchase of a new hair product, makeup, car, clothing, etc. We all want love and we are seeking the inner truth that we are that. We are embodiments of the grace of God. Major corporations knowingly and unknowingly do not promote this truth. Why would you spend money on a product, if you didn't need it to fulfil an empty void?

When we're afraid we buy things that comfort us and delude us into feeling whole and complete. We're never satisfied because these products are not fulfilment itself. We need to nurture our spirit in such a way that we feel safe, lovable, loving, and loved.

War is a product, same as cosmetics. There are many companies heavily invested in the path of destruction, arms, military, oil, etc. When we feel unsafe, we become malleable; it's easier to sell us an idea, construct or product. Television teaches us good, bad, right, wrong, and can lead to severe judgements, on ourselves and others.

Once again, through your belief in your own light you can change the world. If big corporations realise we will no longer allow the veil of deception to sell us junk we don't need, they'll look to what we are needing and try to sell us that instead. Selling love, compassion, and truth.

Row, row, row your boat gently down the stream, merrily, merrily, merrily, merrily, life is but a dream.

Life *is* but a dream. In life as in the dream state, we can change the tone of the extrasensory experience through the power of thought. The key word, *gently,* applies to the way we move through the current of life. When we are gentle on others and ourselves life becomes much more bearable. When we're in deep sleep and unconscious to the awareness we are dreaming, we can suffer from nightmares. We can be eaten by sharks, mauled by tigers, and speared by enemies. In the dreaming state when we become conscious, we experience feelings of bliss, fulfilment, and peace.

The key is to stay present. When we guide our thoughts not through excessive control, but flow down the stream, to a better feeling thought, and another better feeling thought, we act as our own love guides. Journeying to places that are vibrant and loving.

There are awakened beings projecting thoughts of compassion and love and their joy is infectious. When you surround yourself with miserable people, it's easier to feel low. If joy and sorrow is contagious then it becomes very important who, what and where you focus your energy. Images and stories of violence, grief, negativity, and pain plummet our energy levels. Every time you read something, meet with a friend, or watch a movie ask; How does this experience, make me feel? Do I feel empowered and safe?

We're living in a dream, and we can change the channel, float down the stream or sink in bleak, black misery. Nothing can harm us, but the feelings surrounding darker paths can be trapping and excruciating.

The mind cannot differentiate between fact or fiction. That's why we become so emotionally entwined with characters when reading a good book or watching a movie. Our subconscious mind is involved and wants to know the outcome. We all want happy families, yet how much misery and suffering will we force ourselves to endure?

I'm not saying throw your television in the bin. Just be aware of what you're observing. Is it pointing you towards a higher state of awareness and consciousness? When we feel cheated by life, we often look to others to justify our perspective. This leads to a negative downward spiral.

Choose peace, choose love. There are individuals who float in plateaus of love, and ecstatic states. Regardless of what they are visually seeing or experiencing. They've reached a level of conscious where they are aware of the dream. Until you reach this point in conscious evolution, focus the mind towards feelings of love, self-acceptance and wellbeing.

Drugs and alcohol can induce love and ecstasy. Just like watching the television. They're another way to escape our present day reality. A way of trying to change the channel because we're not content with life and the emotions we feel. People become addicted to many things, caffeine, sugar, bad news, disappointment, money, self-harm, and yes drugs and alcohol. In part, they trick the mind to make it feel relaxed. A roller coaster of positivity and negativity, the trap of duality. When what we really desire is to feel a state of love all the time, to *know divinity*.

The high states of ecstasy experienced whilst taking drugs feels real. If you were experiencing the divinity of your nature through conscious awareness these feelings would never leave. The mind becomes depressed when we're taken out of the high. We can reach points of bliss, without the fear of having a negative drug related experience. When we know the truth of our being and release our mental tendencies and desires, we have bliss to keep. An acquired habit, of joy.

It's very important to claim your power and not to let others disturb your peace of mind. People often expect when they are feeling miserable, hurt, or angry everyone around them should know about it and become involved in their pain.

There are times when we become angry, hurt, and aggressive. It's part of our nature as human beings. As is peace. Still, you don't have to lower your consciousness surrounding yourself with people who are emotionally destructive; even if you love them. It's important for your own wellbeing, self-esteem, and safety to change the channel and say no. This is being gentle on yourself.

It's not compassionate to serve another out of fear. Be there for people, but learn that *you too are somebody and are deserving of love, peace, and respect*. Sometimes until we learn how to say no, we keep ourselves stuck in experiences which induce suffering. Give yourself time to go within and heal.

When we're surrounded with positive loving vibrations we become lighter and feel lifted. Life flows harmoniously, another individual's problems do not have to be accepted as our own. We can offer help to those suffering as long as we are not caught in a net of darkness and destruction by doing so. Forgiveness is a gift you can offer even when you're not in the presence of the individual you feel has wronged you.

When you tune into the channel of bliss; pain dissolves as does suffering. Choose channels of love, joy, harmony, and compassion for yourself. When you protect yourself, it empowers others. You cannot protect children and innocent ones if you do not shelter yourself first. Protection comes first through the choice to live a life guided by love. Positive affirmations guide love, positive television shows guide love, meditation, positive books and people lift our vibrations to states where we unite with peace.

When we choose not to forgive, fulfilling our hearts desires is halted through fear and resentment blocks. Once you allow yourself to move through anger - the self-protection barrier created in attempt to avoid fear - your perception of reality shifts. Moving into forgiveness, love, and grace, you release light into the world, which illuminates the path. It allows you to see through the dark and walk the path of light and love.

If we refuse to forgive, through extreme fear, stubbornness, the wish to be right, or suppressing our need to feel anger we halt our path and spiritual progression. Forgive yourself for being where you are right in this moment and forgive others for the hurts inflicted on you. Also remember that this moment is perfect, it is in divine alignment with your soul and the best place you could possibly be to forgive, practise compassion for yourself and others and to discover the divine light of love that breathes through your being.

When we choose not to forgive, a fork can be created in the road ahead. For instance, if a woman is cheated on by her spouse, divorces him, and chooses not to forgive; it's likely the next path in her road to recovery will be with another man who abuses trust. Even if it feels like a different experience, it's just a fork in the road. Until we learn to forgive and release the need to create experiences which we find hurtful.

These experiences are not here to hurt us, or tell us we are wrong or bad. They are here to help guide us to the light where we forgive. It doesn't matter how long the journey takes, as long as we reach our destination. Everyone is headed to the same place, love based awareness. So we can spiritually evolve and step forth into a magnificent state of happiness, and a life filled with joy.

We're like floating specks of dust illuminated by the light. Lit within from the glow of universal synchronicity and harmony.

Allow yourself to float and flutter absorbing the safety of the air that holds you buoyant amongst this Earthly plane. Drift through existence, letting your light shine bright.

If you do use electronic media devices, turn them off before eight pm, or an hour before you go to sleep. This allows your mind to unwind and for your creative juices to flow. It allows for detachment from the outer world and for inner awareness to be present.

Meditate, read a book, stare at the stars, drink hot herbal teas before bed. Read positive affirmation cards and value yourself. Your footsteps on this planet are valued and important. You are here because you deserve love.

Consciously choosing the people you associate with, the shows you watch, and the forms of social media you engage in can affect your mood and sense of wellbeing. If you surround yourself with people or media forms that scare you, or bully others, it's hard to feel safe. Especially if you feel scared from traumatic childhood memories.

Remember that verbal and mental manipulative abuse can be just as destructive as physical. Associate with people who care for your wellbeing and enhance your health, in body, mind, and spirit. When you do this you make way for healing past betrayals and hurts, creating room for love-based awareness.

Removing a favourite television show, social media, and people from our lives can be difficult. However, it is doable! First, meditate on cutting cords. You don't have to tell someone why you aren't as available, as they may try to manipulate or guilt trip you into association. You know when you are afraid to be in the presence of someone, listen to this inner voice. Also when you feel pain in your body, in association with an individual you are most likely being manipulated. Guilt seeks punishment. If you're being severely mentally or physically abused then please seek psychological counselling and assistance.

When we release negative self-esteem habits that allow individuals and the media to manipulate and bully us we re-enter the social arena from a safe vantage point. It's very important your inner child knows it's safe. That you are willing to listen to its cries and protect it whenever necessary. Listen to your heart.

Practise meditation, positive affirmations mentally and verbally in front of a mirror and do things that support your spirit. This may include arts, crafts, going for a walk in nature, visiting art galleries, places of worship, ashrams, yoga, laughing, reading etc. Write a list of things you can do that make you feel great, safe, empowered, and happy. Bring them into physical manifestation.

Be gentle with yourself. We sometimes love to cling onto things, even if they are not lifting our spirits, or making us feel good. This self-sabotage can become a war in the psyche as our heart fights our mind. We don't always make the right decision, or do the right thing. Self-punishment can be the biggest and most excruciating form of bullying. Learn to stay centred in the heart. Witness your life through eyes of love and compassion.

Give yourself the space and time to learn - like a baby taking its first steps. When we truly love the self, we release the need to associate with, and or attract people who inflict harmful energies on us. When we walk, talk and breathe love, especially self-love, people and places that openly love and respect us will be magnetically drawn to our aura.

Learn to listen to your intuitive nudges. A voice in your head, is guiding you with love if it's saying things that make you feel safe. If the voices are bitchy, weary, worried, obsessive compulsive, or misleading, delete them and reboot with positive programming. When we give our power over to negative mind chatter, we lose vital chi, energy in the body which helps us stay grounded, present, and vibrant. It takes time to learn a new language, so be patient as you learn to associate with media, magazines, music, environments, and people that raise your vibration.

There is a lot of talk these days about listening to your body, and following your intuition and gut instincts. Sometimes we jump out of our body due to trauma and become severally disconnected with our body. As we begin to heal and come back into our body we find it can be filled with pain, everything can feel like the wrong path. Try to become connected with your heart centre through meditation, yoga, or reading or listening to your favourite spiritual teachers.

As you become more comfortable with your body it becomes easier to feel the grace of your heart. This comfort can take years to achieve but it doesn't matter, just try to listen to your heart and gently the universe will guide your conscious awareness to this loving, guiding presence. It can also take only moments! Live open and receptive to the grace which lives inside your heart.

When you are kind to yourself, you naturally attract people into your reality that reflect this point of grace. We are always our own biggest critics. Buried within our ego is layer, upon layer of hurt, rejection, and isolation. The deepest fear being that we are truly separate from all that is. When people are cruel or unkind towards us as individuals the first thing to note is that the desire to be judgemental always stems from a point of self-hatred, so however bad 'they' have made you feel, this anguish lives within their own psyche. Even if it's been buried and ignored.

Somewhere deep within we believe we are unworthy and unlovable, people trigger this so that we can heal on deeper and more profound levels. This isn't a bad thing; everyone has perceptions and conditioned layers of unhappiness even if these fears are not being currently examined. You are in the right time and right place, when rejection, cruelty, or bullying occurs now is the perfect time to heal core wounds. Even if we believed they weren't present until 'they' hurt us, they were just buried deep within, so hidden we couldn't see or feel them. The good news is that once we heal the pain we no longer need to react with suffering and can connect deeper to our true divine nature.

Everything that appears or disappears on this planet is part of the illusion. For all the suffering, discrimination and bullying we endure it is not a permanent experience. Breathe through the pain, and allow it to act as medicine. Healing the deep wounds, that once remained invisible to the conscious mind, but on some level cut at our core being whilst we remained unawares.

The gentler we are on ourselves the easier it is to dissolve fear, guilt, remorse, and regret. These programs have been running on loops since childhood, and through many past lives. You are a beautiful, empowered, glorious being of love. As your walls of fear dissolve, you step into true empowerment, which is heart based, vibrant, compassionate, aware, and loving.

A simple switch in the mind, allows you to see the beauty of you. You are magnificent. You are made of the stars, sun, earth, and light. You are beautiful, whole, and complete. The light of the sun shines bright within you.

My body is a vessel
Spirit the mortar and pestle
You cannot crush me
I am already free
It's just a matter of dissolving reality
A spice is malleable,
that doesn't make it any less valuable
I am open to change,
for life to rearrange
The structure you've clung to,
doesn't define you
I surrender my soul, to a story untold
Life is divine, I am but a speck amongst mankind
Sometimes I feel small, like I have no worth at all
I am the wind,
the grass,
the being,
the mask
I take God's hand,
as I rediscover
I AM

-    Trust

CHAPTER SEVEN

The Lost Shamans

Ancient cultures for centuries have revered, and sort guidance from shamanic healers, medicine men and women, monks, saints, gurus, healers, witches and wizards. These wise ones were acknowledged as essential souls that helped communities flourish and function. Today these healers are almost bereft from Western society, and each one of us can feel the cut and wounds caused by a lack of spiritual guidance.

Many ancient spiritual teachers and beings who have come to raise the consciousness of Earth have incarnated into a world where their teachings are presently considered irrelevant. Some of these beings were saints, sages, and monks in past lives. They also may come to Earth from different realms of consciousness or solar systems. These sensitive souls that once would have helped to lead society are pushed to the fringes. They need to learn the value of their true essence before they can re-emerge. To reclaim their self-worth.

You know how aware spiritually someone is by how they make you feel. In their presence, is your awareness of your connection to nature, bliss, and happiness enhanced? Do you acknowledge that you are one with source? Pure light, radiating bliss, harmony, and unity? Sometimes a spiritual teacher can raise to the surface all of our subconscious fears and memories, but in their presence through divine guidance these begin to clear and heal.

There is a spiritual teacher born into most families. Often these are the intuitive souls, who do not quite fit society's standards. They often don't understand the need for hunting and gathering. Sadly, many end up living under bridges, in unloved environments, or completing mundane life paths that don't encourage them to express their gifts to the world. To share the essence of magic and wonder at their fingertips.

Many have also suffered extremely traumatic childhood abuse, ill-health, neglect etc. If you are one of these souls, allow yourself to accept yourself right where you are and then piece by piece tap into your magic and recall ancient gifts. Once this is complete, you will learn to attract abundance, respect, and help many other souls on their pathway to enlightenment. Or if you know anyone in your family who is walking such a path be there for them, offer support where you can.

If you are one of these sensitives, you can be very vulnerable to psychic attacks and judgements from others. Often people will use you to dump their own insecurities, as you are a healing soul who has the ability to transcend these emotions. Major issues can arise in the unacknowledged healer as the damage inflicted from residual dumping can manifest physical wounds in their aura. Especially when they feel responsible for the transcendence of the perpetrators issue.

It's important you learn to detach from trying to take on the suffering of others, compassion is important but you do not need to carry the burdens of your family and those that surround you. When you give people the freedom to heal their own pain, you empower them. Don't beat yourself up to help someone else. Love yourself. Love them and accept others as they heal and grow.

As these lost shamans abilities have not always fully developed, or they are unaware of their spiritual gifts they are aurically vulnerable. To allow yourself to heal practise cord cutting meditations.

Wearing black tourmaline with mica creates protective psychic barriers. The mica reflects back negativity to the one who has imparted it so they must learn from the outbursts they are projecting upon another's soul. Breaking the karmic cycle so that one can transcend into peace. Or use crystals such as selenite to raise your awareness to pure light.

Healers are needed on this planet more than ever now. Wake up to your true power. You don't need to do anything, or go anywhere, just bring love awareness to your day. You are already enough. Your presence graces this planet with peace, love and light and I thank you for your existence. This willingness to share love, to be open, heals everyone.

Many spiritual teachers have incarnated here to learn that money is not bad. As this form of worship overtook their place in society, it became resented and despised. Money is a means of exchange. Monks take poverty vows and these need to be released even in subsequent lifetimes. Many members of religious groups took chastity vows which can be reflected in subsequent lifetimes as frigidity and the feeling of sexual acts as 'dirty' in adult life. Remember, nothing is good or bad, our judgement calls in lessons so we can learn the truth of unconditional love.

This is a message from an angel I received: *Anything that isn't permanent isn't a reality, only a concept of the mind. Only consciousness beyond the mind is one true reality. From where does this reality arise?*

When we forget something, it loses its power - its impact on the world becomes minimal, if not non-existent. As society has forgotten the ability of these energy healers, their power has depleted. You need to reclaim this power if you want to embrace your gifts. There are people who would have you suppress your abilities. They are afraid of the light you bring and the peace this can create. Connect to your inner light.

Forgetfulness creates epic changes in society. If we were to forget the devastation and impact of war, it would become a shadow on the conscious field of existence. Not a powerful magnetic thing that could change the structure of Earth, as we know it. We watch images of killing over and over again, and we are taught the dates of wars. Justifying the need to kill, rather than embracing wonderful humanitarians such as Ghandi, and the power of love and unity. In school, when we are learning about past wars, our mind wanders, facts seem dry - this is intuitive higher guidance. We need to learn about peace, to create a peaceful world.

When we think of chocolate, or a favourite food, we feel hungry; we remember taste; desire floods through our being. Cravings have power. They symbolise the power of remembrance. If you reflect upon someone who hurt you, you feel physical pain in the heart. Love consciousness helps pain dissolve from our lives with grace.

If we learn to look within, we can attune to these gifts and these lost shamans and healers can be supported on their spiritual paths. So every family and tribe has someone who has knowledge and access to their spiritual gifts with whom to seek guidance.

Love can be the guiding light, enriching healing. Instead of being marginalised and living in poverty, these lost shamans can be revered for their innate capacity to love. It's not about finding a new modality of healing; it is about forgetting everything we have learned to be true about life, and at once discovering our true essence, the Self.

If you are wandering the planet looking for a purpose, or if you are worried about a person who seems unable to function in the world, please relax. Go gentle on yourself and others. The purpose of life is not to accumulate vast wealth or things, to win a race, or even be a polite person. It's to learn divine love, to discover who you are. We can do this by being gentle and kind, and allowing our own inner light to shine. Compassion, generosity, and kindness flow the more we tune into our soul's true nature.

Humans are quite a fickle race, and it can be easy for us to turn against one another. Even the purest soul, may lose touch with religion of the heart if they live in anger towards those souls who create pain and suffering in the world. Do not surrender your own light for the resentment felt when you've been hurt. The only true form of power is love.

We're all driven by self-preservation, thus our beliefs and present lives are perceptions and reflections of our present point of attraction. We hide behind the confines of our families, neighbourhoods, and cities. Even when we move away from our hometowns, we're still guided to people and places that reflect similar circumstances and safety zones constraining us within these pathways.

You wouldn't be reading this book if you didn't have a deep burning wish to let your light spread throughout the world. This light burns bright and creates a pathway for others to follow under your wings. You don't need to do anything, simply embrace the magic, wisdom, and love that resides within your heart. Your presence is a gift to the world. Your existence is enough. You are a divine blessing.

Release the need to be normal and allow the knowledge that your true essence is good, whole, and pure to come forth. Attract a life of peace, security, and harmony. When we feel peace from within our core, life reflects this and a life in harmony with the divinity of our spirit manifests. Conscious evolution is not needed for we are already the light we seek. It is only our point of perception that needs to be changed.

No matter where you've been or what you've done or haven't done, forgive yourself. Forgiveness releases all karmic ties and bonds. You are goodness simply because you exist. Even if you believe you have caused suffering to others and are so ashamed and believe you can never be forgiven, this is a trick of the mind keeping you trapped in fear, illusion and despair.

When we are out of touch with our true nature, experiencing the world through duality, we are more likely to cause suffering to ourselves and others. You are forgiven. You are a beautiful manifestation of peace and light. When you forgive yourself and others you become the ultimate healer and light being.

We don't have to act from states of peace and harmony all the time. Be gentle on yourself! It's perfectly fine to have fears and to experience resistance, we all do. However, it's now time to remember your true nature. To claim your hearts truth. You are nothing but love and when you live from this awareness, you bring infinite peace to yourself, others and the world.

Thank you for your presence. Thank you for honouring your heart. Thank you for existing. You are love, loved, supported and accepted, right here and right now. You are whole and complete, just where you are. You are a magnificent being of light and unconditional love.

I sparkle and shine
lit by the divine,
When the world feels hollow
I'm the one to follow
From the top, the world is a giant rock
a current, a swirl
watch it twist and twirl,
A light in the night
I shine bright
Surrounded by nothing, supported by the ether
I weather storms, of all shapes and forms
A reflection
A resurrection
My light is the spark
hidden in your heart
Let go
There's nothing to follow
You are complete, life is sweet
Release all fear, wipe away your tear
There is nothing but love
I shine this truth from above illuminating the dark,
recesses of your heart
Feel the light within
start to spin
and you'll see you're a star
shining your light upon me from afar

-    *Life as a Star*

CHAPTER EIGHT

The Power of Meditation

Meditation is the art of guiding the mind towards inner peace. It creates space to acknowledge the stillness within, and the spark of divinity that surges through our essence. Being present, whilst allowing our mind to still creates deep, lasting peace. Through the hardest times in my life, I've found meditation creates a space where safety can be found. For looking at the divine light within, allows divinity to reveal its hidden location inside the heart.

Meditation and positive visualisation creates a platform that can elevate your conscious evolution. Embrace self-love, and release the need to feel bad and sad. Attract forth feelings of love, peace, wealth, harmony, and security.

Through conscious evolvement, you become peaceful with what is. If you are hiding behind failure, as a method of disguising what you perceive to be past faults and mistakes, you need to realise you're already whole and complete.

When you connect to inner stillness, peace creates space in your heart. Meditation makes the journey from suffering and pain to love so much easier. All it takes is to acknowledge infinite space, the silence, and stillness from where all thought arises. Sometimes when we choose to heal our past hurts that we've been suppressing rise like a great tidal wave to the surface of our consciousness. Meditation is an empowering, free, and self-taught skill that can help us to look within to heal our deepest sufferings.

Ask yourself; 'Who am I?' Let go of the mind and watch from within where the first 'I' thought arises. If interfering thoughts come forth ask, 'From where do these thoughts arise?' Your mind will answer, 'From me'. Ask yourself, 'Who is this me? Where does the 'I' come from?' And watch as the self emerges from the heart. Feel heart space awareness.

Right here and now you can allow yourself to feel and fill the void before you. That sense of emptiness, before you take a leap of faith. There's a point of consciousness that comes before our thoughts, here we are at peace with who we are in this moment. When we think about the future from this space, we are free to connect without judgement or expectation and to live from our own inner truth.

Meditation and visualisations help to slow the mind. They help us to gain access to inner wisdom and to connect to source. You can use moon cycles during your meditation, a waning moon is a great time to practise release work and forgiveness. A new moon is a wonderful time to connect to and attract, that which you desire.

We can also create a sanctuary at home. Set up an altar filled with leaves, shells, crystals or images of things, people, Gods, Goddess's etc. that help you connect to love and feel safe. Your alter can change to reflect the seasons. An alter can recognise your inner transformation on an external level. Create your own retreat centre by leaving the telly off, lighting candles, spending time outdoors, and eating wholesome foods.

Visit people you want see, not those you feel obliged visit. Release the guilt of feeling as if you're acting selfishly. If someone is not right for you, then the relationship isn't right for them either. Sometimes no matter the amount of self-love we shower ourselves with, the best thing we can learn is to say, 'no'. You're not necessarily going to feel strong enough to say no every day, but honouring your need to say no is a start. A sign that you are willing to listen to your heart and put yourself and your needs first.

When you say no, it allows others who are being victimised to assert that *no* can be an appropriate option. Once we've said no, we have to acknowledge the bitterness and resentment we feel towards others and to clear this from our energy systems. You can also practise mirror work, Emotional Freedom Technique and let yourself know you are doing well and are safe. We are all doing the best we can with the knowledge we have.

When we pull back from environments a new pattern of love manifests around our being. Remember our loved ones know how to push our buttons and reflect to us the deep fears and hurts we bury in our subconscious. These perceived failures can be hard to hear out loud. When someone voices your fears you have the choice to say; "I hate so and so", or "I hate myself", or "How wonderful! I'm learning about my fears that equate to not loving myself. I now choose to let this go with love". Your reaction makes a huge difference in your life. It doesn't mean you instantly release pain and trauma, but you give yourself permission to surrender and let it all go. When you associate with people who make you feel afraid, this gifts you the opportunity to heal and grow. It doesn't have to leave a permanent sting in your psyche. Consciously acknowledged pain can transform your life for the better.

A good time to visualise is early in the morning upon awakening, or last thing at night before sleep. It's hard to focus on positive visualisations and daydreams of your future if your mind is blinded by dramas from your favourite television show or negative comments dumped on you during the day. Or if you're left discerning the climax of the latest novel you're reading. Replace these forms of information sources with positive ones.

Make time for yourself. When you do this, you become more grounded and centred. Once you've claimed your sacred space, in whatever way you feel safe and comfortable it's important to reprogram with positivity. Send love to the perceived perpetrators - who are highlighting where you need to love yourself more - and practise meditation. You *are* worthy of love and kindness.

A guru once told me it's necessary to spend at least one hour of the day (this can be all at once, or in two parts) in meditation, to shift focus and lift awareness. It may not seem to be making a big difference in your life, however one day you will have a divine experience, and you'll know the effort you cultivated in nourishing your mind and spirit, created space for magic.

Meditation has been the single most transformative healing tool in my life. When we're present with our thoughts, and learn to watch from a place of non-judgement, and compassion we create room for goodness to grow. We become still, and realise the thoughts we perceived to mask our suffering, hid the magic of our being.

It matters that you listen. That you give your heart and emotions the space to surface and be accepted in stillness. Often just sitting, eyes closed in silence, focusing on your heart centre can be so powerful. *Letting thoughts wash in and out, like ocean water lapping the shore.* At first it feels like you want to grab each thought, however as the mind stills, so does your thoughts. It is practise and simplicity rolled into one. When we listen; our inner light guides us and holds our hands in this physical experience.

If you have question, sit down and meditate, on your heart. When you're connected to your true source, you shine bright with the light of love. Answers come from a state of peace and inner harmony.

If you ever hear negative voices, you're not connecting to divine love. You may burn a white sage smudge stick over your aura, clearing any negative entities interfering with your auric systems and consciousness. You can also sage your home or meditation place to clear the energy and play light chanting mantra music. Sometimes there may be darkness or entity attachments residing in your aura that need to be purged, before you feel your light. Auric cleansing is like taking a shower and washing away dirt; it helps us plug into peaceful alignment.

Sometimes the negative voices are the stories you've adapted into your definition of Self over your lifetime. Rather than trying to escape them, simply watch the thoughts. When you don't try and fight them, the strength of their essence releases its grip.

The voice of love always feels pure and good, because you are brushing shoulders with source. It's like entering heaven on Earth. When you step beyond the light of bliss, you merge into pure consciousness.

When the collective consciousness of people, a place, or city you're associated with isn't harmonious with the desires you have projected forth into your life, guided meditations can be helpful to unlock the bonds. We attract people, places and circumstances to us that vibrate with us even if we feel stuck, scared and out of balance. Our higher self has chosen a life path associated with these environments so we can learn and grow. Our biggest life purpose is always to know God, Spirit, and the truth of our existence. We are always divinely aligned and in the right circumstance to develop and grow.

Accept where you are, who you are friends with, what you do, what you don't do or have, and the words you use to define yourself. You cannot trick yourself into thinking you love your environment and current point of attraction. You need to do this for real. Forgiving yourself for the life path you've chosen. No matter how painful.

Time is often regret, remorse and pains greatest healer. Once you can accept your situation you can place love there. Every time you judge yourself or life circumstance, say "I bless this with love and hand it over to you God/Source". Acceptance and love are both beautiful barrier dissolving healing gifts.

Remember spirit doesn't judge. You are eternally loved. You are love. You emerge from the source of creation. When you acknowledge you're here for a greater purpose, *to connect to your true nature, unconditional love, the truth of your being,* you see how life reflects to you that which you love and that which you do not love depending on where you're placing the most energy. This is so you can heal. If you didn't know where you were resisting love, you wouldn't know where you need to acknowledge love.

Love is a powerful force, and so is hate. If you learn to let go of the need to hate, love will conquer and become a beacon of guiding light in your life. If you are based in a fearful community, surrounded by prejudice, fear of lack, anger and resentment, coerced by feelings of powerlessness, you need to embody love, acceptance, and forgiveness. Armed with these weapons, you can move mountains. Look at Ghandi; he achieved monumental feats with little material goods, guided by the desire to serve from kindness and compassion.

Many people create a collective consciousness. When a belief is present in any environment it can feel easier to be swept into the stream of the herd mentality. However, if this group is living lives unfulfilling to your soul's destiny you'll become repelled and may even feel physical pain. No matter how fast you are moving in the stream surrounded by this vortex of consciousness. Often being repelled can feel like depression.

When we rebel, we push against the current and swim back up the stream. Those who we're rebelling against battle and plummet their way down the stream and they may hit us as we pass, causing suffering and pain. As we learn to let go and forgive, acknowledging the discontentment and discomfort we feel we float gently downstream until we are gently guided to the shore. Here we can remove ourselves from this current of energy to a place of positive alignment. We don't need to become swept up in drama.

Dislodging from energy currents often means saying goodbye. In death, we leave the world and we must surrender family, places, and physical experiences. In life, cutting our cords can be painful, as we do not know what the future will bring us. We have undiscovered places left for us to explore and this can be daunting. That's why it's a good idea to remove yourself from any circumstance or group consciousness with gentleness and ease. Comfort zones can be broken, but they don't have to be shattered.

When we remove ourselves from the stream of the current consciousness that surrounds us, we step onto higher pathways and sometimes people will reach out and try to pull us back. This can happen through negative comments, abuse, manipulation, and fear tactics. If this happens to you, acknowledge that a part of yourself is rebelling and swimming back up the stream. It's not a bad thing, however, if you can learn to let go, forgiving yourself and others, you can once again divert yourself onto the path of love.

If people are reacting to you albeit positive or negative, know it's because you have taken conscious steps to remove yourself from their pathway. On some level, this makes them feel uncomfortable as it breaks the balance of the collective conscious. You are learning to surrender and if you follow your inner guidance a new path of love will forge forth for you. You also pave the way for others, who, on an unconscious level would like to remove themselves from the slipstream of the collective conscious and return home to divine love.

When you take the time to practise meditation, you slip into higher levels of consciousness. Falling into streams paved by monks, lightworkers, angels, and intuitive guides. Connection to these streams helps nourish our spiritual bodies and physical direction. When your mind is at peace, you are given the opportunity to create new beautiful pathways.

Meditation is empowering as it allows us to see clearly. To set our mind on a pathway of manifesting a joyous, creative and happy life. Giving yourself the space to go within, takes only a few moments and is so rewarding.

Dissolve the mind, and discover truth. You are good, positive, loving, compassionate, and emanate kindness. For you are love consciousness itself. You are that. No matter where you've come from, what you've done, how you feel about yourself, you are a child of divine love.

Meditation is a simple practise. The goal of meditation is to quieten the mind so you can discover who you are. We want to dissolve the mind, let go of all thought and let the grace that permeates all to be recognisable by our being.

For all meditations:

☆ Find a quiet relaxing space.

☆ Sit crossed legged, arms relaxed, or lie down. The key is to feel comfortable, safe, and be away from distractions.

☆ Close your eyes and tune into your heart centre to relax.

☆ Start a daily routine. Once you've been meditating for a month or just over, it becomes a habit.

☆ Meditation is a way of plugging into source, of acknowledging that we are more than our minds.

☆ Allow what needs to come up to surface. When starting a meditation practise you may tap into buried hurts, rejections, fears, and insecurities. Sometimes the need to simply cry arises, this is all okay and part of the healing process. Our fears remain no matter how well we bury them so allowing yourself to be present with, and watch your inner emotions is a wonderful experience. Pain can lesson when we acknowledge its presence.

☆ Be gentle on yourself, you don't have to be perfect. When you can be present and content in this moment, no matter what you've achieved or feel as though you've failed at, you gift yourself the grace of self-love. From a space of inner-kindness we become accepting of others and ourselves. To create world peace, we first need to feel peaceful in our own skin. You are enough exactly as you are right now.

☆ Our brain likes to run the show, and often it leaves us feeling exhausted, unworthy, depressed, and terrible. Meditation puts your higher self in the driving seat and makes way for transformational inner change.

☆ You may like to hold a pair of crystals in both hands. This isn't necessary but it can be a fun way to connect and let your body know it's meditation time. Crystals help us relax and unwind. This can really help to highly charge your crystals and they become powerful tools of focus, relaxation, and strength of purpose.

☆ Meditate because you're worth it! You're worth the time. You're worth the effort. Realise that there is nothing but grace. You were put here by the divine and life is really so simple. We just need to learn to see it for what it really is, a divine experience of love.

Meditation Techniques

Technique 1:

☆ Focus on the brow/third eye. The space just above the point between your eyebrows. If the mind wanders, pull it back to this point.

☆ Allow your thoughts to arise, watch them but don't expand upon them. Just keep pulling back to the third eye.

☆ Start for 10 minutes a day; build to 30, then an hour. It gets easier the more you practise.

☆ This is such a simple technique. You don't need anything, or to go anyplace special. For me it's the most effective way to calm my mind and transcend beyond mindless, obsessive thought.

Technique 2:

☆ In this mindfulness meditation, we take our attention to the breath.

☆ Focus on the point between each breath.

Technique 3:

☆ Self-Inquiry (for more information on this technique read anything by David Godman on Ramana Maharshi or study the work and satsangs of Robert Adams or Papaji (Sri H. W. L. Poonja).

☆ Continually ask the question; Who am I?

☆ As thoughts arise, question the thoughts. To whom does this thought/feeling come? (The answer is always: It comes to me, 'I' feel/think it.)

☆ Who am I? Watch for the answer.

☆ From where do I arise?

☆ Who am I?

☆ Taste bliss!

Technique 4:

☆ Use a meditation track, or music, which is calm and nurturing. It can be nature sounds, classical, mantras, sitar music etc.

☆ Binaural beats are used in some meditation tracks (you'll need headphones), these beats help to release stress and improve relaxation. They help to slow brain activity and guide you into a state of deep meditation. Aligning to natural rhythms, which help enhance mental clarity.

☆ This is a great way to relax in meditation especially when the mind just doesn't want to settle.

☆ Allow the vibrations and tones of the music to help you relax, meditate, and unwind.

You light the dark
An infinite spark
Oh how you glow
filling the cracks that feel hollow
You're a messenger of the divine
You are sublime
You light the way
so we can see
what it is to be free
You're nothing but bliss
A ripple across the ocean of infinite consciousness
I salute the light
Surrender my soul
I watch my heart
release fears of the dark
To the story untold
the abyss of gold

-      Papaji

CHAPTER NINE

Protection & Auric Cords

In life, we attract. When we release our fears and step into the oneness of all-encompassing love, only good can come. However, if we ignore our connection to divine love or live in discordant environments, the shifts in our thought patterning can attract negative energies. This can create havoc on our energy system, due to adverse effects of psychic attack, or energy cords, which traverse between us and another entity.

Anything we are fearful of is created through divine love. At some point, it will recognise the source of its nature. Due to the experience of free will, we create and experience fear. The more we align with the source of our being the more we attract safe, comfortable, loving environments. As people realise their source, divine love, we create a peaceful planet.

Fear is a part of the illusion. Just as life forms from a dream, as does fear. Love, bliss, the silence of your being, is reality. We must slip into the place of divinity to eradicate fear. Find the place from where you arise, the silent emptiness will reveal you to yourself and you shall be free.

Whilst we live and believe in a dualistic reality, we may deal with fears. These fears maybe yours or they may be projected onto you from loved ones or entities. Thus, it's important to use ancient tools to connect home to the heart. For the safer we feel, the more confident we are to discover the source of our being.

Fear itself is the strongest form of psychic vampirism. Fear energy manifests as light energy being leaked from our etheric body. Which then affects our physical body and can leave us feeling tired, hungry, empty, and alone. When you allow fear into your life you become distracted from the greatness you already are. Forgetting the infinite source of your majestic, harmonious nature. We need not tend to anything that creates this illusion in our reality.

Worry is fear. When you worry about others, the past, or the future, you are emitting a fear vibration. Some of us are raised in environments where it's seen as caring to worry about people. This encourages the projection of fear. A healthier attitude is where we offer to help, and aim to feel happy in our own hearts. Feeling the flow of happiness creates a much nicer environment for all. It doesn't push people away with fear. It opens our arms to friendship, kindness, and true compassion.

Chi, prana, or life force energy is vital for our survival. The more we embrace its presence the more we experience, joy, and happiness, and are open and receptive to prosperity and a peaceful existence. When we connect, we become unhindered by darker forces, which may wish us harm or feel the need to suck our energy because they cannot find their own light.

Realise what makes you happy and sad. Learn to set boundaries that create a safe environment where you can flourish. When we're afraid, our mental, physical, and spiritual health is affected. We appear to disconnect from the universal energy that feeds us optimism, hope and aligns us with the true source of our nature, eternal love.

Psychic attack, or psychic vampirism, is an illusion of the light, for we are one with all of creation. However, as we are living a physical, dualistic light experience we sometimes feel separate from all that is. We are one with creation, yet we perceive this as a veiled illusion.

The brighter our light, the more we attract. As we awaken as light beings we can pull to us dark energies which (consciously or unconsciously) also wish to merge with light. This can be overwhelming when we don't understand how to handle the energy.

As you raise your vibration, you cut off lower entities. When we feel sick, depressed, or eat foods which lower our consciousness etc. we allow more energies both positive and negative into our awareness field. These energies can be so subtle we don't recognise their presence as they simply reflect in the way we feel. As you heal and lift your consciousness to higher plains of reality, negative energies fall away from your experience. So caught in the dark they cannot stand a light that shines so bright, it burns.

When we surrender our ego to the divine, fear leaves us. When we discover the source of 'I', we are magically set free. Until then we witness all from a dualistic perspective – seeing everything as separate from ourselves.

When you learn what may feed off your energy and why, you can best learn to protect yourself. This gives you sure footing to step forward into life with ease and grace. Through depression, drug and alcohol use, sadness, resentment, and bitterness, we create a feeding ground for lost souls (see following for description) to descend and harness our energy in ways we wish to avoid. Just because we don't always see what is happening this doesn't mean we cannot feel tugs at our psychic heartstrings.

Energy protection can be as simple as taking the time to brush your teeth. Creating safe psychic protection barriers makes sense when we interact with so many people. Intuitives are automatically drawn into the thought field consciousness of those around them and can be particularly receptive to others thought patterns and behavioural influence.

Often intuitive people, (one who has high levels of sensitivity) feel a distinct yearning to help others, this can lead them into all sorts of uncomfortable and abusive relationships where they want to help raise other peoples energy so they may feel more peaceful. Intuitives become very disturbed, as they are intricately aware of the suffering of others. They literally *feel* their pain. Always make sure that you honour yourself in helping others. Give with compassion and non-judgement and gift yourself by doing your best to associate with people who respect, love and also support you.

You don't have to be psychic to feel the energy of others. You need not be able to see the future, have visions, speak to angels, or even believe. However, it's good to understand how energy from spirits, angels, fairies, family, friends, entities, spirits and the thought field conscious vibratory rate etc. can affect our daily life.

You are the creator of your reality. When you claim this power, you remove walls, and can open doors to a love filled life. When we lose sight of this truth, we become battered and broken, falling into a stream where we perceive we have no control. This belief allows others to lower our vibrational rate and for us to cling onto people who may not promote inner love or safety.

Our consciousness shifts, like the tide moving in and out. Shielding yourself from embracing negative thought waves, which can be incredibly destructive, helps to allow your own light to shine.

We know to feed ourselves good food, to look and feel our best. But what about our etheric bodies? What are we doing to nourish our spirit and make it feel good? Meditation helps to fortify our minds extrasensory perception and brings confidence inner peace.

☆ Protection Prayer ☆

You may call upon Archangel Michael, Quan Yin, Ganesh, Buddha etc., or any being that you relate to and that helps you to feel at peace.

I call upon my angelic guides to protect me now, and remove any cords or negative attachments that lower my energy.

By universal law, I decree that the only beings allowed in or near my energy field are those of peace, love, and acceptance that help me to feel safe and recognise my divinity.

Thank you for your protection. Thank you for filling me with your love and light and giving me the courage to shine bright.

Thank you, I surrender all to love.

☆ Cord Cutting Prayer ☆

On every level of my being I call my power back to me now.

I am whole and complete in this moment.

In this moment I release the need for all internal or external contact with people or beings who are interfering with my energetic and physical body negatively.

Only white light, positive loving energy is allowed in my aura.

By universal law I decree this as so, and say no to any energetic or karmic contracts that interfere with my energy field and wellbeing.

☆ Lost Souls ☆

Lost souls are entities, which have left our world and have not yet past onto the next. They are Earth bound, even though they no longer reside in their physical body. These entities are not visible to most, unless you've developed strong clairvoyant abilities. However, like mobile phone signals and radio waves their energy is there, and can be of influence.

Negative Entities and Lost Souls are beings trapped in the essence of despair, lack and limitation. They can range from aliens, spirits, demons, curses, thought forms from malicious people, ghouls, to creatures trapped in fear.

On one level they exist in our reality because we believe the physical form is real. Until we surpass the state of duality, it is important to be able to protect yourself.

As the darkness doesn't allow you to naturally expand into your power negative entities must feed off the light of others to survive. They are beings fuelled only by fear. Essentially, they are energy parasites.

Most lost souls have refused to cross over. Embracing the sacred passageway of life to death. This may be due to unresolved life issues, family members begging them to stay when their time has come to die, etc. It will be a reason connected by fear. Sudden unexpected deaths, suicide (not always), shocks, demonic beings leading souls astray when they cross over etc. These deaths don't always lead to the creation of a lost soul; it depends upon the individual's soul path.

For loved ones that have died that you feel may not have crossed over to genuine light you can help them on their journey. Sit in meditation, call in high vibrational spiritual beings you are connected with or know that they felt comfortable with whilst alive. Visualise them, say their name aloud, call upon them. When they appear in your mind's eye wrap them in light. Reassure the person that you are crossing over that they are safe. See them surrounded by light and have the spiritual guide surround them in light until they dissolve into the light together.

You can use all the protective mechanisms listed at the end of the chapter to protect your energy field. Also, if you experience any lost souls that you have never encountered before you can show them light through visualising enlightened beings or angels coming to see them being taken across to the other side. Make sure you guide lost souls and watch them fully dissolve into an abyss of light. Ask your guides to cut any negative cords to your body and to fill you with divine light.

Some lost souls are simply lost. The friendly wanderers that have lost their way. For example, an old man that didn't want to leave his wife and refused to cross to the light. Other beings refuse to cross the bridge of life and death. These beings lose their inner connection to source and try to feed off the light of others. They may even want people to join them in their despair.

Some beings (especially demonic) will try to prevent light from being shared in the world. As you awaken and speak your truth, you may become under psychic attack, as for their own reasons these beings do not want light essence filtering through the Earth's astral planes. They literally can see your light in the astral realms. As you claim your power and turn your light on, they can see you as they hover over the Earth. This is why it is very important to protect yourself daily with prayers etc. to make it very clear that you are a being of light and love and not to be interfered with. Often these beings approach anyone with cracks in their auras, who are newly awakening or who have a very strong light presence on Earth.

There are also ethereal soul beings that can approach you with the best of intentions. Some beings due to karmic ties (many ties being reinforced through surprise deaths once more) stay bound to the Earth. These beings are similar to angelic beings, but they can be more ego driven. Often these beings will have a positive role to play. They may help people who are depressed and considering suicide, struggling with financial difficulties, family relations, or ill health. These beings often appear in dreams, and at moments of personal crisis and are here to help. There are highly evolved beings that clear the astral pathways of demonic entities and lost souls and can help you if you are ever being harassed by darker energies.

Calling in enlightened beings is generally the fastest and most effective and reliable way to cut any negative energies from your being and shield your personal space.

Lost souls can cause havoc. Sometimes they become so lost they don't realise why they are still Earth bound. If we're unprepared or have fragile auras, they can attempt to step into our physical body to gain control of their own lives and to become a physical force in this dimension. As they are trapped in darkness, they attach to beings of the light as an inner sense guides them to cross over to the light, even if this isn't their conscious motivation.

You can tell if a lost soul may be attached to someone, or yourself, through these basic forms of identification:

☆ The individual may have changed familiar personality traits and be acting out of character. Alternatively, they may have sudden urges and desires to do uncharacteristic things.

☆ Hearing thoughts that are particularly malicious. These beings can often shuffle through your thoughts and experiences and pull on triggers that bring you down into depressed and fearful states of awareness.

☆ Feeling as though someone is going through your mind, as though searching through a filing cabinet and regurgitating all your most painful and fearful memories.

☆ Repetitive night terrors or terrifying dreams. Dreams that are particularly fearful and violent may indicate possible etheric attacks.

☆ Sudden emotions of extreme terror.

☆ When you look in the mirror, you see other faces superimposed on your own.

☆ A voice outside the mind telling you to do something negative, or destructive. Or that you are not enough.

☆ Sporadic unexpected arguments with loved ones or friends. Especially after you've left a crowded party, pub or gathering.

☆ Faces and monsters appearing on walls. (This often can occur around children who are very psychically sensitive or open.)

☆ Physical appearance may suddenly change.

☆ Thoughts of suicide, dying, death entering your aura, whether you think you have conceived them they may or may not be yours as your higher self only connects you to life, light, and love.

☆ Hearing songs or music in your mind that you don't know, yet feel familiar with, but suddenly you seem to remember all the words.

☆ Strange cravings, i.e. feeling like a glass of wine and a cigarette – when you're sober and don't smoke.

☆ Feeling drained, lethargic and tired.

When you tune into your higher self, atman, you know that love resides at the core of your being. If you are under severe psychic attack tuning into this force may appear illusive or impossible. This is a sign you're connected to something other than your own energy force.

There is a stream of white light that flows through your crown chakra right down and into your body. This stream is the one that makes us feel joy, bliss, and alive. Sometimes lower energy consciousness, will try to attach onto this light and feed off it. Stealing it for its own survival. When these cords link, you may hear negative thoughts about yourself; or feel afraid, or anxious etc. They can become twisted repetitive patterns. These thoughts come into your being because as your higher self struggles to release itself from this trap it loses connection to the light that is feeding your infinite nature, the expanse of your eternal creation. You become trapped in your mind and watching the mind can be likened to watching television. Sometimes it's brilliant and inspiring, other times you keep changing the channels to be bombarded with junk or fear based propaganda.

When under psychic attack your higher self keeps feeding you more and more light, but you're trapped in fear. Darker energies feed off the fear and you lose connection, what feels like, to the light at all. All you see is blackness, repressed fears, and negativity. You cannot expand or grow when you're so afraid.

Drugs, alcohol, extreme fear, traumatic events, food allergies (especially to genetically modified foods), large arguments, negative texts, horror movies, the news, can all lead us to try to escape pain which can be experienced on Earth. We jump out of our bodies, which unfortunately makes us easy targets for negative beings. We become controlled by fear.

Become aware of the light of divine love, source energy, flowing into your mind, and into your body. You'd never truly seek to harm your own self. Your higher self resides in light based high vibrational stratospheres; you can reconnect with your true source of power, aliveness and inspiration.

We switch off to the power of our true essence through our cultures desire to be inundated with fear, shame and guilt. When you perceive that your soul is good and that you are an energetic, immortal being of the light you live from a higher level of awareness. These negative entities lose their grip on controlling your consciousness.

Call in your guides, guardians, angels, and light beings to help free you from the bonds of fear. We are one with all creation. When you know that you are all powerful and that nothing can interfere with your essence unless you *allow* it to do so, you begin to feel at peace. Powerful to create the life of your dreams, powerful to experience happiness, powerful to attract that which you desire. This life is yours by divine right and universal law. Proclaim that only good and light can enter your energy field!

Awareness that all is a reflection of divine love helps to clear illusions of fear, fear based beings and energy attacks. Stay focused on the source of yourself, discover the light and bliss before the 'I' emerges. When you feel the silent space from which breath arises, you dissolve the need for fear-based experiences.

We are all learning and developing, as we flicker between heart based awareness and living in a physical fear based reality. We can experience different emotions and energies.

Love dissolves all, even our worst nightmares, so it is best to simply continue to reconnect to the heart. Especially as we slip into fear based programming and awareness. The more people who tune into this heart space the easier it becomes to align with. It's good to be aware of light and dark energies as we can dissolve illusion through knowledge, shifting the screen of our perception. With this awareness, we can clear our energy and step into a safe and loving life and environment.

♥ Loved Ones ♥

Many parents, and or guardians, feel they own their children. They have raised them, groomed them, shaped them, and taught them how to behave, how to be. There are households where this may not apply, however we shall look into this attachment perspective first.

There is a certain expectation that floats through many parents. They've spent so much time grooming their prodigy that when their child acts in a way different to the parent's beliefs, they may be perceived as uncouth, disloyal, unrewarding, unreliable, and unrealistic. But you cannot simply return a misbehaving child and upgrade as you would a car. We've been marketed the concept of upgrading over and over again that we somehow think we have a right to project this desire for 'the best' onto our families. Sub-par or differing experiences are deemed as unacceptable. Yet these projections are of the mind, they are not reality, and they do not celebrate the divine and unique nature of each individual beings experience.

We're all divine children of the universe. Created through love. We are source energy manifest in physical form. We are all connected, all one. What did we come here to experience? How did we hope to learn and grow?

Only wanting the best for your family and no one outside this unite, is a limiting, fear-based mindset. It can be a hard habit to break as we have deep connections and bonds with our loved ones. To be truly of service we need to share our love and compassion with all. Everyone on Earth is your family.

When you are true to yourself, despite the judgements and criticism of others, you create the brightest pathway for your inner light to shine. Your purpose unfolds in a way where you allow yourself to be guided by the universe. Becoming the truest version of you is the greatest gift you can give to the world. This flows out beyond our immediate family and creates a ripple effect allowing the consciousness of the entire planet to rise. Acceptance of the self is by far the most unique and powerful healing tool. You are a vessel of love, light, and freedom.

When we plug into our connection with source, we are given access to unlimited power. Not simply the power generated by another soul and their connection to source. When we believe we gain vital energy from others, we seek approval. This limits our natural source of energy.

Manipulation occurs when we believe that others *are* our source of light, wealth, creativity, love, happiness, success, etc. When you plug into universal love, the manifestation of these desires becomes *unlimited*.

There are small cords that flow between us and other beings. We're trained to suck upon these cords for energy. The love you receive is what the cords allow back and forth. There is however, an all-pervading life force energy that allows the existence of love, life, and creation on the Earth plane. When we tune to this energy and allow it to flow, the love we have access to is unlimited.

Distractions in life can pull us outside of ourselves. We're left wishing to unite with inner peace. This yearning to connect can leave us feeling empty, isolated, unsupported, and alone. When we become aware of divine peace in this moment, we unite with the infinite truth of our eternal soul's divinity. From this energy, creation is born. Love is a marvellous thing, ever-expanding, limitless; it releases fears of good enough, nice enough, deservedness and opens us up to the true force of limitless all-connecting oneness.

It isn't through living up to expectations that you create happiness. You need to look to your heart and connect to the divine. Even if you don't know what to do, the first step is to discover you are already happiness itself.

Cutting cords to those which love us, and care for us can be a form of protection. This is because the ties that bind us with family, lovers, friends etc. are some of the strongest etheric bonds that exist. For example, if a lover leaves you, your heart may feel as though it's shattered into a thousand pieces. An emptiness engulfs your aura and you feel you'll never love in the same way again. You're left feeling they have stolen something from you. A piece of you now resides with them, but you cannot access it.

That which you are experiencing is the cutting of cords. The releasing of bonds forged and constructed through love, lust, and fear. Fierce, tightening and binding. When a soul releases its tether and steps away from us, we feel the severing of ties between two physical souls. Through embracing all channels to love you welcome divine love, which is all pervading and ever present, to be acknowledged and felt by your being. You don't need to 'get love' from another person, when you are that love, and when recognise you are infinitely connected and supported.

It's so important to forgive our parents and caregivers, whether they are dead or alive. To release patterns of resentment, guilt, shame and blame. You are enough for creation and so are your parents. Parents are not much older than their children. We all have a limited time on this plane of existence and sometimes we expect our parents to know everything and to be there for us in the way we wish, yet this too is a form of control. Some people become lost in trying to be the perfect prodigy for their parents, forgetting they are already perfect, whole, and complete simply because they exist. You are always enough for universal spirit, the divine hands which created you, as are all beings.

Energetic cords may also be created when we cling to a family member who we don't wish to die, is ill, mentally unwell, or depressed etc. If someone in your family is suffering, without even realising it they may tap into your life force energy. This sounds parasitic at worst yet when we care deeply for someone, we'll do anything to keep that person alive because we believe they are a source of our happiness. Even if it means sharing our light with them.

There is nothing wrong with a constant sharing of light essence; we do it every day when we interact with beings, and our beloved pets. It can be rewarding and uplifting. If you're constantly worried about another whom you love, you may be allowing your energy to flow into their auric field. Problems occur when you receive no light or joy in return and aren't plugging yourself back in through meditation, rest, universal awareness, etc. In this circumstance, you become drained as you consciously or unconsciously allow your own vibration to lower to continue the relationship.

Physical symptoms may occur through, fatigue, discolouration of skin (no rosy cheeks), a bleak outlook on life, empty feelings, or a deep sense of inner hollowness. They result from the deep sadness experienced when you think of this person. It's sad that they are suffering. *You need not suffer to help another to feel good.* This creates a drop in energy for everyone involved. It is vital you stay empowered in your own energy, when in contact, and when you're thinking about them, in order for your natural radiance to return. You are always of the best service when your own gateways to divine love feel safe enough to remain open.

Light consciousness is available to all. Sometimes we forget the magnificence of our being. Especially when we encounter shock, trauma, abuse, and neglect. Deep wounds can become the greatest catalyst for healing. Our pain is resolved as we realise that it's not up to others to save us, for we already are complete in this moment. We are love itself.

No matter the bond, you hold no personal responsibility to raise another from the dark. When you try to shift another person's energy you can sometimes unconsciously block their personal power, as you attempt to shelter them from feeling pain, and suffering. It is very important that we support people. It's also important that we allow them to heal. This is where inner empowerment is found.

You know when it is not in your highest good to be lifting others, it's a gut feeling, and happens when we try and force someone to change, this is not supportive it is simply an attempt to control another as we believe when they are happy we will be too. Attempting to change another person - especially due to our own guilt - creates resentment, depression, and a stagnation of blocked energy.

Be present, be there, and allow them to be guided to claim their own power. You can be a force of light and help them lift their energy, a magical gift. Nevertheless, the best gift to first give is to take wonderful care of yourself and your energy system. This empowerment will help you embody light.

You are in no way responsible to change another or to interfere in another's relationships. Yes, you can consciously give advice when asked, but how often do you energetically become heated, angry, or upset, just by thinking of the pain, manipulation or suffering another being is going through? We instinctively try to act like mamma and papa bears to our loved ones, or people we care for but most often its best not to try and change someone else or their experience. To be responsible for the emotions we have entwined in their problems, and to claim back the energy we've allowed to drain into the other person's problems. Be there, be present and available. Stay calm, happy, and well in your own body. This is the best help and service you can be to the situation.

You can still be kind, generous, giving, and thoughtful. Compassion makes anyone align with their heart and is a lesson we all need to learn deeply on this planet to prevent wars and major global suffering. This is to say be of service but honour yourself, your feelings, and monitor your emotions. Relationships become toxic when we place *our* negative thoughts and controlling instinct into the mix.

Be present. Be love. Be peace. You are of best service when you take care of yourself. Sometimes we try to fix others when we are attempting to escape our own pain and life. The stronger you become the more you can support others and yourself.

Beautiful affirmations for these scenarios include:

☆ I release all need for interference and lovingly claim my power.

☆ I claim my power with love and light and release the need for energetic meddling.

☆ I am whole and complete; my light is bright and lights the world.

☆ I attract all love, all good, and joy.

☆ My family is loved and supported and so am I.

♥ Toxic Relationship ♥

High-energy light beings bring love and their angelic blessings to the world. *This is you if you are drawn to this text.* You shine a bright light that others gravitate towards. Friends, family, lovers, people don't always understand the high vibrations emitting from your being - this vibration can come through any individual, regardless of past, race, wealth, education, religious background etc.

There are different levels of conscious present day experiences. We're all unique and divinely connected and at the same time we experience different perceptions and emotions. It would be weird if the entire world felt hunger at exactly the same millisecond. We are all having a *vibrational* experience on Earth, every emotion, and sensory perception is governed by a vibratory rate.

People drawn to high vibrations of light may wish to emulate it; in short, they want what you've got. They may try to pull what physically appears to be your essence into their own being. Emulating the way, you dress, speak, walk, talk, or what you do, in attempt to receive a ripple of your good energy. Through Neuro-Linguistic Programming we are taught to emulate others to make them feel comfortable and to mimic in order to create the life we want. Babies learn this way. Copying is healthy, it helps us expand, and it's how we grow. It becomes a problem when an individual is so blinded by another's light they fail to see their own.

You may have karmic bonds to people who try to suck your energy, or feel obligated to help increase their happiness. Through this desire to almost become another person, a decrease in their own self-love and rejection of the good available to them through their unique essence occurs. They no longer want to be themselves, to learn their own lessons. They simply want to take your experiences as their own, to shell you out, and grow into your light.

This is a subtle and manipulative form of psychic attack. It can be intentional or unintentional although it does happen. Look at the great scientists who had their inventions stolen. You cannot steal another's light, but this is what's being attempted.

By taking someone else's life. Living a vision that was never theirs to begin with, these people live a half-life. Never connecting to their own true destiny. Emptiness comes when we try to live through the eyes of others. The body moves forwards but a void remains. We have greater destinies than we can imagine and to tap into this provides an infinite resource of hope.

If this has happened to you, firstly you need to learn to forgive the other person. This can be hard when you feel they've *taken* something from you. Secondly if you've ever attracted this form of psychic leaching, you've probably suffered from poor self-esteem, or didn't feel worthy of your angelic light. You may not have understood how to protect your energy field. By seeing the situation for what is sheds light, this illumination can help to reduce fears of it happening again and forgiveness of the past so you may trust once more.

You can take something and possess it, but you still haven't learnt how to draw it into your life. It's much more positive if we attract things through feelings of goodness, without the guilt that shows our lack of trust in universal law. Guilt shows us a space where we need to shine more love and forgiveness. Be gentle with yourself. Make sure your relationships are reciprocal, that you are encouraged and nurtured by family and friends.

Sometimes the ties that bind us through love, to our mother, father, lovers, children etc. can be driven by love, but undermined by fear. For example, if you wish to move to another country and confide this desire to a trusted loved one, they may become afraid. Worried for your safety. Fearful that you will outgrow them. Scared they'll lose contact with you. Afraid of their imminent loneliness. Fearful you'll leave them all alone for good.

These fears can be placed into your energy system through cords that bind. Love strengthens cords and your auric system and thought consciousness may become tampered with fears, worry, and concern. Hence, the manifestation and coming to fruition of your dreams is put on hold until you:

a.   Clear your own fears and doubts.

b.   Release the stress and hidden fears from those meaning you only good, but causing you harm, through their well-meaning fears. A well-meaning fear is simply a fear, and it needs to be released for freedom to be felt by the soul. (Simple acknowledgement of fear attachments begins the release process.)

c.   Step into your own power, forgive yourself, and forgive others. Learn the lesson and let go. We decide karmic lessons before arriving on Earth. No matter how painful, it's good to learn to surrender all to divine will, this can bring enormous relief.

Cutting cords can be painful, as no one likes the thought of losing out on love. We're afraid of lack, when we are already that which we seek.

We all crave a mother's touch, kind words, and safety. However, we must recognise where we are holding ourselves back for fear of lack of love. Rather than experiencing the truth of unconditional, unequivocal, all-encompassing soul love. Love which knows no fear, no bounds. Love which nurtures your hearts, brings you freedom and recognition of your divinity.

Clinging to fears holds us back, and those whom we love. To cut cords you can meditate and visualise white light emanating through your auric system. Bring a large sword down about your person; let it cut through your etheric field. You can pray to your guides or whichever deities bring you to a state of peace for help during this exercise. See cords releasing between you and those you love and see them and you protected in white light. A light separate from yours, but safe and whole.

We can also use crystals such as black tourmaline; worn on our body at all times to protect ourselves and release the need for etheric bonds holding us back. Cleanse the tourmaline regularly whether it be through a light bath under a full moon or a salt bath.

☯ Karmic Reflections ☯

We are all instruments of the divine. When a harp plays, musical notes vibrate and touch our hearts. We are cosmic instruments, dancing through life to the music of divine love.

Sometimes when we think we're under psychic attack; we are simply feeling a direct result of karmic backlash. If we judge another, we feel the sting of that judgement. This doesn't make us bad; it just means we need to realign our heart space. Sometimes we judge to self-protect. To hide from feelings of failure, shame and guilt.

Most often, these reflections occur when we are feeling afraid, at work, the supermarket, school, and around people en masse. We need to learn to accept ourselves and others. Not everyone will act in ways we believe to be appropriate. We cannot control another's responses, actions, thoughts, and emotions. We may feel they are not of a high vibration or have negative energy. But we can accept their actions with compassion. We also have the choice as to how we handle their freedom to express their view and perspective of creation.

By judging or criticising another, be it ethereally, mentally or aloud, we:

☆ Invite them into our reality sphere. Which stimulates law of attraction i.e. we step into alignment with this being.

☆ Choose to lower our own energetic vibration.

☆ Judge ourselves. Judgement of others is always reflected in the amount we are able to love and accept ourselves in the here and now. Someone truly at peace within, does not judge.

As soon as we lower ourselves to focus on energy we dislike, we allow these judgemental feelings to boomerang and hurt our energy system. Not only do we project our fears we also become controlled by these fears.

When you see something you dislike, *bless* the person or situation with *love*. Most likely, it's a direct reflection of things you've suppressed or fear within yourself. When we move into alignment with love, and stop feeding the fears we pull towards us abundance, hope, and happiness. Feelings that uplift us can help us move forwards with courage and confidence. If you can learn to project love instead of resentment and anger, all that's boomeranged back is love.

Thus, it's important we're conscious of our own thoughts. Is the negativity we feel a projection from within the self? If it's from an outside source it can be cleansed, released and we can practise cord cutting. Please note; even if it's coming from outside, it will still reflect subconscious yet undealt with issues or karma. Spirit projects where we aren't witnessing through eyes of love, so we learn to bow to all through the grace of oneness. A simple switch in our own thought projections can have instantaneous healing and releasing effects on negativity forged from conscious feelings of anger and resentment.

When we feel rays of universal light throughout our body everyone becomes reflections of divine love. Surround yourself in environments and with people wherever possible that reflect love and nurture your soul. You can be pulled down by group energies.

The more we embrace love, the more we step into the true essence of our being. Projecting and feeding judgemental thoughts creates instant karma - you begin to feel dark. When you project love, you immerse yourself in divine bliss.

No one person's actions can steal your joy, unless you allow it to be taken. Create a perceived reality of love. Through the excuse of, 'They made me feel this way,' be it anger, judgement or resentment, we give our power away. We need to heal wounds of the past.

It is more than okay to process your painful emotions. To honour them and give yourself true permission to feel them and express them. Once they have been acknowledged and felt it is wonderful to reach a state where you feel peace, calm, and equanimity. Sometimes we find it difficult to truly face our inner fears and this leaves them hovering at the periphery of our thoughts. To release something it is imperative that it is acknowledged, heard, accepted and forgiven.

Accept that you're a divine being of light and love. Perfect just the way you are. Release the need to blame others for negative, uncomfortable emotions. We use our judgement as an excuse and controlling factor for why we are not allowing love into our reality. We are responsible for our thoughts and energetic projections. Our power returns when we choose to live in the light.

☆ Comparison ☆

When we compare ourselves to another, we hand over a vital piece of our energy. Our chakras stream energy towards the being (or thing) we're observing. The angst, jealousy, and pain we feel is created by our energy leaving our system and becoming attuned to that which we don't possess. It's like eating junk food; it looks good, but can make you feel sick!

For example, when you compare yourself to your partner's ex-lovers you can be left feeling insecure, not enough, ugly and ashamed. You are putting negative feelers out. For no one who feels really good about themselves and loves their soul with complete openness wastes time judging others. When you judge you are harming yourself and literally giving the other person your time and your energy. In effect, it's as though your psychic attack has rebounded.

The word comparison holds the lexigram of prison. We imprison our creativity and progress when we succumb to comparison. The only people comparison benefits are those who profit from individuals feeling so badly about themselves that they will do, or buy anything they believe will make them feel worthy, whole and complete. Comparison is a wonderful manipulation tool that is so ingrained in our psyche it can sell us virtually anything.

Comparison sometimes feels like fun. We've been taught for many years to sum ourselves up alongside our fellow man. But what is the point? So we feel low, bad and hope to buy a product that'll make us feel better about ourselves? An instant high or feeling of wellbeing?

We've also been taught to worship and compare ourselves to celebrities – movie stars, singers and sports stars etc. The more we compare and worship the more we literally give our life force energy away. Staring at a screen in worship of an illusionary God is emotionally destructive and leads us to becoming self-critical shadowed by feelings of worthlessness. Even though at the time we may not consciously recognise the dissolving of our internal positive power, we literally give it away as we compare and idolise that which is purely self-serving - serving the being who is accumulating the energy of worship.

Comparison serves a purpose. It makes us want to be more than we are; we need to realise we already are enough. We are more than enough.

Instead of leaching energy onto those whom you wish to be better than, or who make you feel as though you haven't achieved enough, bring love awareness back into yourself. Learn to meditate, talk about things that interest, and inspire you. Remember when you were a child making sandcastles on the beach, or playing in a garden. Call upon happy memories, ones that make you glow. Where life is focused on peace. Calling your energy back through peaceful focus and intention is so simple and it can make miracles manifest.

☆ Removing bullies & verbal abusers ☆

Love is all pervasive, all-powerful, and can transform connections we hold with others. A bully functions by first hitting on social, physical, economic or other issues we fear, bringing them to the surface so our fear energy increases pulsating in self-defence.

The added tension, self-defensiveness, and distress we feel when we think of a bully feeds their egoic self. It gives them a feeling of empowerment. Power created through feeding off another's fears. Only a person suffering from self-revulsion with a lack of personal inner strength will resort to this form of energy leaching. They feel it's necessary to put another down to feel good about themselves.

It's important we learn to stand up to bullies. Often bullies feed off our reaction, so it's best to forgive and forget. Try your best to avoid being around bullies, they are not worth your energy and time. Some bullies are simply looking for a reaction. When you don't react they lose interest and don't claim that powerful hold of fear over you that they were hoping to achieve.

Often bullies are attracted to our own inner judgements, lack of acceptance and criticism of the self, often we are our own inner bullies. Has anyone ever been more critical on you than your own mind?

It can be hard to understand why someone would choose to become a bully. Maybe they are jealous, or feel so badly about themselves that they bully others to deflect attention away from their perceived flaws. Many bullies are extremely fearful; they attack in an attempt to avert unwanted attention away from themselves. Pray to your guides and angels for help. You can also contact any authorities that can have them removed from your world. Seek people who know how to professionally handle abuse.

Bullies live in mental environments which house dark energies. They are literally unaware of their own light and seek light, or 'feel good energy' from their prey. Oblivious to the fact that the power, validation, and self-esteem they are seeking already lives within them. They are the light shrouded in the illusion of darkness.

Most bullying starts in the home. Then as we go out into the world if we are already afraid, or feel broken, we attract others who feed off this energy. Say no, stand strong, stand tall, and find a way to remove yourself from the situation.

We can choose to embrace the world of the bully and believe their judgements. We can also choose to forgive and forget. Building a life and a world in a safe and nurturing environment.

You are worthy and deserving of love and support. After bullying has occurred, it may take time to rebuild trust in the world. Trust comes by acknowledging your own divinity. Allow your angels to nurture you as you rebuild confidence and courage. Practise positive affirmations and seek people who support you and love you unconditionally.

Self-love Affirmations:

I love and accept myself as I am now.

I love myself and allow happiness.

I only attract positive feeling experiences into my reality.

I am worthy of all love, light and good.

I am safe and loved.

☆ Unconditional Love ☆

When we connect to unconditional love, the basis of creation, all other platforms for clearing our energy systems become obsolete.

Love is the most powerful cleansing force on the planet. Divine love is the purest, highest vibrational frequency emotion. Everything else is a distraction, and can lead to suffering.

Even our reactions, to situations which appear to be out of our control, can create more suffering. Sometimes we need to realise that something bigger than our ego and thoughts is driving our life. That we are being divinely guided every step of the way and if something happens that causes us deep trauma, and hurt there will be a reason for the suffering. It is time for us to wake up to the divine truth of our nature. To come home and rediscover soul truths once more, remembering that we are divine reflections of bliss and love.

Love can be defined as a strong feeling of connection between two physical beings. This limited perception of love brings us to a state of awareness that love can create pain, suffering, be unreciprocated and can be broken. This kind of love is best defined as lust. A temporary boost of adrenalin that makes us exhilarated and excited. Like a drug, it can leave us with a hangover or feeling terrible when things don't work out as anticipated.

It can become confusing as we interpret true unconditional divine love with other descriptions of love. It's like those adverts where they say, "It looks like butter; it tastes like butter, but it's not butter!" When we become enveloped in the truth of divine love, we become magical powerful lights.

Love perceived from an egoic vantage point is aligned with turbulent emotions such as jealousy, hate, rage, lust, desire, and fear, which is why it directly reflects these emotions. Anything that feels like love and leaves us feeling empty and hollow, is not the universal divine love of which we speak.

We tend to store that which we experience as love and reserve it for special people. For our Nana's, for our lovers, for our mothers, our children and pets. We feel and have been taught it's somehow wrong to share our love. Confusing true love with trust and lust.

Often in relationships we bury emotions, confusing love with lust - when they are two different things. Shutting ourselves off from unconditional love only causes pain, suffering, and fear.

You can tell the difference between love and lust. Feeling love for a neighbour, for the Earth, for the grass under your feet is very healthy. Lust when used in a way that is betraying another leads to guilt, shame and regret. Divine love leads to a life of wonder and peace. It releases all judgements, guilt, and suffering.

We need to give ourselves permission to feel divine unconditional love all the time. We've been twisted to perceive it in alignment with lust and fear. Feeling the pain we endure when lust (perceived love) isn't reciprocated, from our lover's, etc. we start to shut down our heart chakra. Believing it's responsible for our suffering when in actuality it's the tool that will clear all pain on this planet. Unconditional love is the true essence of creation and the core of our very being.

We are always looking for divine love in every action. We reach for emotions that make us feel better in the world. In every moment we are reaching to experience more love. Fearing deep within that we are unlovable. When love is our true nature.

Even if we feel we are completely worthless nobodies, we are acting out of love for humanity as we feel this world would be better off without us. This action is resonating with a direction towards love as we are looking to benefit humankind by the lack of our presence. We are also looking to travel to a place where we will feel better than the nothingness that encompasses our soul. Not realising that through embracing our trauma and pain we are literally standing at the doorway to inner wellbeing.

When we embrace our fears and dissolve into the nothingness, we discover that the barriers to love were constructed by our minds, not reality. Divine love is found when we let go. If we were all aware of the truth of our nature, there would be no need for suffering on Earth.

When we feel true love, we are open to helping others. We have empathy for their suffering. We become generous. We share our ideas, our food, our hearts, our homes, and lift consciousness in the process. Becoming more humane; less defensive, and more open to life. That which we fear holds us trapped in judgement and blocks the flow of good into our life.

So what is true love? True love is the essence of creation. It is what we are made of and from. It is the truth of our being. We are made of love, light, and bliss. We feel true love when we tune into our heart chakra. When it's open and radiates warmth. When we are one with divine love, we're receptive to all the good that's in the universe.

True love is also reflected through unconditional compassion. Buddhism talks a lot about compassion; to me it's another word for unconditional love. When you are compassionate, your heart is open, it's not driven by lust, or sex, or greed. The warmth of your heart that is unconditional, generous, and all pervasive drives compassion.

"Thousands of candles can be lit from a single candle, and the life of the candle will not be shortened. Happiness never decreases by being shared," Buddha.

The light that shines in our heart is a powerful force. The light of love fills our hearts. When we tune into this energy all that radiates from us is pure source, it cannot be extinguished. Sometimes we forget our candle is already lit. As we open to this awareness, we allow for the inflow of pure goodness into our lives. We shift the axis of the universe and pave a path that will bring good unto others and us. Our desires and perceptions may shift aligning us to true happiness.

It's safe to share the light of love in our hearts. When we fear its power, when we suppress it to fit in, when we deny it's all pervasive force; we suppress our bodies, our immune system, and our wellbeing. You can suppress this conscious field when you're not awake, but if you deny yourself your true nature, you allow others to step in and take advantage of the light you possess. Deluding themselves that they are not made from the same fibre. Without giving yourself a glimmer of affection, you create a way for cords of fear and doubt to latch into your energetic field. Tuning into our hearts, we create a pathway where the negativity that polarises our existence and current limited beliefs of love can be dissolved.

Compassion is oneness. It dissolves illusions of them and us. If all beings can learn to let down the walls that block their hearts, we can create everlasting peace. When we use love as our guidance and first point of reference in communicating with others and see everyone as reflections ourselves, true harmony will manifest in our world.

Fear guides us off the path of love. It disconnects us from our emotions. Various levels of fear can shut down our bodies, immune and emotional systems. In shutting down, and turning off our inner lights we create suffering for others and ourselves.

The only reason we become afraid is because we see things from a dualistic perceptive. Everyone physically dies at one point. We all come from a source of energy that is governing the whole of creation.

Opening our heart chakra feels scary, as we fear we may get hurt. But from already living in a closed perception of reality we're hurting ourselves. Transmuting our fears, we open to a world where we attract love, peace, wealth, and harmony.

Evolving and connecting to love is a learning process. Remembering the truth of our being can be a journey. It's okay to walk forwards in love and then close up and walk in the other direction. We can never truly turn away from love for it is the fibre of our being. We can simply open like a lotus flower to the light and gently become more and more aware of our true nature.

In loving ourselves, we choose to be around people that reflect the love within. Sometimes if our light is shining bright, it may make others aware of their own suppressed emotions and sense of separation. It's okay to hold out your hand and offer help. If someone wants to stay at a lower standpoint of judgement and negativity, you can let them go. Self-worth manifests through heightened perceptions of love.

Whenever you face potential confrontation go to the mirror, look deep into your eyes and say, "I'm here for you. I love and approve of myself. All is well."

Sometimes when we're scared or anticipating the worst, our spirit jumps out of our body. In our adult place, the little child steps in feeling frightened, scared, and alone. This is okay, reassure yourself that you are safe and that you love, approve and accept yourself. Take deep breaths and focus on the heart. Tune into unconditional love.

Life mirrors our core beliefs. If we've wandered off our path, we need not lose ourselves further by taking on the judgements of others. We also need to remember that where we are is a stepping-stone to moving in the direction of where we want to go. We are never stuck, even though we may feel held down by toxic emotions, and core beliefs about who we perceive we are. Remember that we are witnessing life through a keyhole. Our perception of reality is limited to the vision that we have. Sometimes as we learn to step into our own power, this can disgruntle loved ones and they may manipulate, or become angry to try to get us to fit their structured perception of who they think we are. We are boundless beings of love and infinite possibility.

People can knock our path of love off balance. Most often we're affected by the bonds between our families. These are very strong karmic ties we chose to deal with when we incarnated on Earth. Even if they are not in our vicinity or we've broken ties, the thought of them, their voices, can still shake our core. As until we love ourselves, we look for approval, love and acceptance from others. It's not bad or wrong to look for approval, it's in our nature. However, becoming aware of divine love helps us move forward with grace.

True freedom comes when we walk the world without burdens of fear, guilt, shame, jealousy, and judgement. These emotions rise to the surface and need acceptance as we heal. The power of our focus on love serves to dissolve the blockages that have kept us bound to suffering, hatred of the self, and fear of the unknown. To walk in love is complete freedom.

☆ Identifying & Releasing ☆

It's imperative to transmute our awareness so we can be in the world and release the need to carry another's burdens. When we allow for this release, we step into infinite potential.

Mindfulness, compassion, and being willing to step into higher frequency vibrational states are strong forms of defence against psychic attack. Divine love has the power to dissolve all cords and help us embrace the now. To identify painful arrows in our energy fields and aid in forgiving and releasing those who we allow to cause us pain and suffering.

When you're unwilling to step into higher states of vibrational awareness, you create openings where you may endure painful experiences. However, benevolent forces influence us all. These help wake us up and guide us in aligning with our higher purpose.

As we begin to acknowledge our inner light, we awaken into this world fresh as a newborn. We swaddle babies with blankets, kisses, cuddles and cribs so they don't fall and hurt themselves. It's only appropriate we take the same care of ourselves as we open to new states of awareness.

Remember your light, the spark that made you, is the gift you bring to the world. You're divinely created. Awareness helps create a new pathway for humankind.

When we allow ourselves to be guided by our higher intuitive awareness, we create a vibrational pathway where we connect to like-minded individuals. When we surround ourselves with people who say they are open to change, but stay stagnant in negativity it can manifest as physical pain. This is a direct effect of psychic attack and or unprotected psychic cords and energy currents.

When we are first tuning in to higher energy, we may wish to help everyone, and at the same time feel the need to isolate ourselves. Places like bars, restaurants, and shopping malls churn with different people's vibratory consciousness. If the collective consciousness is happy then we uplift one another. If it's sad, confused, or simply lost, then this misery enslaves, pulling upon our heartstrings, bringing us collectively down to lower states of consciousness.

Desire to release the need for attachment to fear and lack, creates pathways from where answers of truth arise. They may manifest in forms of simple conversation, on signs, number plates etc. For example, you may be wondering about moving home when a butterfly lands on your shoulder. This is a positive indication that you are moving in the right direction.

To interpret signs just look at how they make you feel, good or bad? What emotions do you associate with the signs you are being presented with? The universe always explains things to us in a way that we can understand; we just need to learn how to interpret.

Feelings and emotions are our best guide. When my Granny died, on the day of her funeral a double rainbow appeared over my parents' house, this was a positive sign that she was watching over those she loved.

Everything is a direct reflection of source. Our angels want to help us, and always guide us to discover our inner light and peace. So we may plug in to prosperity, bliss, joy, and inner calm. Asking for divine guidance can shift your energy instantly.

If you feel afraid, lonely, or resistant to change, don't force these emotions to get out of the way. Simply be aware that source is guiding you towards higher truths, to peace and love. Through awareness of our true nature, all fears, doubts, and negative programming can be healed. We can transform.

The physical pain we feel can result from neighbourhood pain and suffering. As we open up, we become aware of the suffering of others. We may become a psychic sponge for all that's troubling neighbours, friends, and family members.

If you're particularly attuned to family or friends who stay in lower vibratory states, you may feel this pain through thought association. This is okay, it's our body's way of guiding us when we are being pulled off our path and are allowing ourselves to take on another's hurts.

When you see someone suffering, what do you see? A victim, or a beautiful angelic being trapped in a body, hoping through despair to awaken to the inner light within their soul? When we lift our point of focus, our vibrational consciousness shifts.

Suffering often manifests from our beliefs and wish to help carry another's burdens. When we let go of hurt and denial, burdensome feelings that permeate our being, we transform. Love and acceptance create a pathway to grace, abundance, joy, happiness and good health. From this point of attraction and reaction, we resonate with the truth of compassion, understanding, and non-judgement. This bestows a ripple of love and peace in the world.

You cannot alter another person's destiny or karma. However, through eyes of compassion, not pity or judgement, you can offer support and love. We are never truly locked in one predicament. Life floats about us like a swirling dream and at one point our predicament, our life, will change as we die and move on to explore more adventures.

Whilst we are present and aware on this planet, it is important that we listen to our heart and follow the guidance and wisdom that comes from within. Your heart always forges the way towards compassion, forgiveness (of yourself and others), and surrender. Your heart is not laced with feelings of shame, regret, or guilt; it is the embodiment of true inner peace. Connecting to your heart is the greatest gift.

Our individual thought field consciousness affects the whole universe. Don't look to others for guidance. Seek the light that shines within to allow your true nature to bless humanity and create a path of freedom for the entire universe.

We need to learn to share our energy, with ourselves and with the world to light a path of peace and non-resistance. The light and the dark may battle but we can rise above and shield our energetic field through our point of focus. By choosing what we allow into our conscious reality and through our simple will to align with love and know God, peace and joy within.

Psychic Protection and Preventing Psychic Attack

How to strengthen your energy systems and protect against psychic interference:

☆ Meditation is a wonderful way to calm our auric interactive field. It opens us to angels, enlightened wisdom, and guidance from source. When we connect with love consciousness, we release fears, and judgements, which appeared to protect but only held us back.

☆ How many times after an argument with someone, have you declared you'll never go back? Only to find yourself in the same situation? This is because we resist the flow of love and fight fear. If we say, *I choose love before succumbing to the fears of another,* whether it be their projections or a reflection of self-rejection, we allow empowerment. If we bless the person and situation with love, we allow ourselves to forgive and forget. We make room for change. Not simply a replication of the cycle of fear and rejection.

☆ If you have any inkling inside that you don't want to do something, or attend an event allow your fears to guide you, not torment. Fear is present for a reason; it's up to us to listen. Until we still the mind and hear what the fear is trying to say, where it's serving us, it may overcrowd our thoughts. A simple question is will this event, these people, raise my energy?

You are of best service to the universe when you live from a high vibrational state of being. Past fears may torment you, and these may need deep healing. This is okay, we don't want to be driven by terror, but it is also important to honour our fear and then find the most healing way to act that creates a sense of calm, safety, inner peace and freedom. Simply stuffing our fears down only creates more resistance and can create a volcanic effect of terrifying emotions and proportions.

☆ To release negative energy, spellcasting, or imprints from the words of people who have crushed your self-esteem visualise someone who has hurt you. Place yourself in a position where you are taller than them. See the darkness or arrowed words that they have sent towards you and say, whilst bringing your palms into a stop position, "Right back at you".

You can leave it at this or reprimand the person projecting the painful energy towards you as a stern teacher type figure disciplining an unruly child would. Such as, "I no longer give you permission to interfere with my consciousness. Go away! Get out! I prohibit you from interfering any more. Now leave!"

You may afterwards want to practise some forgiveness exercises to release any painful bonds. But this is an excellent way of standing in your power and saying, No! Without having to go through the drama or pain of direct confrontation.

☆ Be brave enough to turn in a different direction. Your body will guide you. It may be time for a change. Often the thought of changing our circumstances brings forth fear, guilt, and shame. Try to meditate in acceptance of these emotions or to consciously practise healing methods (such as past life regression) that can help you move forwards.

Blessed angels and spirit guides follow your every move. Ask them for help. This can speed up or smoothen your pathway to love, healing, and abundance.

☆ As a conduit for light the more you connect, the more you hear, smell, see and receive divinely guided messages. Divine messages are always delivered with love, and it's up to us to act. That little positive dream that's been whispering in your mind is your spirit guide's way of saying, "Take this path!"

☆ Create healthy boundaries. Understand that people may react when you change patterns you've followed for years. Choose healthy life affirming affirmations such as, *I am divinely protected,* or *Life supports me, people support me and I choose harmony.*

☆ Often when we open up spiritually, and really affirm that we are ready to connect to the light and love within a whole heap of suppressed and fearful emotions surface. You aren't being energetically attacked you are simply viewing your deep, painful, buried emotions, for the first time.

Give yourself time, and space to heal. Perfection isn't found in simply being peaceful all the time. Embrace your anger, shame, and regrets, allow them to be there without judgement. Love the negative emotions and find peace through lack of resistance.

☆ When we allow our ego to guide us, we step into fear. Sometimes our egoic mind will project fear thoughts on top of creative or inspirational ideas. Learn to identify these thoughts and release them through humility and the ability to serve others. Here we learn to surrender. Thus, we can step into more light filled, peaceful, and prosperous experiences.

☆ Wear a large quartz crystal to strengthen your aura along with black tourmaline, kyanite or obsidian. Cleanse these crystals regularly.

☆ Selenite is wonderful for attracting light consciousness awareness. It naturally attracts light, and is sometimes referenced as holding the energy of 'liquid light' solidified. Placed in water selenite will slowly dissolve. If you want to feel energetically lighter, this is a wonderfully precious gem.

☆ Sleep on your back with a large crystal - any natural crystal you connect to - placed just below the ribs.

☆ Place tourmaline, or a bag of crystals under your pillow. Note: Tourmaline can reflect your own negative thoughts and hidden fears and can feel aggravating when you're suppressing your shadow side and acknowledgement of personal self-worth. It is wonderful for shielding from negative energy if it's being projected onto you from an outside source.

☆ You can also grid your room, desk, bed etc. with quartz crystals, black jade, tourmaline, selenite, or any other crystals you feel attracted too.

☆ Have your living space designed according to Feng Shui. This ancient scientific art enhances environments. Good energy is allowed in and negative energy is released. It creates spaces of wellbeing, longevity, and prosperity.

☆ Clear out your closets of any clothing that no longer fits you, or items that clutter cupboards and you no longer use or love. Letting go, allows space for new memories, healing and abundance.

☆ Listen to positive music that aligns you to spiritual realms, raising your vibrational frequency.

☆ Silk is wonderful for energetic protection, it helps to remove unwanted thoughts, be them from yourself or another. It can also protect crystals, tarot cards, etc. from negative energy.

☆ Burn white sage throughout the home, and over your body. Be careful not to burn fabrics. Carried over a saucepan whilst smouldering prevents sage embers from scattering. Keep doors and windows closed as you cleanse and then open to release. Repeat mantras or positive affirmations whilst cleansing and then see white light filling the space or body.

☆ See a waterfall of light flood through your body then shine out. This helps to cleanse your energy. You may wish to extend your light and clear the stagnant energy in your own body, home, office, school, gym, city, country, the world or across the entire universe!

☆ You can give yourself a light bath morning and evening to protect your energy. Visualise a waterfall washing over the top of your head down through your fingers and toes taking away any dark or stagnant energy. See yourself diving into a pool of white light, which flows through your body. Water can help cleanse the soul and etheric body.

Visualisation practise strengthens over time as you become more confident. Premeditated protection is wonderful for avoiding destructive situations and can be used after confrontational experiences to cleanse the aura and to release anger and resentment.

☆ Visualise yourself grinding a sceptre into the Earth and see protective light spill out all around you.

☆ If you feel someone, or a spirit entity steps into your etheric field, you may say, aloud, "Out! Leave now!" Asserting your barriers prevents entrance into your sacred space.

Call upon your guides, angels, guardians or sacred spiritual masters and proclaim; "Only pure positive energy has permission to enter my energy field. I command by universal law that only positive energy be one with my spirit."

☆ Visualise stepping into a protective bubble with mirrors that wrap round the outside deflecting negative energies. Alternatively, step into a reflective pyramid with a solid floor.

☆ Visualise a safe space. It may be a room with two beautiful dogs standing guard. A practised visualised safety space creates a sacred place where you feel safe and sheltered, which is easy to find when you need it most.

☆ Affirm: *I claim my power through love. I deserve positive experiences. I release the need for interference.*

☆ It's important you remember you're one with source energy. This allows any lower levels of consciousness to be eradicated from your thought field. Fear promotes fear, and when you connect with the divine, you become aligned to love and light.

☆ Take a cleansing bath. It feels wonderful to cleanse our energy bodies, whilst giving our physical body time to relax. Soaking in a tub with three tablespoons of sea salt, ½ cup of baking soda, three drops of ethically sourced Palo Santo essential oil, and a couple of drops of lavender essential oil, helps to clear the spiritual body. (If you feel really out of balance add more salt.)

☆ If you feel unwanted energy on you, have a warm shower and wet your hair. Then turn the shower to cold. Let your hair soak up the water and then shake it all out, releasing and letting go. This helps remove memories and patterns from hair membranes. Afterwards dress in white.

☆ Bathing in the ocean is a wonderful way to release negative energy cords and attachments. Salt water purifies the body.

☆ Spend time with animals. Animals are wonderful healers. A loving animal aligns us and teaches us the truth of our nature. Animals love unconditionally, it's powerful to recognise that we're worthy of this love. Their love has no bounds.

☆ Spend time with young children. They are so connected to the earth and the moment and even when you are taking care of them, they are healing you. Reminding you of innocence, happiness, boundless joy, unconditional love, and how to process emotions.

☆ Wear a pendant filled with vervain and cinquefoil. Bless the pendant with wishes for protection.

☆ Take your shoes off and walk in nature. Walk along the beach and through soft grass. This strengthens your spirit reminding you of your connection to all.

☆ Qigong is a wonderful practise for strengthening the heart and energy centres.

☆ Yoga helps to squeeze out and stretch our chakras and remove unwanted blockages.

☆ Avoid consuming sugar, caffeine, chocolate alcohol, and drugs. These can place cracks in the aura and allow your energy system to be easily penetrated. Consumption can strengthen anxieties and create fear blockages.

☆ Go to bed at sunset, whilst arising at sunrise. Falling into sink with nature strengthens your energy field.

☆ Upon rising and before going to sleep rub vetiver oil on the back of your neck in a circular motion. This essential oil is wonderful for psychic protection.

☆ Read positive books and meditate before going to sleep and upon awakening. Don't watch the news or read the papers, or compare yourself to people on social media - just prior to sleep and awakening you are very energetically open and vulnerable. Use this openness as a gift, not as a time to pressure yourself or to distract from your present point of wellbeing.

☆ Have crystal healing, Reiki, past life regressions, or energy work sessions with people whom you trust. You can even share energy healing sessions with trusted friends.

☆ Call upon your ancestors to protect and guide you.

☆ Tune into positive thoughts. Repeat affirmations and mantras.

☆ Learn to love and accept yourself. Self-worth denotes that we deserve only positive vibrations in our energy field.

☆ Accept yourself. In this moment, you're worthy and deserving of love.

☆ Connect to love, the highest vibration of all! When you see divine love reflected in all you dissolve fear and interface.

Honouring Your Divine Nature

Sometimes we're so afraid to be different we try to hide ourselves. Disguising the truth of who we are in the projections of others and the projection of our self. We want to fit in, to be loved, because it feels safer for the survival of our physical being. Love is really what we are all always searching for.

It costs us financially, physically, and mentally, as we suppress our soul and our being, to be more 'lovable'. This love, is not true love, it's fake and thus the rewards for embracing it are docile. Through acceptance of the eternal nature of our being, the facade of fitting in drops away. The magnificence of our essence is left.

Sometimes we deny our spiritual truths, to try fit in with our family and social circle. This is like pretending you cannot speak English when you're fluent. Or wearing trainer wheels when you can ride a bike. It's not to say you need to push your beliefs onto another. However, it's healthy to speak your inner truth when you feel guided. We often suppress our gifts to appease others. This can lead to you feeling dominated as you suppress yourself and allow people to flood you with the intricate details of their life.

When you let go, you allow others to share your journey, not hold you back from taking flight. If someone has a problem with you being you, this is cruel, fearful, and not coming from love. Learn to love yourself and watch them drift away from your life, or change their attitude. It's taken lifetimes to get to this experience, so why deny your true nature? Allow beings into your world that lift you to light.

When we experience illness, blocks in creativity, deep depression, fear, anxiety, worry, we've forgotten true nature. All these emotions are guiding us back home to our heart. We want to be in a state of peace and love that's why it's so uncomfortable when we feel restless and insecure. These feelings are literally pulling us home to our hearts.

Some beings incarnate on Earth from higher dimensional planes to be the light and lift the consciousness of humanity. They come with the sole purpose of letting their light shine. When they enter the vortex of the Earth's sphere, they often forget past programming, arriving with amnesia of sorts. It's a dangerous task as they are often blinded by the influence of those that would suppress the light. When they incarnate they often sign soul contracts that also protect their awareness. For example, if they deviate off their path, they may have the desire to terminate their mission. The reason these light beings become suicidal, depressed, sick etc., is because they know they're going down on the rungs of higher consciousness. However, it is a paradox in a way as checking out (suicide) does not release us from karmic bonds, and the pain of life that we haven't consciously gone beyond. As until we realise we are one with divine love we are stuck with all of our emotions (positive and negative) and karmic bonds, whether living or dead. As life carries on in the astral planes, and on Earth until we dissolve our minds rigorous programming and our structured beliefs of reality.

Regardless of pre-programmed agendas, everyone in life is travelling the same path; we are all seeking the truth of the self. The discovery of who we really are and unveiling of our divine nature as we merge into light, grace, and love. We never truly deviate from the path of love, no matter the mistakes, pain, or suffering we endure. For life is love, and so are you.

We are here to learn, to embrace love, the truth of our nature and experience this planet in the process. You are on planet Earth for a reason. The experience is not permanent so you may as well enjoy it as much as possible. Earthly life is a gift, no matter how challenging. It doesn't last for anyone no matter the rewards, failures and successes. There are many wonderful experiences you can have simply by changing your physical and emotional circumstances. Changes help to start the healing process. When we are willing to look within for the answers (to the emptiness) at the same time as making physical changes, we can transform our lives.

When we drop our vibrational consciousness to fit in, sacrificing our light in the process, protective instincts kick in, and either we'll have a spiritual awakening or may break down, physically, mentally and emotionally. Pain and suffering is simply a reminder to get back on your path. To release judgement, fear, shame, and guilt and remember your true nature, love, light and peace. Have you ever noticed the more pain you feel, the more you crave love? Pain can be a gift that makes room for no distractions, for nothing but peace found in the heart. The discovery of your true nature is your divine destiny.

Yes, not everyone may like you on Earth. But this comes from limitations, distrust, jealousy, and masking of the self. To judge, hate, or violate is to retaliate against the purity and simplicity of our true nature. Trapped in a cage, with the door wide open, we have the choice to fear life and the projections of others, or to progress into the truth of our being. It's okay to feel scared, this is part of living, part of the experience on the journey to discovering your true nature.

Only when we allow the stillness of creation to flood our bodies, do we release fear. Projections are fear. Touch no thought of the past, present and future and you allow yourself to release the bonds of karma. Quietness of the mind creates inner peace.

"There is no word for the silence within."
So my guru said
I took this thought to bed
Feeling a state of love so deep,
I fell asleep
Upon Awakening,
all conscious thought began breaking
Love, Consciousness, Bliss
The desire for peace has led me to this moment,
God's kiss
Relationships are projections of the mind
Release all thought, surrender, unwind
So it would seem,
that every thought,
experience,
voice
is all but a dream
Silence within
is the place from which,
the truth of life shall begin

-     *The Silence Within*

CHAPTER TEN

Healing Emotional Pain

We can live from a state of love awareness, experiencing good feeling emotions such as gratitude, joy, happiness, and bliss. Alternatively, we can live paralysed by fear, embodying hatred, anger, regret, jealousy, and resentment. When we feel love, we come closer to our inner truth and our path becomes easier. When we are choosing thoughts that create fear - this may be conscious or unconscious - our life can be thrown into turmoil. Even being still becomes a task as we're constantly looking to fulfil our desires and needs.

When we learn to be still, and live in a state of unconditional love, our true purpose, and genuine desires on Earth are revealed. Through intention of service, rather than personal gain it's easier for us to be guided by spirit. Karmically this pathway opens us up to receiving.

Our purpose becomes masked and shadowed in a world where we believe we have to get this, or do that, to experience being loved. All it takes is to realise the fact that our essence is love so we can let go and allow our inner journey to unfold. Once we find inner peace, our outer world mirrors the love we feel inside, and life flows.

The first affirmation we need to use, and connect to is, *I am love, loved and lovable because I exist*. When we get this and really begin to believe it as a universal truth, it becomes a law for our existence. When we love and approve of ourselves, we attract good and life becomes easier.

It doesn't matter if the affirmation, *I am love, loved and lovable because I exist*, feels true to you in this moment. There are times when all of us feel more connected, disconnected, worthy, and unworthy. No matter what you think about yourself, you are still unconsciously gravitating towards feelings and experiences that lead to divine love awareness. Using tools that promote this knowledge simply guide us down a gentler pathway. Until eventually the tools slip into the folds of life and we discover our divine nature, naked in its vulnerability and beauty. We don't need to have a total life shakeup to step closer to love awareness; we simply need to be open and receptive to love and forgiveness.

As we genuinely feel loved and aren't afraid of outside influences affecting our peace; what we were sent to do on Earth gently unfolds. The easiest way appears and instead of pushing through brambles and walking on an uncomfortable dirt road, the way becomes clear. The sun shines on our journey and we can smell the roses as we embark on the adventure of life. It's important to recognise that right now you are in the perfect place to heal and grow. To simply be. To exist.

We are all on Earth to awaken and discover the source of the 'I', individual or perceived sense of self. Wherever you are in life is the perfect place for you to recognise your divinity. You are in the right place, right now, to discover the magic within.

We're on Earth for such a short amount of time. Learning techniques for making our vacation here a pleasant one, are well worth acquiring along the way. God dwells within each of us, the answers are within us. We're made of consciousness. You weren't just put here to nod politely and say, "Yes. Yes. Yes," to everything and everyone whilst feeling your soul crush.

If we listen to and do what everyone tells us, we become engrained in their definition of happiness. Moreover, everyone is taking advice from this person and that person and then they die before even realising the simple joy of life. The answers are already within you! You are the answer. You know what makes you happy, and what makes you smile. You know when you feel sad, depressed, and lonely. You know yourself better than anyone. Within you is a pathway to peace.

If you want to change your life but can't see a way out don't worry about it. You are in the perfect place for healing. Make peace with the now, before trying to resolve your future and escape the past. Deep down you know why you came to Earth, and what you hope to get out of your experience here. How you wanted to learn to feel more loved and safe.

When you enter life from a loving perspective, you can rewrite your own script. You can choose loving people to have beside you who make you feel fabulous. The audience, those around you, are blessed by the light you bring to the world.

Anger is not bad; it informs us where we're resisting love. When we experience and release anger - in healthy ways - we allow ourselves to understand the truth from where it emerges. We can see the people, places, and circumstances that have allowed fear to seep into our energy field.

Creating safe environments to openly express our anger, allows our inner child to speak. Past hurts may arise and even repressed memories of which we weren't aware. When these thought forms come into the present, we are granted the freedom to move through them, express them, feel them, and let them go. When we acknowledge our pain, and feel the void of consciousness all around, we create a space where we merge with love.

Holding onto anger as a protection layer often holds us back in life. Sometimes there are memories, people, and experiences from years ago where the energy is so fierce we feel upset, guilty, ashamed, and angry when we remember. We sometimes regress to these thoughts repeatedly as we use them in an attempt to prevent more soul suffering. Programmed warnings that remind us not to let down our barriers.

Guilt is another way we suppress our destiny. We use guilt to hide from our desires. If we feel guilty enough, we sometimes believe we will be 'good people'. But guilt is only a shadow of illusionary protection. When we realise, we are beings of love, we surrender fears of being judged and serve from love consciousness.

Learn to bless these experiences with love and reprogram your mind with positive affirmations. We can refill our consciousness with positive thoughts. Remember your soul consciousness is divine love and bliss. Positive vibrations attract good into your life.

As you step into realms of love, you release the need to be afraid of your own magnificence. Which can be quite terrifying. It's okay if you take two steps forwards, then a couple back, you will reach your destination. It doesn't matter what anyone else does or thinks.

Shining as a bright light in the world doesn't mean you have to be famous, or well known, or have the world's best career. It means you take the time to nurture your own soul. Whether this entails spending the weekend in bed, going to the beach and enjoying the sun's rays, or stepping out into nature and feeling the grass between your toes. It can be simple or extravagant. Create an environment where you feel safe and loved, so your inner light can show its magnificence. So you can feel and experience the beauty of you.

Affirmations improve the quality of our life and can help us reach our divine purpose in comfort and safety.

Affirmations are navigation tools that set the precedence of our life experience. They need to be spoken in present tense to make them most effective.

To begin practising affirmations you can sit in front of the mirror and begin by saying nice things to yourself. Loving all of your being and talking as though you are already in possession of your hearts desires, be these emotionally fulfilling or material desires. Watch and see what comes up. Do you feel worthy, deserving and happy when affirming that you are living the life of your dreams?

For example, if you were in front of a mirror and stated, "I am now experiencing an abundance of prosperity." You can watch your response to the affirmation. If you feel good, and a little scared at the same time you can assess, what is it making me feel scared? Maybe you heard as a child, "Money is bad."

You now know the negative affirmation that has been imprinted on your subconscious and that is creating resistance. This negative affirmation can be reprogrammed with affirmations such as, *Money is good. I am a good person. I deserve all good.* (Even if you don't believe these statements.) You are reprogramming your mind to create new perceptions of reality and pathways of joy in your life. These new affirmations bring alignment with wealth and abundance in a way that feels safe and secure.

Affirmations repeated many times over reprogram our mind, and connect us to all good that surrounds. We no longer create protective blocks, as this habitual pattern is unnecessary for our continued preservation. Tailor affirmations for your individual needs. This helps to reach core issues that have affected your entire life. Affirmations allow us to grow and as they are personally adjusted, they can have positive outcomes in our life.

Also when you look at another who you judge or dislike, reflect this in yourself and see where you're rejecting yourself.

Create affirmations to release the judgement. For resentments held against others, fester deep within our own soul. Pulling us out of alignment with the truth of our being, love.

I like to sit on the floor in front of a large mirror to practise my affirmations, whilst staring deep into my eyes. Or repeating them as I drift into sleep. Sometimes after I've been practising an affirmation repeatedly, I begin to feel as though I'm hypnotising myself - which in a way we are.

I turn a timer on for ten minutes and don't move until I've finished practising my affirmations. This means I'm not as tempted to get up and walk away during my practise. I also like to use mala prayer beads to flick over my fingers with my thumb as I practise each affirmation, they feel supportive. At other times, I'll say my affirmations whilst tapping or massaging the meridian points used in EFT (Emotional Freedom Technique). This action drills the affirmations into my core and is very effective for fast assimilation.

Bring in good and release all you've clung too so tightly to shelter yourself. Fears and energy blocks interfere with your happiness, compassion, and ability to feel the love that you are, the truth behind your existence. Understand that old patterns and practises are outdated. People who are unhappy and insecure hand negative habits to us. We adopt them as truth as they vibrationally match our subconscious or sometimes conscious beliefs about ourselves. But we can move through our patterns and transform our lives.

In the end, we are all travelling the road home to love. In each experience, we attempt to find inner peace and happiness. We are all doing the best we can with the knowledge we have.

Everyone wants to feel love and bliss all the time - especially when you know these experiences are available. If we reach higher states of consciousness naturally, as we merge into divine love we retain this awareness much more viscerally.

A note on drug use: Often when people take drugs, they see life from an alternate perspective. Viewing life from a point of altered consciousness. A different perspective of what is truth. Taking drugs may raise your consciousness and open your mind to different realms of existence. Just because this level of consciousness isn't experienced by the majority doesn't mean it is an illusion.

You can reach all states of consciousness and peace through inner development. Give yourself permission to live in the conscious point you are at until your vibration rises high enough to feel ecstasy or bliss. The problem with using drugs to alter consciousness is that they show you worlds you're not yet immersed in on a daily basis. This can lead to insanity, dissatisfaction, and deep depression.

Feeling good, often appears as a temporary state of being. It's quite an addictive feeling, like having an orgasm! Hence why sex works so well in advertising. The problem is that it doesn't last longer. I like to call this the feel good flame. We light up, and our whole world expands when something good comes our way. It's liberating and addictive, the reason it's so addictive, is because there's reality in the temporary elation we feel. For a moment, or longer our being lights up, like a candle, our inner light shines bright.

We want the flame to never flicker and die. The only reason it seems to leave our body is because we think thoughts, which lead to feelings that affect our very being. Our mind is the flames butcher, and it controls us. When we allow the mind/ego to dominate our thoughts can become skewed, unclear, and fearful. Stepping into the present moment allows our mind to still.

Rest and allow any thought, to surface. Excellent, now cuddle the thought, put your arms around it. Embrace the thought with total acceptance. Smile, and allow it to be. What do you feel? What do you think? I find when I practise this the thought takes a back seat; suddenly it's not controlling my emotions. I am instead, embracing love and inner peace.

Our words and thoughts are powerful. We want their dominant presence to be stilled, centred and at peace to attract good into our lives. We need to learn not to react to our thoughts, or the projections of others. Living from this state of being takes patience, but is possible.

Sometimes it can feel difficult when you watch your thoughts and speech, especially when you realise the garbage you've been holding onto. The stories that make up our existence, defining our interpretation of ourselves create the hardships and joy in our life. The only requirement is that we learn to surrender. It is, in essence, so simple.

Most of us feel as though we're not enough. No matter what achievements someone has tucked under their belt. There is a disease in society that pierces the soul, it's called the, I'm Not Good Enough disease.

A dis-*ease* takes away our ease and makes us feel uncomfortable. So why do we insist on hanging onto our thoughts? Because we are under the illusionary veil that thought defines reality, when existence, time, and space are far greater and wider than our minds perspective. We allow our mind to rule over us like a dictator. Until we release the need to be dominated and controlled, we will be held under the authority and spell of the mind.

As our thoughts expand beyond our world, the people we know, our favourite television shows, the hunger in our bellies etc. we tap into the extensive reality of thought field consciousness.

Our bodies are our shell, a home to rest our spirit. Yet they are not the definition of our existence. Neither is our things, our friends, or our families. We are universal beings of love. Living at one with the Earth. Our manifestation on this living, breathing, planet represents the love and worth we all have to exist. Knowing you are worthy, gives you limitless power. It sets you free.

Everything we have, do, become, and experience, reflects our point of attraction. You are like a tuning fork, whatever vibrates at the same frequency vibration as you, manifests into your reality. What we attract into our life is a direct reflection of how we *feel* in the present moment. Our feelings are expressed through the way we hold ourselves, the clothes we wear (a superficial expression), our perspective of life, and the words we speak.

Words are like arrows; they shoot out of our mouths and hit the target ahead of us, even if we are not paying attention. Are your words poison tipped? When we use our words not as weapons, but as prayers, we aim towards things we love. Our targets bring forth positive events, lifestyles and circumstances.

It really doesn't matter if you've attracted uncomfortable circumstances into your life. You are still a good person! You are goodness because you exist. Sometimes the control freak part of our being can try to run the show forcing only positive thoughts and experiences. Surrender to your destiny. Letting what will be, be and still doing the best you can to raise your conscious point of perception. Being human it's natural for us to have both positive and negative thoughts, it's just a matter of tipping the scales to a more positive perspective and surrendering what will be to the hands of spirit.

The words we speak and the thoughts we think are little spells or intentions floating from our being. They can take the shape of sparkling gemstones, or be dark and dank, casting shadows upon our world. The universe is on our side. We are creating our own heaven or hell on Earth in this very moment. Positive affirmations spoken aloud, or practised repetitively in the mind are thought based projections. They affect our current mood and state of well-being. When we affirm or use prayer in the present tense, we command that which we wish to be brought forth. Thinking, feeling, and speaking as though we are in possession of our desires helps create pathways for them to be delivered.

When we don't project an exhaustive amount of energy over that which we desire materialisation appears in briefer momentum. This is because we don't have so many attachment cords and insecurities that are brought forth to clear at the same point of attraction.

Negative seed thoughts can reside in our subconscious awareness. Sometimes these seed beliefs are hidden behind mental blocks of – *I am afraid to be noticed. I'm unworthy. I'm afraid of judgement, etc.* Counter them with positive affirmations such as, *I am loved and supported in everything I do,* and *The more I have, the more I can give.*

Accept your blockages, they are not bad. They are a part of you and when you love yourself fully in the moment the ties that bind loosen.

Some may fret over negative sayings, thoughts of people and situations, or past experiences that play in repetitions through the mind, seemingly with no control from the observer. These hurts and prejudice, which may feel hard to let go of can be released through the words *cancel* or *out.* If every time we open our mouths and want to say something negative, we simply say *cancel,* our mind will gravitate to greener pastures. Another technique is to clap loudly three times. This can help us to snap out of it!

We can also embrace our negative thought patterns with love. Lack of resistance to fear based thoughts can release the pressure of a repetitive negative mindset. Our perception naturally changes to a place where words feel fresher. The stories align with our inner most being as we accept a new foundation of truth.

The human mind has a strong ability to hold onto pain and suffering. Repetitive mind circles of events that traumatised our soul can have a major effect on our ability to live happy, healthy lives. Sometimes these events are very vivid and we talk about them and see them playing in our mind's eye like scary movies. Sometimes they're buried deep within our subconscious; masking fears of why it's not safe to partake in the world.

It doesn't matter how we cover these events or replay them, the horrors of childhood, and the fears suffered by abuse victims be it verbal or physical can corrupt our present day perception. If reality is a reflection of our experiences mirrored back to us, until we find a state of inner peace and completeness, it makes sense to create an environment where it's safe to heal. Then release, and realign our being with the pure infinite source of divine love that is within every atom, every fibre, and every vibratory being. The essence of creation that surrounds us and is within us.

Arguments and anger form a protective shield where we don't allow the true light of success and self-acceptance to step forth. There can be environments where it's not safe on a physical and psychological level for us to remain. This also includes relationships where you just don't feel comfortable. Listen to what your body tells you. Often we put up with feelings of rejection, terror, hurt, and resentment in order to please others.

For these situations, the best thing to do is retreat, and make sure everyone involved is safe. Put down our weapons - mind and thought - of self-defence and create an environment that's a direct reflection of love, compassion, and self-trust. Learning to say *no*, is an affirmation. It affirms what we're willing to say *yes* to and what we are opening our arms towards and accepting into our lives.

Saying no can create a space where people may get angry or upset. This is because you are shifting your boundaries and the physical expectation of consciousness - be it positive or negative - that you allow into your reality. Babies learn, 'no' and are then made to unlearn the power behind the word. Now we need to relearn. If we want to stay safe and create an environment in harmony with our mental, physical and spiritual wellbeing.

Saying no takes practise. It doesn't matter if we make mistakes along the way, or say no, where later we think we could've said yes. You are always making the best decision you can in the moment for what you feel serves your greater good, and that of your associates. When you say no to something that isn't right for you - coming from an intuitive, gut feeling - it is also not right for others involved.

We need to understand that saying no creates an environment for us to heal and also creates room for change in the lives of those whom we need space from. If we say no, then feel guilty, we are being manipulated. As manipulation stems from a fear of guilt. It is worthwhile remembering this so we may make stable, loving, decisions that best serve our higher selves.

When we find peace, embracing our inner light, we create a ripple of love and harmony throughout the world. Peace within your soul is the best gift you can give to humanity.

Whenever you find yourself in a situation where people are arguing over sensitive issues, go within your heart. See how the energy projected leaves you feeling. Do you feel calm and confident? Do you want to jump in and have a rough and tumble? We cannot save the planet by speaking through aggression. We are simply contributing more negativity. Remove yourself from the situation, or suggest, "Let's talk about something that creates space for peace," or "I'm angry right now and don't feel I can respond in a calm manner. Let's have this conversation later." Going back to a conversation once we've cooled down and calmed uncomfortable situations. Just remember to have the important conversations and not to use this as a tool to avoid them totally, unless this is what you truly believe is best for your state of mind.

Choosing peace in an argumentative environment can seem extreme and can give rise to suppressed anger. Yes, we need to release any bottled emotions we hold within, however we can choose when, how, and with whom. We all go through times where we explode, or feel furious and this is okay. We need to love all of our emotions and heal our suppressed fears and traumas. Being conscious of our thoughts also leads us to being conscious of our environment and others.

Choosing peace is powerful. Even now, I sometimes find it a task as I have a quick temper. Yet I find it takes away from my personal power of creation to choose fear. Days spent muddled over he said, she said, are days lost. You don't have to agree with everyone and everything, and you also don't need to associate with everyone and everything.

Choose friends that uplift, inspire, and help your heart soar. We all carry pain, suffering, and memories we'd rather leave hidden. If we can learn to nurture them and ourselves with love, then it may be possible for our perception of the world to change.

Trauma can block our energetic pathways. Our conscious or subconscious mind can become locked on repetitive negative affirmations because a part of ourselves is desperately trying to keep us safe. So we do not have to endure the pain and suffering of the experiences our childhood or life. Sometimes atrocities committed on the soul in physical form can be so damaging it feels easier to forget, to shut off, and to shut down.

Trauma occurs when the soul is left feeling unsafe and unloved. Be it from physical violence, sexual abuse, neglect, verbal abuse, or bullying. Sometimes seemingly insignificant events shake the core of our being. Our bodies may also retain past life memories and these may freeze our spiritual development and split our soul.

Our conscious ability to process trauma in a way that it can be released from our aura, affects the destruction and havoc it may play in our life. Trauma can halt our conscious progression to accepting all good into our life. Sometimes our life's progression seems to suspend in time. From the point of the traumatic event our material and physical evolution may become frozen. Deep trauma causes the psyche to freeze. Our karmic bonds to the event release when fear, is replaced with the acceptance of the universal presence of unconditional love.

Sometimes a traumatic event will be life threatening, or violent, breaking through the conscious acceptance of love in the bodies temple. When we lose faith in love, our life may turn into a chaotic mess, of fear and doubt. **Each person and event attracted into our consciousness from this point will:**

☆ Be a mirror of what we need to surrender, to become aware of divine love. The events and individuals magnetically drawn into our evolution may be terrifying, unpleasant, or difficult.

☆ Blocked to the extent that we cannot function from a standpoint of love, which causes obstacles appearing across the spectrum of our existence.

☆ Turn our perception of love into fear, despite the soul's wish to let go. If the trauma is not released into a consciousness of love, the engine driving our soul's ability to connect with the Earthly plane will feel broken and unresponsive. Resulting in the connection to life being ground to a halt in temporary paralysis. Note the word temporary. Everything can be transformed and as we dissolve the ego we realise universal, all pervading love.

When life seems blocked, this is usually created by a fear response to trauma. The only emotional awareness, which can transmute traumatic experience, is that of love. People experience all levels of what appears to be self-sabotage. This may materialise in circumstantial life experiences such as money blockages, lack of romantic love, painful or no friendships/relationships, uncomfortable family relationships, weight issues, etc.

Sometimes an individual excels in one part of their life and *appears* to fail in another. Note: There's no such thing as failure only the arising of such feelings to invoke us into creating a love based response. Many times, we forget traumatic events, or do not place importance on their significance for fear of the pain that will be experienced when they are mentally relived.

The mind cannot discern between physical reality and mental experience. We always want to heal and without proper knowledge of how to heal, we turn to that which appears to help. This may include burying our emotions, drug and alcohol abuse, worry addiction, shopping, sport, television obsessions, career obsession, eating disorders, and focusing on sensations of lack.

Sometimes we become obsessed with becoming winners or something outside ourselves for fulfilment. To fill the gap of emptiness which resides in our life. Losing touch with the gift hidden in our hearts that will help us reach peacefulness. Masks are a temporary fix; we will never truly heal until we reach a state where we're ready to let go and totally accept ourselves and our life as it is right now without judgement.

It's very important we have compassion for every individual around us, no matter where they are in life. We cannot dive into someone else's brain and release or comprehend their traumas and the events which have shaped their life. Judgement causes more suffering for ourselves. Every soul is on an individual journey, this includes yourself.

This doesn't mean we have to associate with people who try to bring us down; it can mean forgiving and forgetting. If you do want to help someone, the best you can do is offer love and acceptance. For love is the antidote to all wounds. When we feel loved to the depths of our soul, we are much abler to process pain and resolve emotional trauma. We become stronger and braver as love pervades deeper levels of our consciousness than ever experienced.

No matter how deep we love someone, it's not until this soul is willing and able to heal that they can heal. Remember our greatest responsibility is development of the fluidity of divine love experienced in our own consciousness. Wanting someone to heal is not love. Loving them the way they are is, and we can only do this through the amount of love we allow into our own existence.

When trauma arises offer support to individuals if you can. The quicker a trauma is released the less devastating affects it has on one's life. Remember, sometimes people need to bury their pain to function. Sometimes it's so great they cannot handle the affects if it was all to come rushing forth into their present reality. Forcing something out into the open air can be like picking a scab before it's ready to heal. It may cause festering, inflammation, and more suffering. Thus, do not pressure yourself or another to heal, accept yourself and try to create a space where you feel safe enough to let go of pain.

Your guardian angels will know when you're ready and the healers and teachers will appear. You deserve love and support. Finding this book is a symbol of the self-love you are willing to open to and experience for your soul. You are never truly alone, I love you, just the way you are. Mother Earth loves every fibre of your being that is why you have permission to live here and to breathe. Mother Earth loves all of her children. You are a child of universal spirit, and for that very fact you are worthy and lovable.

To release trauma, a person may withdraw from life. Losing friends, cutting close connections until they are essentially living a hermit style existence. This is okay. It's not giving up, even though it can be perceived as this whilst we experience the isolation and loneliness of our hearts.

Sometimes we need to retract to a place where we feel safe enough to heal. Once we feel in a place where we are safe, we can allow the terror thoughts to rise. With help, we can begin, to move forward. It's always a safe idea to keep trusted friends, families, councillors, or spiritual healers that are reliable nearby. So when repressed emotions surface, we can release them with support if needed. Call upon angelic guardians or spiritual deities that you connect with if there is no one physically accessible.

From the core of our pain, emerges light. Darkness does not last forever, just as the sun rises every morning we can wake from the thoughts and memories that have been haunting our souls. This is so important to remember, the greatest and most compassionate healers and leaders in our world have often experienced this darkness. The fear, and sometimes the desire to escape from this existence altogether. We cannot escape because what we fear is really an illusion of the mind.

Yes, trauma and traumatic experiences scar our souls. However, the core basis for our existence on this Earth is love. Love that is unperishable no matter how dark, real, and tormenting our suffering has been.

When the soul splits from extreme terror, what essentially is happening is that part of the core, unique makeup, that which makes you whole, is hiding. It hides so well you cannot even feel its presence, or be consciously aware of its existence. When the soul fractures, we are left to partake in the human vessel experience from an abject and dissolute conscious standpoint. So it's impossible for us to live fully, to feel fully, and truly understand our inner being. The radiant light of love which flows through every aspect of nature.

For the healing to begin, we need to feel 110% safe so we can come back into our bodies. Even when we seek outside therapy, our soul may not reveal hidden parts at the time of intervention. Normally we wait till a point in our lives where we feel secure enough to witness events of the past, whilst we reconnect with the present moment.

If broken parts of our soul try arise whilst we don't feel truly safe, or understand what's happening on a spiritual level, this re-emergence can be much more difficult and painful. Our psyche doesn't understand the need for painful emotions to be filtered and the re-grounding that is taking place on an astral level into the physical. This can churn up physical suffering such as unwanted illness or disease and create relationship blockages. These are just that; blockages of the soul being allowed safe passage as it descends into our physical conscious existence. A true merging of worlds. It can feel like coming on land after floating at sea for months. It takes time to find our land legs and be able walk with ease.

Tools such as meditation (including guided audio meditations), practise of compassion to ourselves and others, walking in nature, Emotional Freedom Technique EFT, resting, yoga, forging relationships with animals, self-enquiry, allowing ourselves to be present, etc. can help as we allow shattered parts of our soul to re-emerge and connect again, like the building of a jigsaw puzzle. So we can return into our body and for our healing to begin in safety. This is very important as it makes the journey a much smoother ride. Seeking help from others we trust may guide us on our inner journey. Appreciation for the gifts we have in our life, allows these positive reflections to grow.

As we go through the healing process, we realise we are whole and complete in the present moment. The part of ourselves that was lost in time, suspended in fear begins to show itself. As we heal, that part of ourselves comes back into our body. Our conscious awareness perception shifts; life becomes more vibrant. Our feet are grounded to the Earth and we aren't left trying to hide a part of ourselves from our perception of existence.

The fear that was buried and suppressed unveils and is accepted into conscious reality. We may experience flashbacks, sadness, and depression as we acknowledge that which we felt we lost, and all we hid from.

Parts of our soul may burst through, springing back into our conscious existence like a jack-in-the-box, when we step into the present moment. This spring like affect can leave us feeling disorientated and sometimes a little scared. Practising self-love, compassion and allowing ourselves time to heal and feel safe creates an environment where we can bloom. Letting light guide our entire existence.

Remember the past does not control us. Nor does fear need to define our future. Instead of feeling rejected, neglected and abandoned when we acknowledge our inner blocks we become stronger and more confident to take part in the world. When you step into the path of life with love, you allow others to do so, raising the consciousness of yourself and all other beings on planet Earth.

Through these experiences, we are connecting to love. The knowledge that we're infinite beings on a pathway to love that is already us, makes us ponder the fragility of life. Why are we here? What do we take with us when we leave this planet? Our thoughts, our actions, our social motivations can be expanded upon, as we embrace the gift before us: we are infinite beings of love. The realisation of this gives us one purpose, to become consciously aware of the presence of love pervading all.

Life is love, and acceptance of ourselves and others is everything.

Sometimes we reach points in life and we wonder how we came to be where we are now. We reach these fear-based points when we've been struggling through life through sheer determination, or brute force. We set out on the road with good intentions and we wind up feeling scared, alone, and ashamed. We have not achieved our definition of success and/or feel isolated. Unable to move forward or backwards. Trying desperately to connect to a world which flashes by like a whirlwind. The problem is when we try to fit in; we pull away from our strength and generosity. Through the acceptance and love of our own unique character, we create inner harmony.

At times, it feels like we give up when things seem too hard. This image of *giving up* is the force of our being putting a full stop on our momentum. Past traumas and significant events in our life can weigh us down like anchors. Whether you feel as though you're moving too fast, or are unable to begin the rest of your life, even though you desperately wish to achieve something, anything. It's important to note that we've reached this point through the sum of our thoughts, past karma and pre-ordained destiny. You are worthy and valuable, always have been, and always will be, no matter what you believe to be true about you. You are a divine expression of consciousness, this in itself is enough.

Suppressed emotion's often control our life even if we don't realise it. Pain, guilt, anger, anguish, and regret have taken hold of the steering wheel. When these emotions take over, we're blindfolded to all good that surrounds us. Our direction has gone off course and it can literally feel like you're driving a car in reverse, to get from Alabama to New York. A recipe for disaster.

Loving ourselves and totally accepting where we're at without judgement is incredibly important. At times we push up against feeling present moment love with extreme resistance. This is because we're unsatisfied with our present circumstances in life. We resist loving ourselves for fear that if we do, we'll stay stuck. Feeling that if we don't push on forwards, we will never reach career fulfilment, get the car, the body, the holiday, the lifestyle, the relationship, the positive recognition, etc. Using fear as a drive to achieve greatness is not productive. Believing we cannot accept ourselves in the now keeps us stuck.

Yes, it's wonderful to have, be, do, and achieve your dreams. But being able to love yourself right now, no matter how difficult, helps you progress towards goals that much quicker. Experiencing life from a loving and accepting standpoint allows peace through trust, wisdom, and clear insight.

Omnia Vincit Amor ~ *Love Conquers All*

When you allow yourself to sit still, and to breathe, creating a safe environment around your soul you connect to the life that's meant for you. By this I mean, the life you were born to live. Where you are nurtured, self-assured, safe, empowered, prosperous, loved, loving and confident.

To clear our negative thought patterns, we need to release, let go and accept where we are at. Honouring the shadows and the forgotten painful memories that have closed our souls from embracing the divine love which defines us. So we may look past the dark and into the hidden light, glowing within our hearts.

In our world, we often compare our life to the lives of our friends, families, and celebrities. This drive of the most successful is inhibiting the truth of natural and fulfilling self-love, compassion, and care. Once we've created a safe platform, we can clean out the remaining debris of self-deprecating stories we use to cause harm, and inflict suffering and punishment on our being.

Love is the most basic human right. When we live from love our entire world flows in harmony. Abundance issues are cleared, illness is healed, hatred turns to compassion, and inner peace is rectified. We create a world where all wish to live.

Affirmations pull us to a place of self-love and acceptance. They build a deep lifelong sustainable relationship with the most important person in our lives, ourselves. When you truly love yourself you're able to love others. You become an auric beacon spreading compassion, forgiveness, prosperity, and joy. Your life becomes a mirror of the goodness you feel. You are set free to shine and encourage your light to radiate throughout the entire universe. *I love and accept myself now,* is a beautiful and powerful affirmation.

Affirmations are key on this path as they bring light into our world. They give us the opportunity to create new pathways of prosperity, growth, and joy. Practised daily, on repeat, they can bring unprecedented joy and good fortune. They create walls of strength, love, and support around us and new walkways of spiritual growth. Becoming released from the frozen gates of internal hate allows your light to illuminate the entire world.

You are safe. You are loved. You are free. When you water tiny seeds of good thoughts, roots sprout, strength grows, and you become the wizened oak tree. Supporting life, supporting yourself, gently reaching for the stars and sun. Whilst their light nourishes you, feeds you, and keeps you whole, loved, and safe.

Even if you feel stuck and unable to consciously release past and present hurts, that appear to have damaged your soul and life, you can use positive affirmations to create future life experiences. Repetition of positive affirmations, verbal and mental into the subconscious plant seeds of change into our existence. They create pathways where positive people can enter or the right book appears. We become open to the guidance that has always been present but we refused to see.

We're taught to compare, compete, and succeed. Often we compare and complain. Especially when our dreams have not yet been realised. Sometimes this makes us feel so poorly that it's easier to escape into the downward spiral rather than embrace own our feelings of despair.

As children we often envision we will grow up to be our idols, the singer, movie star, billionaire, model, sports star etc. When we don't attain these aspirations our self-esteem drops.

Obviously simply desiring 'their' success is not enough to achieve similar outcomes in our own life. Hours spent adoring others can deflect our energy from looking within.

To truly succeed we need to love ourselves. Give yourself this gift right now. You were created by a force so powerful it is responsible for the manifestation of your heroes and heroines. It's not what you do, it's what you feel and believe to be true about yourself that is important. The people that you idolise, that you aspire to 'be like' were created by the love and infinite bliss that manifested your beautiful being. You emerge from the one creation. You are worthy, valuable and loveable simply because you exist. You are a good person.

This is not vanity, it's honouring the divine. There is nothing more sacred than soul worship, than self-love and acceptance. For in loving yourself, you love all of creation.

We are all on our own journey. When you compare, you push away from the wonder of creation you already embody. Every individual has unique gifts and talents. Whether we live on the streets or in a mansion, we are all unique vibrant beings. For the love and radiant energetic sparkle to be unleashed from each individual all that needs to be unlocked is a connection to Self. From deep self-love and self-awareness stems true happiness and wholeness.

Competing to justify our validation of being, looking down upon others to make oneself feel better stems from deep self-discontentment. When you become filled with gratitude for your existence, you harmonise with your purpose on the planet. Our eyes instead of being blinded by judgement (which feels like staring at the sun) become wide open to compassion, love, and understanding. Affirmations help to release the need to compete and instead be happy with who we are, in this moment.

Advertising is a wonderful example of the psychological effects of repetitive learning. Almost every individual in the entire world understands the meaning, image, and products of big named food brands, the colours, the labels, everything. Why? Because they've been repetitively drilled into our brain. The core of our being believes in the power of branded junk food, its accessibility, taste etc. Even if we do not consume the food when we think of it, we feel positive. Our subconscious has been programmed by advertising savvy into understanding the pleasures involved with its consumption and material acquisition.

The same goes with major brands, all create an image via advertising repetitions. These companies do not spend billions of dollars a year on advertising because it's not effective. Why would they? No, they understand the potency of repetitive programming. How it makes the body react, feel deserving, and attract their product into our consciousness and then into our lives, and money into their pockets. If we understand how advertising works, we can understand how affirmations affect our entire reality.

The one thing these corporations lack is the ability to control what we watch, where we go, and most importantly our every instantaneous thought. We are in control of the most powerful advertising tool of all, our brains, our consciousness, and thus our subconscious.

When you choose to see the world from the perspective of your inner glory, you bring joy into your conscious reality. And into the reality of all those who you encounter. Yes, we've been trained to entertain our minds through outside thought projections, television, internet sites, social media, the books we read, the projections of others, and the images we see on a daily basis. However, only we have the power to change our focus and choose our thoughts.

When we promote and advertise all the wonders of the world to ourselves our existential existence, our dreams and hopes are brought forth to the centre of our reality. We can thrive; living full happy and healthy lives just by learning to train our minds into positive cycles of repetitive affirmation sequences.

Our body is in physical form, however we all know we can gain weight and lose weight, but from where does this weight appear? Just because we don't see the rolling hills of life's journey in the mirror in front of us, doesn't mean that through visualisation techniques and balance of mind, body, and spirit, our life path will unfold in a different matter to that of weight, gain or loss. What we now feel to be our emotional reflection can be altered by a single thought. All it takes is the willingness to let go and our whole destiny is recreated in the blink of an eye. Feed yourself a diet of positive thoughts, self-reflection, and uplifting words and you shall shine!

All we ever have to do is be willing to change. Our spirit guides, angels, and guiding lights will guide the way. They will nurture and care for us as tiny seeds until we're strong enough to partake actively. Just as the earth supports a tree so are we supported by the divine. When we're willing to change, our eyes open and teachers, healers, videos, and forms of communication are presented that can help our journey to move forwards with renewed joy.

Old patterns often re-emerge as the universe gently nudges us to see if we've released our past's shadows. This is okay. If we act as the witness we can release and re-frame our conscious existence and the cut between what uplifts us and what drains our energy and pulls us down becomes swifter, more empowered and defined.

Be sure all you allow into your energy system is that which makes you feel loved and nourishes your inner being. Practising affirmations in congruence with this awareness is like following a compass that makes it far easier to move in the best direction, for you.

You are always in the right place at the right time. Life is a river guiding you towards bliss, peace, and enlightenment.

Surrender to the moment, to where you're at. You a divine being. Awareness is our spirits wakeup call guiding us towards a peace filled existence. Harmony in the mind, equals harmony in our thoughts. You are loved, safe, whole, and complete exactly as you are now.

Escape the haze,
created by the minds maze
Those you fear, are only here
because the scared part of your soul allows them near
Everyone is a guest in your reality
even your own family
Let everything melt
Forgive the cards you've been dealt
Close your eyes
Watch the demise
of the reality you thought to be true
as you discover you're not even you
Rest your head, soul, body and breath
Feel the illusion, acknowledge the conclusion
You're made by the magic of love
Everyone you meet, it's you, you greet
Open your eyes,
unveil the disguise
Fear shuts down our heart,
the only place to start
Take a bird's eye view
Watch the pain controlling you
Ask, who am I?
Follow the last breath
Let your soul rest
Feel the happiness within
Let your heart swim
Into the ocean, like a droplet you fall,
as you merge with all
For you are the one sending blessings from above
A spark of the divine
I am you, you are mine
Everything, everyone, is sublime
Nature holds the key to dissolve reality
Sacred breath helps trees to grow
In your heart discover it's true,
the divine breathes through you

-     Divine Breath

CHAPTER ELEVEN

Crystals & Stones

Crystals have magical powers and the ability to transform lives. Crystal and stones are vibrational tools that guide us to experience life from a new vantage point. Just as positive affirmations and meditations can change your conscious perception of life, crystals can guide you to new levels of positive wellbeing. I like to see crystals as living souls, who carry good wishes and love to share their energy with all who encounter their grace.

We can use crystals that vibrate with love to draw love to us. They can release negative energies, raise our consciousness, draw in abundance and help release karmic patterns, increase our psychic abilities, and heighten our intuition.

When life's paper castles collapse, spirituality can help plug us back into something that feels wholesome and meaningful. The connection to source and the knowledge we are eternal beings who have forgotten that our true nature is love. This is a higher truth.

Connecting to source energy you become a bright light. An electrical current of wellbeing turns you on. No matter how detached, empty, and vacuous you may feel in the world, you can always plug into source. The true light from which you manifest. When your switch turns on, currents of universal energy flow through you and peace becomes your nature.

No matter how much you may feel that others are better than you or have accomplished more, they have manifested from the same space as you, from the same source. They are present due to the same grace that flows through your body. All beings are equal. Emerging from the infinite into this planetary conscious wave of existence.

No one is better than or worse than. The human mind likes to make judgements. We are collectively wonderful at judging ourselves. The problem is that we forget our source. Our origin. We all arise from infinite consciousness. Something beyond your brain, beyond your conception, beyond your doubt and insecurities has made you manifest.

You don't have to trust yourself, or even like yourself. But the hands of pure divine consciousness created you as a glorious, holy, and worthy being. Trust in that power. Even if it's beyond comprehension, it's reliable. After all, it is responsible for the creation of reality.

Take a blender. It's new, the latest model, stainless steel, powerful blades. You know it can dice kale, spirulina, bananas, turmeric, maple syrup, and ice into a luscious smoothie. But when it's sitting there on the bench it appears still, rock solid, lifeless. When you plug it in, and allow the flow of electricity, it jumps into action creating delicious beverages. Humans are the same. We all want that good feeling, life-creating juice. We're looking for that *on* switch. It doesn't matter how long we've been sitting on the shelf, when you plug into source energy, you create miracles.

Everything is energy, everything. Be it a pair of scissors or a rose. The unique thing about crystals is we can program them with positive intent. They also come pre-programmed with divine earth or intergalactic energy. They absorb vibrations and each crystal holds its own unique vibration. Every object holds energy currents.

A kinaesthetic (touch based) intuitive person can hold someone's car keys and tell you about that person. Even if they've never met before. People with this gift demonstrate how objects can store vibrations. This is one way that the metaphysical properties of crystals are discerned. We all have latent psychic abilities, whether we are aware of them or not. The energy held in objects can affect our mood and sense of wellbeing. Crystals with positive vibrations can enhance our energy.

Crystals have spent millennia growing and forming in the Earth's bed. They are wise, ancient, and alive and can help to tune us. If we have issues with letting people in, we can use rose quartz, which holds the vibration of love. Pink tourmaline is also a love charged stone that is very protective (wonderful for bruised hearts). Crystals can help plug us back into universal energy.

When a crystal is vibrating to a more positive, harmonious vibration than our own, as we carry it with us its feel good vibes begin to rub off. It's like if you were travelling with people who never stopped arguing. Eventually they'd get on your nerves and you'd drop your level of enthusiasm. If the same people were always happy, like a giggling baby, you'd feel uplifted every time you connected with them.

When a crystal is charged with high vibrations, that consciousness, can shift your own. Sometimes our energy can be lower and the crystal helps to absorb this energy, hold space, and create balance. That's why crystals need to be cleansed - although there are some crystals that can transmute energy.

Crystals may carry other people's or our own bad vibes and like all of us need a wash and a helping hand to transmute this energy every now and then. Allow yourself to be still and to share in the energy of the crystal. They are gifts from Mother Nature and wonderful tools that can help elevate your consciousness and shift your mood and life experience.

Healers charge crystals and embrace their strength to help draw blockages from the body. We're all universal healers. As your inner light turns on and your awareness awakens, you lift the consciousness of the planet and help to heal the world. Creating a loving and nurturing world for future generations. If you identify where you're not letting love flow in your universal daily existence, you can use crystals reflecting the positive charge of this state of being to help you let go.

If you look at Doctor Emotos incredible work, you can see how he has used crystals immersed in water to create beautiful water crystal images. Crystals change the water's vibration and structural makeup to one of grace, beauty, and wonder. Considering that our bodies are made of mostly water, we can now see when we hold crystals close to our body how they can change the structure of our makeup. Allowing us to realise our connection with beauty, light and all good.

Life-giving white light flows through you, connecting you to universal life force. This vital energy is well recognised by many healing systems. The Chinese call it *chi* while the Indian Ayurvedic system calls it *prana*. When this light energy becomes blocked, disharmony is caused between the body, mind and soul and a state of disharmony or disease follows. These blocks of energy are caused by modern stressful lifestyles, bad diet, lack of natural light, exposure to abuse, self-hatred, non-movement, judgemental thoughts, negative reoccurring thoughts, fear based prejudice, suppressed emotions i.e. fear, resentment, jealousy, anger etc., and various types of astral and physical pollution.

When I was a little girl, I lived next door to two neighbours, named Mr. and Mrs. Treasure Rock (I never actually knew their real names, and the above was what I always called them). This couple travelled to many crystal fairs, and they had a crystal tumbler in their back garden. Their front driveway was made of tiny churned granite stones. They'd throw crystals into it, so when I walked past I could discover beautiful treasure rocks.

It's funny how life is always supporting you and guiding you on your path even when you are so young. Feel the nurturing hands of the universe, your soul guidance mother. How could I've known I'd come to love the metaphysical properties of crystals? To be guided by their amazing energies? We are always being guided and are in the right place at the right time, for whatever it is we need to learn and grow from. All is well.

I used to place special crystals under my mattress as a child. I knew if they were kept under my pillow, they'd be moved, so I would place them in specific positions under the mattress. I know they helped me to sleep better and improved my dreams. However, no one had explained their gifts. I feel so blessed to have experienced the magic of crystals at such a young age.

There is such a large variety of uses for crystals. They are soothing to hold during meditation, and specific crystals can be used during times of stress. Protection crystals can be held during travel, outings, family gatherings, difficult phone calls and through situations where we may feel uncomfortable. The strength of the crystal can permeate our being and bless us with courage and protection. The more open and receptive we are the easier it is to allow the crystals loving energy and spirit to slip harmoniously into our environment.

Carrying crystals is a wonderful way to rebalance and call in guidance for all of our pursuits whether they be material, spiritual or physical. They help charge the body. Just as eating good food can make our bodies feel lighter, crystals can help our etheric bodies release unnecessary tension. They unite us with love and place us on the path towards wellbeing and energetic lightness.

Holding crystals during the day and sleeping with them under your pillow at night helps to align you with their positive energy. They can help protect your aura, strengthen self-esteem, and build confidence. *The Crystal Bible*, by Judy Hall, is a wonderful reference book which describes the metaphysical properties of many individual crystals.

Crystals, gems and stones are living entities. Their powerful vibrations can heal, balance, unite, and attune the body, mind, and spirit. When we meditate, we allow the inner self to flow with ease, relieving mind interference. We enter pure states of consciousness that help us to let go, forgive, and find stillness and peace in the present moment. Crystals are tools which can help elevate us to inner peace as they enhance opening of the mind, and connection to the spiritual astral realms.

How to cleanse crystals and gemstones:

☆ A full moon bath where you leave your gemstones outside overnight under a full moon is an excellent way to cleanse crystals. It's particularly good if you have any precious metals attached to the crystal as it prevents tarnishing.

☆ Crystals can also be cleansed by being left to bath in the sun's rays. The sun infuses them with its glorious warmth and vitality. The sun helps things to grow and blossom and its energy enhances your crystals vitality and radiance. Some crystals can fade in the sun (such as amethyst) so be careful with the crystals you choose to cleanse in the sun's warm and nurturing light bath.

☆ A solution of sea salt and filtered water left overnight on a bench can cleanse crystals. Salt is psychically neutral, and after sitting in salt water for twenty-four hours your crystal will be clear. Just add a couple of tablespoons of salt per cup of water.

Make sure that the water is cool to the touch as crystals can crack in hot water. Porous crystals cannot be cleansed in this solution as it can damage the stone itself. However, for suitable crystals it's a powerful method of cleansing. You also want to be careful with crystals set in metals as they can tarnish.

☆ Place crystals and jewellery in a bed of dry sea salt and leave for twenty-four hours. This can still damage sensitive gems and may tarnish jewellery. However, it's a lot safer than the wet method.

☆ You can place crystals inside an amethyst cave overnight to cleanse them. Or on a block of selenite.

☆ Cleanse your crystals whenever they start to feel dense and heavy, or you are no longer attracted to their radiance. If you've been in a particularly stressful environment, or associating with people who make you feel uncomfortable or scared cleanse your crystals. I like to cleanse the crystals I wear once every couple of weeks and the crystals in my home on the full moon or every couple of full moons. It really depends on how you feel, what's been happening in your life and how comfortable you feel your crystals are.

☆ If you feel your crystals, gems or jewellery have absorbed a lot of negativity, or they have broken and you want to keep them wrap them in white silk or fabric, and bury them in the ground on the new moon. Collect them the day after the full moon has passed.

Underneath an ancient and strong tree is a good place to bury them as the tree can help to remove stagnant energies. Make sure you ask the tree for permission. It'll tell you through how you feel, or it may speak to you confirming if it's okay to burying your crystal nearby.

Allow your inner guidance to choose a suitable place. Remember where they're buried!

☆ Pure spring water with a few drops of Bach Flower Rescue Remedy will help cleanse and raise their vibrations.

☆ When a crystal breaks it has often played its part in protecting you. It may be overwhelmed with energy. Be sure to thank the crystal. Cleanse, if you choose to keep it. Sometimes, if it feels right, it's time to return this crystal back to Mother Nature's hands. A fast running stream, the ocean or a forest is a wonderful place to return the crystal. Thank the crystal and let it go.

☆ Bathing crystals in a fresh running stream will help to cleanse crystals and attune the energy to the high vibration of raw nature. Hold on tight!

☆ Place your crystal on an image that represents peace and love to you overnight. This can be a deity, God, Goddess, a picture of beautiful scenery, or even something fabulous that you'd love to manifest. This helps to imprint the crystal with new vibrations.

☆ The power of intention and positive thought, can cleanse crystals. Place the crystal you wish to cleanse in your left hand. Direct any points away from the body, as you wish to direct negative energy away from yourself. Still your mind, then ask your angels and guides for the stone to be purified and cleansed. Visualise any negative energy being sucked out and pulled away from the crystal.

Once the crystal feels clean, you've created a vacuum like effect. It's now ready to imprint. Focus on your heart centre and feel love spreading throughout your body and into the crystal.

☆ Once cleansed keep your crystal near to imprint your own energy and to allow it to heal your auric body. You can keep it near your skin, in handbags, or under your pillow at night.

☆ To programme a cleansed crystal hold it between your hands. Take a deep breath in, hold the breath and ask the crystal for that which are seeking support i.e. relationships, heightened intuition, protection, abundance, peace of mind, academic skills etc. Breathe out and feel the crystal fill with love and this support flow throughout your being. Keep the crystal close so that it can help support your wishes, goals, and dreams.

☆ Gem Elixirs ☆

We can use our gems and crystals to create elixirs. Gem essence in a spritzer bottle can make a wonderful room cleanser for when you need to concentrate, and to re-balance calm, loving feelings into a home environment. Gem elixirs are wonderful as quick remedies to cleanse an environment and to relieve stress. When you have them easily accessible they are a wonderful remedy to create calm.

You can use citrine to attract wealth. Black tourmaline, onyx, and obsidian for protection and to remove psychic attack. Rose quartz and pink tourmaline to create loving vibrations. Just a few examples to help start your magical alchemical journey. Research crystals and decide whether you feel as though you'll benefit from the vibrations they naturally emit.

Gem Essences - Nature's gift to help balance mental, emotional, and spiritual well-being.

Ingredients:

Crystals

Spring or distilled water.

Clear alcohol i.e. vodka. This is to act as a preservative if you prefer not to use alcohol you can use vegetable glycerine or distilled water.

Essential Oils (Optional)

Utensils:

Glass spritzer bottle.

Labels

Glass jar

Cotton cloth or plastic wrap

Elastic Band

Instructions:

Place a crystal in the glass jar and add spring or distilled water. Bless the jar with love and say a healing prayer over it. Cover the container, with the cotton cloth and elastic band (or plastic wrap) and leave it to soak in the sun's rays for several hours, or under a full moon.

When the bathing time for the stone has finished, fill your spritzer bottle with 50% gem water and 50% drinking alcohol. You may also add in a couple of drops of essential oils i.e. lavender for a calming effect, lemongrass to uplift or sage for added protection etc. Label the bottle with the gems or crystals used to produce your elixir. You can even write down the most beneficial properties of the crystal.

A lovely idea when using your gem essence is to give yourself a positive affirmation to go with it. The affirmation can be practised throughout the day. It will aid in setting up a repetitious pattern of positive thought waves that will strengthen and reinforce the action of the elixir. Gem essences also make beautiful gifts!

☆ Crystal Properties ☆

Here is a list of crystals I've found very beneficial and am currently enjoying. Naturally, this list is always growing and changing! There is a wonderful array of amazing crystals we can collect and experience.

When we choose to experience a crystals energy, it also must choose us for the union to be complete. You know when you connect to a crystal as when you lay your eyes upon the crystal, or hold it in your hand you feel an instant connection. It's a bit like falling in love! Twin souls coming together, at the right place and time, intertwining, connecting, growing, and sharing the flow of beautiful energy.

Amazonite: A stone of courage. When you're blessed with the grace and wisdom of this crystal, it guides you in the best possible direction and encourages warrior like strength to embrace the human spirit.

Amethyst: Amethyst caves raise the vibration of their location. I once purchased several caves and as they left my home to go to new owners as gifts, I felt a dramatic shift in the rooms where they'd been residing. It was as though the magnificence and power of these caves had swept an enormous bubble of love, peace, and protection around my entire home. It felt as through a physical presence left as each one departed.

Amethyst truly can turn a house into a home. It creates a space where people feel safe and are open to connecting to their deepest feelings and emotions. I recommend this crystal to anyone in the healing profession. Amethyst can help to pull back protection layers so you can expand your own unique light of love out into the world.

Natural Citrine (Also known as Kundalini Quartz.): This gorgeous crystal is used to attract self-worth, wealth and acknowledge universal abundance. It creates stability in the family, at home and renews faith.

Citrine brings good luck, joy, and relaxation as we let go of our tight grip on money and allow it to flow to us. It teaches us deservability and to trust in the universal flow of conscious existence. An affirmation to use with citrine is: *I am a magnet for prosperity and it's safe to prosper wherever I turn.* Or, *money is good, and I am good.*

Many citrines on the market today are heat-treated amethyst. If you look at this citrine in the same way you perceive naturally occurring citrine, it will continue to bring you prosperity and positive growth in all of your endeavours. The vibration from heating shifts it to that of citrine, it's no longer amethyst. Although it will not be as potent as naturally forming citrine it's still a powerful vibrational healing tool.

Dioptase: A crystal for anyone who has been through a rough or painful childhood. Victims of abuse may find this crystal helps one be present with uncomfortable memories so they can be released through acknowledgement. Dioptase helps ground difficult energies and align you with your true purpose.

Emerald: Emerald is an amazing stone that has many metaphysical properties and it has been revered by Sharman's for centuries. I have two large pieces of emerald and several pieces of the raw stone made into jewellery, it's not the high quality gem emerald we are accustomed to seeing in jewellery stores, it's raw and solid in appearance (not opaque). You don't need to purchase the most expensive gems, simply those which resonate with you. Emerald helps with connecting to our true path, and surrendering to our destiny. It may help you feel safe, nurtured, and loved.

Fuchsite: Fuchsite is a powerful crystal that can help to give people who have enormous difficulties in saying no, to be able to do so. It is empowering and releases the need to be a 'healer' and have people depend on you. When really this dependence is serving our own need to be validated as kind and caring individuals. A very powerful crystal for stepping into your own energy and not being so adrift with decision making.

Idocrase: A wonderful and unusual crystal for new age thinkers and speakers. It helps one overcome fears of persecution for speaking their truth. A stone of strength and courage it also evokes the grace of Archangel Michael.

Black Jade: Jade has been revered for centuries. Used in fine jewellery and as a protective talisman in many cultures. Its protective effects are second to none. Black jade has the ability to protect people from nightmares and it can halt remote viewers from interfering with thought consciousness. It is a powerfully protective crystal to have nearby when you're feeling vulnerable. Black jade seals the aura and blocks psychic interference.

Garnet: Garnet is wonderful for energising the body and for strengthening and protecting the aura. It can also be used to soothe nightmares and enhance self-worth.

Labradorite: Labradorite is a true mystic and magician's crystal! It helps to awaken psychic and magical abilities. Labradorite stimulates communication abilities, and is very handy when you need to address a crowd. It's wonderful for auric protection, sealing the aura, and healing energy leaks.

Lapis Lazuli: Is a magical crystal, hailing from Egyptian times, which helps one connect to their inner warrior. It allows you to call upon your higher self, and latent powers from past lives that you may not have realised you possessed. It's wonderful for inner strength and being a guiding beacon to illuminate the true power within. Calling upon ancestors and past lives for wisdom, guidance and protection.

It awakens forgotten mystical knowledge. The knowledge is already inside of us, it's simply a matter of waiting and creating fertile soil for revelation. Lapis Lazuli is fabulous for opening the third eye and deepening your spiritual practise.

Moldavite: This is a tektite, said to have formed when a meteorite hit the Earth. Its energy helps to assist people who do not feel grounded, uncomfortably bound to the Earth Plane, and who may struggle to fit into worldly existence. It holds a high vibration and is wonderful when your mind spins to esoteric planes and you no longer feel at home on Earth. Or if you have incarnated on Earth from another planet, and feel a deep longing to return home.

It instils a sense of peace and is full of the knowledge of light guides who come to protect and guide you on the physical and spiritual plane. Helping multiple fields of existence to unite as one so we may find inner harmony. Moldavite is a true stone of the new age. There is lots of artificial moldavite on the market so try to find someone selling genuine moldavite if you wish to acquire some.

Moonstone: A wonderful crystal for enhancing psychic gifts. It gently helps people who find it hard to focus to feel safe in their present environment. It is calming and soothing. Moonstone can take you over the moon and into far off galaxies! So when you want to stay grounded you may wish to avoid wearing or carrying moonstone. However, it is wonderful for meditation. It is also wonderful for enhancing dreams, especially on the new moon.

Lepidolite: This is a very powerful crystal for releasing depression. Lepidolite has the ability to block negative thoughts. It simply won't stand for them. When you feel an avalanche of negative thought pattering drifting through your mind and you can't seem to get rid of these reoccurring thoughts, even if they have been present for years reach for some lepidolite as it can be a powerful consciousness and thought shifter, blocking negative thought. It is therefore a very uplifting and magical crystal.

Opal: Opal is a very powerful and mystical gem. White opal is particularly effective for anyone who feels as though haunted by demonic entities, cursed, or is under regular psychic attack, especially in their dreams. When programmed it can create a sheath of invisibility around the aura of the wearer; which hides the user on the astral planes.

Quartz Crystal: Powerful quartz crystals repair auric damage. This damage may have occurred from shock, trauma, from psychic attack or from the consumption of unhealthy foods, or alcohol and drugs, all which make our energetic systems weaker. It may take the aura months to heal, but when used with loving intent quartz helps to guide and ease the healing process. It's best to put ourselves in circumstances and situations where our energetic field isn't threatened, however sometimes this is unavoidable.

Quartz strengthens the protective shield of the aura, making it less vulnerable or attractive to potential predators. It imbues a strength of courage and hope. When used as a psychic shield it needs to be cleansed regularly. It is also incredibly powerful when naturally combined with black tourmaline, which amplifies its protective shield.

Quartz crystal is wonderful for programming. When you hold a powerful quartz crystal in the palm of your hands, take deep breathes and tune into the crystal, sense the magical, wise energy. Surrender thought, and begin to feel the quartz lifting your mood. As you start to relax, unwind, and feel more connected to the Earth, inner calm is experienced. Without force burdens lessen and peace is gifted from the crystal.

Quartz can heighten the energy of a room. I have a beautiful plate filled with blessed quartz that amplifies the energy of my writing space. It helps me connect to source energy, light energy. I also have a beautiful piece of raw soulmate quartz with hematite growing on the side. This crystal is wonderful for healing. I find that as soon as I place it on my head, to help soothe a headache, the pain starts to dissolve. If I have any pain in my body, I turn to this crystal as it seems to lessen pain when placed on my body. I find it to be the ultimate stress reliever.

We can use quartz crystals to help our wishes and desires to manifest. Doors that once seemed closed open, and new pathways are discovered. All it takes is patience and intent. Take a special crystal with you wherever you go and allow its subtle energy (or not so subtle!) to permeate through your life. Enhancing peace and harmony. Just as nature blooms, and flowers unfold under the loving warmth given freely by the sun, you too can bloom from direct connection with the energy of the quartz crystal.

Rhodochrosite: Helps to soothe pain from emotional wounds. It helps to gradually surface painful memories so they can be released. Rhodochrosite is a beautiful crystal which may be instrumental in healing fears associated with sexual abuse, childhood neglect and or rape. It gently soothes whilst creating a pathway to acknowledge fears, and forgive and release soul traumas.

Rose Quartz: Carries the vibrational affirmation of unconditional love. It's wonderful to drink spring water that's had rose quartz soaking in it as it is very soothing, like liquid love. It's powerful and subtle as it doesn't strip back your past hurts and make you re-evaluate your entire life too quickly. It simply lifts you gently to peaceful vibrational states of wellbeing, self-acceptance, forgiveness, and love of others.

Rose quartz is a wonderful gem to attract romantic, as well as self-love into your life. A beautiful affirmation to use with rose quartz is, *I love and accept myself, and all those who surround me.* Or *I chose the path of peace and attract an abundance of love into my life.*

Selenite: A pure, high vibrational crystal. Selenite does not need consistent cleansing and can be used to cleanse other crystals. Selenite connects you directly to light consciousness and spreads an aura of peace, light, and angelic guidance throughout the room or around the soul it is connected with. Truly a gift from the heavens.

Black Tourmaline: A protective stone. Worn around the neck black tourmaline blocks negative thought forms being projected toward you and psychic attack. It's very helpful to use black tourmaline when you want to release a habit, psychic attack, competitive energies, clingy energy from loved ones, dark energy from negative co-workers or competitors, or negative thought patterns. Black Tourmaline deflects jealousy projected onto you.

Black tourmaline with mica, which has formed around the tourmaline, is a very powerful combination for energetic protection. Black tourmaline absorbs psychic smog. The mica reflects negative projections placed on you back to the psychic leach, encouraging them to resolve their own mental blocks.

Black tourmaline is so protecting it can sometimes keep you almost in a hermit like bubble. For protection whilst interacting with others you may choose to use a labradorite crystal.

Pink Tourmaline: Is a magical, protective, healing stone. Embedded in quartz, the vibration of pure love is enhanced. Pink tourmaline is very effective for bully victims as it creates a safe space to open the heart chakra, whilst being protective at the same time.

Green Tourmaline: Green tourmaline connects us to feelings of abundance and self-worth. It also helps transmute feelings of rejection projected from fatherly figures.

☆ The Magic of Crystals ☆

Often when you walk into a crystal shop, the first crystal you're drawn to or pick up is the one for you. Crystals have a way of choosing their guardians. It's not necessarily the biggest of the prettiest crystals that will have the most transformative effect in your life.

Children are wonderful at picking up the subtle vibrations of crystals. Many times I've met little ones who speak to crystals as though talking to an old friend. Seeing the living soul consciousness emanating from the crystal.

Crystals are truly gifts from the divine. As they subtly align us with their positive vibrations. Deeply connected to nature, they create a healing pathway for the soul. Shifting our consciousness where we may have become so entangled in modern jungles that we've forgotten sensations of peace, empowerment, and wellbeing. Crystals have millions of years of Earth consciousness, Gaia consciousness filtering through them and it is an honour to hold space with such wise and connected beings.

You don't have to feel the energy of crystals to benefit from them. Their beauty brings inner peace as we connect to nature by being in their vicinity. Just as there is no words to describe a magical forest, crystals are another of nature's gifts that bless us asking nothing in return. Gifting us a deep appreciation for the Earth so that we may become wise and generous protectors of this sacred and majestical planet.

Coming in all shapes, colours, and sizes, they teach us the beauty present in variation and of the wisdom hidden inside our wonderful planet. They teach us of the magic in surrendering to life. As you are created by that which manifested the crystal you are already truly blessed.

The presence of crystals in your home creates balance. Simply the act of bringing nature indoors helps to create an ambience of peace and tranquillity and can help begin inner transformations. Like a beautiful flower crystals bring the joy of nature into our present awareness. Alive for millions of years there is so much we can learn from these beautiful earth babies.

You are nothing but a ball of bliss
Floating through the abyss
You think you're here
that's why you're full of fear
But you're not really there
You could be anywhere
You're a special soul, or so I'm told
by the angels watching your life unfold
You think you have to do something bold
to be worthy of life
But you are worthy because you exist
You're a starburst of bliss, floating through the abyss

-     *Starburst*

CHAPTER TWELVE

Natural Beauty, Wellness and Diet

Inner nourishment promotes true beauty. Compassion, laughter, inner-peace and taking care of others provides nourishment for the spirit. Meditation and higher learning assists in nourishing the mind. Natural foods, essential oils, herbs, and supplements nourish the body. Knowing you are a being of light and love helps your aura glow and creates a radiant glow around your being, not visible to the naked eye but perceptible as mystical, enigmatic radiance.

Humans revere beauty, or at least we think we do. What we really revere is inner light. When we take care of ourselves from an internal standpoint, our aesthetic reflection mimics this. We're blessed with the good fortune of the body's temple feeling clean and loved. The body is a vessel taking us from one life experience to the next so we may enjoy the physical delights, wonders and horrors of this plane of consciousness.

A smile, twinkle in the eye, a rustic glow on the cheeks is the direct effect of our mood and state of wellbeing. A loving, positive attitude, helping others and inner joy reflects beauty that cannot be achieved with cosmetic surgery, through a pill, or the use of synthetic beauty products.

The most inspiring and beautiful people to behold are those who are humble, with generous hearts, not plagued by jealousy or judgements. Acceptance of others and ourselves leads to true beauty. Wearing scars of hard times and negative thoughts doesn't matter for when you truly feel peace you become the beauty of your creator. You embody the beauty of the land, of Mother Nature. In truth, every being is beautiful for we are all reflections of source energy.

Beauty is a feeling we get when we interact with someone. Have you ever noticed how you may see someone as incredibly beautiful though they defy societal norms of what's considered beautiful? I've found the most beautiful people are always the ones who share smiles, hugs, tears of delight or sorrow, who accept their fears, triumphs, and most of all, glow from kind-heartedness.

A person who's bitter or resentful cannot maintain an authentic glow. No matter how much effort is spent on their outward appearance. Negative thoughts, complaints, worry, anger, and resentment scar the face and the eyes. They tarnish our good nature and scour our features with the essence of unhealed hurts, pain, and suffering. It doesn't matter that they do, as any issues we have are there to help us heal so we can step into the truth of who we are, beautiful manifestations of pure awareness.

When our mental consciousness is poisoned by self-doubt and a lack of love awareness, we reflect this to the world. Humans are intuitive beings, when you walk into a room you can be drawn to an individual or repelled. It doesn't matter what effort he or she has gone too to present a beautiful happy face. The pain lurking within is reflected in seconds. Before our conscious mind interrupts and makes superficial judgements.

We don't need every person in the world to be drawn to our individual light. As humans, we connect with people for all different reasons. Interaction with a mix of characters is healthy for our growth and development.

Sometimes a severe dislike of an individual can serve as a warning. It can also act as a lesson for us to learn forgiveness, compassion, and to love ourselves and others more. What we dislike in others usually reflects something we hate about ourselves. A negative voice of internal judgement or a reflection of pain and suffering from our earlier years we've not yet forgiven. These are clues we can use to create positive changes.

☆ Clean Diets ☆

Clean food, shifts our bodies vibration into alignment with light essence. This helps to attract positive emotions, good feelings, release toxins both mental and physical and helps us become more courageous. A healthy, harmonious meal, leaves us feeling vibrant, enriched, and uplifted. When we eat dense, solid, low vibration food, we feel sluggish, lethargic, depressed, and unloved. We feel unloved because we're not nourishing our body and our hearts with positive vibrations.

All food carries vibrations. If we want to lift our mood, it's essential we use food as a tool to raise our conscious point of reflection. A saint, guru, or just a positive happy-go-lucky individual can eat all forms of food and remain at peace. This is because food is not the control panel for how we feel - although through advertising manipulation and food addictions we often conclude it's a source of our happiness. Our vibration will however, most often fall into sync with the vibration of the food we eat unless we override this vibrational charge with the essence of love.

Food comprises of frequency. It can be positively or negatively charged. This charge comes from its physical essence, the process used to manufacture the foods, chemicals, pesticides, herbicides and fungicides used to produce the food. Also from the energy placed upon the food as it's being prepared before it reaches our mouth. We are all susceptible to the vibrations our food emits. Bless everything you eat with love, thankfulness, gratitude, and peace.

Kirlian photography can literally show the life force of food. We want to resonate with light, attract light, and vibrate with light. Food produced with love and light becomes a powerful tool for raising our consciousness.

If you feel highly anxious, depressed, suicidal, glum or unhappy it's important to have a look at your diet. You will intuitively know whether the foods you've been consuming resonate happy vibes in your body or if they are taking you down a dark pathway.

A fulfilling diet begins in our minds. Feeding ourselves thoughts of self-love, acceptance, and forgiveness is a healthy practise. A positive outlook is the most important place to start when shifting food awareness. A self-love diet is one from which you'll never need a detox! If you feel you've lost your inner glow, the first cupboard to refresh is in your mind. When we think positive thoughts, we're guided towards healthy food choices.

There are is an enormous variety of diets to choose from. Here are some examples: fruitarian, raw vegan, vegan, vegetarian, paleo, blood group diet, Jain diet, low histamine, gluten-free, Kundalini Yoga diet, etc. If we remember all food carries energy and we are energetic beings who attune to the vibrations of our food, this can help guide us towards a healthy, soul nourishing diet.

We also have the powerful ability to bless each item that passes through our lips with love so it can deliver positivity into our bellies! We can chant mantras over our food and bless each meal before we consume it. This helps to lift the vibration of the food and increase our own connection to universal love.

There are foods that pulse at high vibrations and can make us feel good, no matter how low our current energy has been. Choosing food that is radiant and fresh makes us feel wonderful. When we eat healthy high vibration foods, we rewire our brain with nourishing goodness. It makes it easier to have a more positive outlook on life. How we feel and what we eat can run in direct correlation with one another. That's why when we feel terrible about our inner self; it can be so hard to clean up our diet.

Even fruits and vegetables can be raised in unsightly conditions. Fungicides, herbicides, pesticides and chemicals concoctions used to grow fruits and vegetables can drop their vibration significantly. I believe genetically modified foods are a low vibrational food choice. Growing food without compassionate consciousness is like bullying a child whilst raising them; one who's been treated with cruelty and neglect is rarely as confident and vibrant as one who's matured in an environment of love.

Biodynamic, organic and naturally ripened is best; picked straight from the garden! If it can't be grown, then don't eat it, is a great motto for choosing healthy foods. If you feel you're not in a place to afford organic food, but would like too, that's okay. Be at peace with where you're at in life. Food isn't everything and we need to be gentle to allow change.

When you eat fruits and vegetable look for ones that use less pesticides that others. There are many great lists online indicating pesticide residue levels. Also, see how you feel after a particular meal. Mono meals are a wonderful way to realise how different foods affect our mood and energy levels.

Throughout my life, I've tried a great selection of different health conscious diets. Carnivore, vegan, vegetarian, fruitarian, and raw vegan. I've held these diets for extended periods and felt the effects of each diet in my body. The best benefit I've felt is that through eating a plant based diet you aren't harming any animals. This compassion is felt vibrationally in your body. Eating kindly encourages you to become more and more heart based. Compassionate eating is a simple way to open your heart and to be more loving towards yourself and others.

If you choose to eat meat give thanks to the animal for giving its life to sustain you. Be conscious that you are consuming a being that was once living and breathing. Rather than disassociating from what is before you.

It's possible to be an unhealthy vegan/vegetarian just as it is to be an unhealthy carnivore! It's so easy to judge our own diets. We put unnecessary pressure on our bodies when we analyse a plate of chips and say, "These are so unhealthy! What a glorious guilty pleasure". We are injecting negative thought forms onto our food before it even enters our mouth. Leading us to intake guilt, resentment, *and* saturated fats at the same time. If we look at the chips and bless them with love and gratitude, their effect is much more positive on our body.

This isn't to say indulge in junk food consistently and think positive thoughts. As this would be difficult due to the negative connotations instilled into our consciousness surrounding junk food core beliefs. Foods which are light on the body and carry amazing and strong vibrations for healing include: sweet potatoes, Swiss chard, berries, mandarins, grapes, seeds, fruits of all kinds, fresh vegetables, water kefir, herbal teas, and pure spring water (un-fluoridated) infused with rose quartz crystals and Rescue Remedy.

Having a list of foods, you know make you feel good can be wonderful when cravings arise. You can turn to foods, which lift your mood, satisfy your appetite, and strengthen your energy. When we have genuine *feel good food* on hand, we're less likely to turn to the unhealthy foods to which we are addicted. Junk food makes us feel as though we're quenching our appetite for self-love, acceptance, and reducing stress, when really it adds pressure and pulls us away from states of inner harmony.

Junk foods seem to dig up states of guilt, rejection, and fear. *Feel good foods* don't have to be the same for everyone and it's best to discover what suit you best. Kinesiology (a non-invasive energetic healing method using gentle muscle monitoring to better understand an individual's state of wellbeing and alignment) is a wonderful way to uncover foods, which resonate in harmony with your body's true desires.

Sometimes it's best to allow ourselves just to be, and see how love, life, and food unfolds in our life. As we connect the dots of inner peace and feeling good our relationship with food naturally heals.

Changes in diet can force us to look at suppressed emotional issues. Often we stuff ourselves with foods to stuff down our emotions. I know whenever I'm a little nervous I head to the fridge to look for an (unhealthy!) cure. When we feel safe, our diet gently heals itself. If you find yourself addicted to particular foods, ask, 'Where do I feel afraid?' and 'How can I help myself to feel safer in the present moment?'

When you do decide to change your diet, watch how people around you react. Are they positive and accepting? Do they support your healthy choices, or do they complain that you're being too restrictive and try to block your progress? Or do they comment negatively about changes occurring in your body. You want people that surround you to support your growth. If they don't, it's time to question the relationship. We want to nourish life's journey with healthy food and nurturing people.

One of the hardest things about changing your diet can be explaining to friends and family why you're eating in a particular way. Especially if it's a little 'different' from normal. I've found it's best not to try to explain, unless someone asks from a point of genuine inquisitiveness. This way you are not attracting an argument, debate or discussion that can make you feel afraid or uneducated or put you off your healthy eating plans altogether. What you consume is your choice and your business, no one else's.

When we label what we eat, as good or bad, vegetarian, carnivore, or raw vegan we set ourselves high expectations. When we label our dietary preferences, or try to explain the way we eat, we can be left feeling energetically drained. Especially if we don't have a dictionary of facts on hand! It's easiest to discuss diet with people who are open minded, receptive, and have a positive outlook. Especially as it can be such an emotional trigger for so many people.

If you want to share but feel a little uncomfortable, you can always recommend books and different resources that have helped your journey. That way you can enjoy your meal without having to justify yourself. When people are friendly and open, share your knowledge. Your intuition will guide you. Just check in and *see how comfortable you feel*.

When we are at peace with our dietary choices, we're much more likely to attract accepting and genuinely interested and like-minded people into our reality. People who support our dietary choices.

☆ Choosing Sobriety ☆

I have not consumed alcohol for many years now. It was one of the most life changing dietary adjustments I've ever made. I noticed a radical change in my relationships, some people wanted friendships that revolved purely around social drinking. These relationships faded very quickly! Other friends said they felt relieved. As even though I'd offer alcohol whenever they visited they often preferred to stay sober saying it was relaxing to be with someone with whom they could have fun with whilst not drinking.

After encountering a few hostilities and feeling a little isolated in social situations I adapted my mental affirmations. I used to believe it was sociable to drink. That I was the best version of myself when I was tipsy! Alcohol was a large part of my 'fun' mentality. So I changed my affirmations to, *I always attract positive, inspiring, sober people!*

I met so many wonderful sober people. Everywhere I went, even in bars I'd be standing next to people who never drank. And guess what? They inspired me! Lots of athletes and very successful, driven people don't drink. I found myself surrounded by people I admired. Not drinking became a wonderful experience! Sometimes all it takes is a shift in perception.

I don't consume alcohol, as I know it affects my energy levels, intuitive abilities, focus, and self-confidence. Every time I drank alcohol, my intention was to alleviate pressure in social circumstances. As a child I loved parties and never needed a drink! I wanted to experience this level of openness again so I gave up drinking. I chose that if I felt shy, I'd allow myself to be shy. If I felt radiant, I'd allow myself to glow! I decided I wouldn't drink until I felt as confident as I did as a child in public.

What I found was, eventually I forgot the feeling of needing to drink before I socialised. Sometimes I still feel apprehensive when attending a social event. Instead of reaching for a glass of wine I'll meditate, or try to clear my energy. I'm not as loud and aggressive as I was when I drank socially and I find I can still be sensitive to people's remarks, and heavy energies. When I drank more, I tended not to care, or would respond with aggression. Now I prefer to work on the issues I have, rather than mask them. Which is what I feel I was doing with alcohol. I also feel being sober heightens intuition and revitalises the mind.

Being sober allows us to be present. As uncomfortable, as this can seem, it really is a wonderful thing. Even if it means confronting inner demons when we'd rather not. Healing our own issues - which can arise when we give up alcohol - is a wonderful gift to you and your family and friends. When you can be present and your mind feels clear, you can support others more than you'd realised. I understand that being sober is not for everyone. However, there are some wonderful benefits to it. I've especially loved not waking up groggy, moving through my insecurities, and being more present with my family.

☆ Food, Emotions & Intuition ☆

Food can affect our level of intuitive ability. As it can overpower our conscious mind, directing our desires. When our body is trying to cleanse itself of toxins, we may become bogged down and our intuitive abilities may feel blocked or non-existent. Things like caffeine, alcohol, cigarettes, genetically modified foods, artificial flavours and sweeteners pull us away from our natural intuitive abilities. Even if you're open to these gifts think how much *more* receptive, you'd feel if you weren't suffering from the closing of psychic channels as a result of food consumption choices.

Sometimes very sensitive and intuitive people crave junk food, and addictive substances as it shuts down their psychic channels. This is a natural form of protection. When we're sensitive and our auras are wide open, we pick up on a lot of emotional baggage and shadows surrounding us left by other people, residing thought forms, entities, or negative surroundings and layouts. These energies can leave scars on the land, in houses and the surrounding environment. In Feng Shui this is referred to as shar chi.

Very sensitive people will find themselves highly distressed from news feeds, seeing others suffer, or even feeling the effect of jealousy or competitive arrows being pointed in their direction. They are aware of the heavy thoughts of others and sometimes things like social media can feel suffocating. So many energies rolled into one platform, with everyone searching for recognition and validation.

Sometimes life in this day and age can feel overwhelming. Especially when you're so busy taking care of everybody else that you forget about your own needs. There are physical and non-physical stressors that can really impact the body and mind. Depression, fear, anguish, feelings of failure, and suffering can all lead to weight gain reflecting a lack of love and disconnection with the self and body.

Excess weight is always linked to our emotions and how safe we feel. When you can look at it as 'emotional weight', that this weight serves a purpose of protecting you from heavy and traumatic emotions it's much easier to be gentle on yourself whilst losing weight. Weight fluctuates with what we're going through emotionally. It serves the purposes of protecting us, helping us to feel snugly and safe. As we gently deal with layers of emotional stresses that can range from childhood issues to present day concerns, we can lose weight in a fulfilling and kind way as we are energetically ready, and more aligned to move through fears and uncomfortable emotions.

If you associate with people, who drain your energy and seem to suck the life from you, or find yourself in negative environments, or trapped by fear of past traumas, sometimes the best form of self-defence is to shut down. Food addiction can become a form of protection. Our higher self knows low vibrational food clogs our energy channels and creates a psychic wall of safety that's very difficult to penetrate.

The complications of this protective wall is that we shut down as unique, happy individuals at the same time, suppressing our inner light. Until we feel through and begin to heal from painful emotional and physical wounds we stagnate in our body. If we strengthen our auras, with protective jewellery and amulets, call upon our ancestors for help, use crystals and stones for protection and peace, align our Feng Shui and practise positive affirmations to lift our point of attraction, we can allow ourselves to be unhinged from ties that hold us back. Whilst blocking the need for energy dropping foods to barricade our spiritual and emotional channels. When we feel safe it's much easier to lose weight, consume healthy, life giving nurturing food, and allow our light to shine.

I've found fruit to be the lightest vibration food. Whenever I consume a diet of pure fruit, my energy levels soar. Fear and anxiety begins to dissipate from my body. It removes you from the collective conscious environment you are in and if you practise meditation, it helps to elevate you into realms of pure light. It's like practising meditation through food awareness. High vibrational foods can help to clear toxic and stagnant emotional issues.

Fruit is love. It's Mother Nature's gift to us. It's delicious raw and streams life force. A diet of pure fruit is a wonderful cleanse to help get you back on track, especially if you've been suffering from mental anguish. Fruit is simple and so nourishing. It's easy to source and better yet, super easy to prepare!

Fruits and vegetables are positive forces for your body. You can eat them fresh and raw - the highest vibration. Or steamed and cooked - also very healthy and nourishing. A diet of fruits and vegetables is optimal.

A wonderful healer in India, taught me that caffeine blocks our Mouth of God. A point at the back of the neck, located just beneath the skull. Known in Chinese as the Jade Pillow or Yu Chen. When our Mouth of God is blocked, we close off our psychic/intuitive channels.

This practitioner only performs healing on people who've eliminated caffeine from their diet, this includes, chocolate, tea, coffee, sweet soda beverages, and certain diet pills, for a minimum of one week before the healing session. This, he informed, is because healing channels and the Mouth of God become much more open and receptive to positive change without obstruction from caffeine.

When we consume animal products, we also consume the vibration that the animal emits at death, and the energy they held in their body throughout their life. Fear, anxiety, and terror of death flood through animals before they're slaughtered is still present in the foods vibrational makeup. Most animals used for food do not die of natural causes, they are killed for food. When we remove fear from our lifestyle, we begin to live in harmony with nature. If you choose to eat animal products, choose biodynamic or organically reared produce.

We sometimes fall under the illusion that our food consumption choices mean nothing, but our dietary choices are incredibly powerful. We can choose a peaceful plate. Are we consuming fear slaughtered animals and crops that pollute our waterways? Or are we choosing light energy foods that promote peace?

Foods have the ability to raise or drop our consciousness - unless we are truly aware that we are consciousness itself. The foods we put into our mouths align us with others that are consuming similar foods. We start to vibrationally match people's dominant food choices. When we release particular foods from our diet, this can create a letting go of old relationships. Those based on lifestyle choices that no longer serve our needs, or match our emotional frequency.

Every time we shift a lifestyle pattern, we open ourselves to new beginnings. Sometimes this is why we are scared to change. Dietary change is powerful as it opens us up to new and exciting relationships with people who chose peace and love on their plates. Becoming a conscious eater helps us to shed pounds and release past emotional pains.

Sometimes as we clean up our diets, suppressed emotions may surface. You may wish to seek a reiki healer, or massage therapist etc. to help transmute these emotions. Just watching what comes up allows us to move through and shed the weight buried emotions have on our soul. Leaving these emotions to fester lodges resentment, anger and guilt deeper into our psyche.

Be kind to yourself, you are a beautiful being. The light of all the stars shines within you. Be brave, accept yourself as you are, and let everything go. Surrender your worries and fears to spirit, God, angels, deities, whatever you believe in and allow the gift of unconditional self-love to nourish you.

As we've incarnated on the planet many times, we've experienced cultural eating tendencies from all over the world and even different conscious realms of existence and planets. That's why everyone has varying dietary needs, and why some people just cannot seem to clean up their diet. If we are clinging to our past life diets and experiences, be them positive or negative, they'll influence our lives subtly and sometimes not so subtly.

Through a past life regression, I learned I was once a monk, thus it's been easy for me to give up alcohol and meat. This is a positive aspect reflecting from this lifetime. I once experienced a life as a street cleaner in China. All I could afford was rice and soy sauce, which I love to this day!

We can also be hindered by harder life path decisions that arise from previous lifetimes. It's a good idea to be open to embracing the new and letting go of old ways that no longer serve us. You can easily connect to past lives if you look at a particular food source you're drawn to that no one else in your family enjoys; you may desire Spanish, Thai, European, or Brazilian foods etc. These cravings can give you hints of your earlier incarnations.

☆ Fermented Foods ☆

Some of my favourite foods and beverages are fermented; these include kombucha, water kefir, and sauerkraut, etc. Fermented foods, have an amazing effect on the body. They are full of beneficial bacteria that nourish the gut and can do wonders for your wellbeing. They are wonderful for helping rebuild worn out bodies. I love that these little known, inexpensive (when homemade) and high quality beverages and foods nourish our bodies from the inside out. Secret super foods we can all enjoy.

Good bacteria in our body is essential to our wellbeing. Inside your gut lives countless organisms that help you digest your food and assimilate nutrients into the body. These bacteria are intricately involved with our immune systems protecting us from harmful microorganisms. Fermented foods can help to boost your body's supply of good bacteria.

Anyone who consumes a highly refined diet will benefit from the added consumption of raw fermented foods. Vegans who don't consume yoghurt or probiotics will also benefit from adding fermented foods to their diet.

Probiotic rich fermented foods may prevent pathogenic bacteria attaching to the intestinal wall. Good bacteria's can also help prevent parasitic infections. With people travelling more and more these days having a healthy gut means we are more resilient to nasty bugs, which we may have never before encountered. Good bacteria helps to strengthen our immune system.

Anyone who has suffered from major health concerns may find benefit from adding probiotic rich foods into their diet. Remember to be gentle on your body. At first a little good bacteria may rock the boat of your belly if you're not used to it, so adding fermented foods to the diet gradually is a wonderful practise.

Due to modern living there is an increasing lack of diversity in our *microbiome* - the word used to describe the combination of our human body and its resident bacteria. Many things cause this lack of diversity: diet, environmental factors, antibiotics, etc. The tangible result seems to be people with more health problems.

Fermented foods like kombucha, milk kefir and water kefir, kvass kimchi and sauerkraut etc. fill our bodies with good bacteria and help us to de-stress, relax and live healthy lives. Humans are comprised of hundreds of trillions of microbes that live on our skin, in our mouths, and in our guts. We *need* these microbes for everything from helping us to digest our food, to feeling less stressed.

Following are recipes you can use to make your own homemade kombucha, water kefir and milk kefir. Through these simple methods, and with just a few ingredients you can make your own fermented foods! Which nourish your soul and belly. ♥

☆ Kombucha ☆

Kombucha is an effervescent semi-sweet tea, fermented with the aid of a scoby. Kombucha is full of probiotics, good bacteria, live active enzymes, polyphenols (which fight free radicals), glucuronic acid (a powerful detoxifier), and other happy things that our intestines love. Kombucha may help boost our overall health.

SCOBY, is an acronym for *symbiotic culture of bacteria and yeast*. The scoby (bacteria and yeast) eats the majority of the sugar in the tea, transforming it into a refreshing, fizzy, slightly sour fermented beverage. The scoby is rubbery and spongy, and looks a little bit like a jellyfish. Brown stringy bits hang from it, and it transforms sugary tea into something delicious and unique. It's weird and fabulous.

There are various theories why the bacteria and yeast form this jelly-like layer of cellulose at the top of the kombucha. The most plausible is that it protects the fermenting tea from the air and helps support a specific healthy environment inside the jar, shielded from outside unfriendly bacteria.

Kombucha Instructions

Ingredients
1/2 cup raw organic sugar (or white sugar)
3 tea bags or for loose leaf 3 teaspoons. The tea needs to be naturally caffeinated. Black tea, green tea, white tea and oolong tea are all good options
kombucha starter culture – SCOBY
1/3 cup strong starter liquid
1 litre filtered water

Utensils
kettle
brewing vessel - glass or oak is good, don't use anything made
of metal
cloth cover or paper towel
elastic band

Steps

1. Boil water. Add purified hot water, tea bags, and sugar to brewing vessel. Allow the sweet tea to cool completely.

   Cooled tea is important as hot tea added to your starter and scoby may kill the good bacteria and create mould.

2. Remove the tea. Take the teabags out by hand or filter the tea through a sieve if using loose-leaf tea.

3. Place your kombucha scoby and starter tea into the brewing vessel. Fill with the filtered cool sweet tea. Allow 1-2 inches at the top of the glass for breathing room, and so your scoby doesn't climb out (joking!).

4. Cover with a cloth or paper towel and secure with the elastic band. Bless your kombucha; send reiki energy, and positive vibrations! Kombucha also loves classical music.

5. Keep the jar at room temperature out of direct sunlight. Leave to brew for 7 to 10 days.

6. It's not unlikely for the scoby to float at the top, bottom, or even sideways. A new cream-coloured scoby should start forming on the surface of the kombucha liquid within a few days. With each batch you brew a new baby scoby will grow. It may attach itself to the old scoby, but it's okay if they separate.

You can leave your new scoby in the fermentation vessel, it simply helps to speed up fermentation and may give subsequent brews an added spicy, tart flavour.

You may also see brown stringy bits floating beneath the scoby, sediment collecting at the bottom, and bubbles collecting around the scoby. These are all signs of healthy fermentation.

7. After seven to ten days, try your kombucha ferment. You can use a straw or if you have a vessel with a tap pour yourself a little taster. When it reaches a balance of sweetness and tartness that is pleasant to you, the kombucha is ready. The longer you leave it, the more the kombucha will taste like vinegar, this is okay to drink, it will just have a real bite! It may be a little too strong for some people's taste preferences and can be used on salads.

   The more vinegary the kombucha the less sugar is present, and the stronger the kombucha elixir will be. When you are brewing for health reasons stronger is best, as it's more fermented and will contain an enormous amount of beneficial bacteria. However, if you have a sensitive tummy a milder batch may go down better. Be true to your taste and sensitivities.

8. Save some of the kombucha tea to use as starter tea for your next round of brewing kombucha. Keep the scoby ready for your next ferment.

9. Drink your delicious elixir!

10. Alternatively, at this point you can bottle the finished kombucha. To double ferment, pour the fermented kombucha into bottles, along with any honey, maple

syrup, juice, herbs, ginger, homemade syrups, cordials, or fruit you may wish to use as flavouring. Adding extra sugars prolongs fermentation and hence encourages potent fizz! You'll want to leave your kombucha to double ferment for between two and five days, depending on the temperature and the tartness you require.

Kombucha can become very carbonated, to slow carbonation store it in the fridge. 'Burb' any unrefrigerated bottles by opening them daily. If you're using glass be careful the bottles don't explode. This is a dangerous possibility! They need to be checked regularly and preferably kept them in a sealed plastic container or in a pantry, safely tucked away.

It may be best to use plastic brewing bottles if you want increase carbonation and lessen the risk of potential explosions. When the plastic bottles are hard after being left out of the refrigerator you know they are ready. Kombucha can fizz everywhere like champagne, so it's best to open bottled kombucha outdoors or very slowly!

Additional Notes:

☆ To store your kombucha and have a rest from brewing simply make a fresh batch and leave it on your countertop or in a cupboard. It will likely be too vinegary to drink by the time you're ready to brew again. However, the scoby will be healthy and the starter tea will be super potent, powerful and strong!

It should last for over a month on the counter top. The longer you leave it the bigger your scoby will grow.

Sometimes a kombucha scoby will create an airtight seal at the top of the jar when left for long periods. This can be an issue and it may need a top up with a little extra tea or for you to gently push down the scoby so it's totally submerged in sweet tea. When not submerged mould can grow.

Storing scobys in the fridge slows down the fermentation time too much and may cause mould growth. The yeast shuts down in the fridge and may go into hibernation.

N.B. Leaving your kombucha for longer periods to ferment can strengthen your starter tea and create thick healthy scobys if yours have been growing weak and thin.

☆ Alternative Tea Options: Black tea, green tea, white tea, oolong tea, or even a mix of these makes glorious kombucha. Herbal teas can have excess oils that may coat the good bacteria and create mould so they are avoidable. Earl grey tea contains bergamot oil and is also not advisable to use.

☆ You can use loose-leaf tea to brew Kombucha. The only issue I've found is that bits of black tea (which slip through the filtration process) like to lodge in the scoby itself. They won't hurt your brew but they don't always look pretty.

☆ Please note, if you are strictly avoiding caffeine, there are caffeine residues left in the kombucha after fermentation. If you want to have a full cleanse I would avoid kombucha altogether, however, due to the beneficial bacteria and probiotic content of the beverage I feel that it can enahnce our wellbeing and gut health which is an important priority.

☆ When choosing a fabric cloth to cover kombucha, (or water and milk kefir) go for a natural cotton cloth. Cheesecloth has too many large holes in it and can allow bugs and fruit flies to get into your brew. A tight weave cotton cloth is best. You'll still need to use an elastic band to tie down a tea towel, fruit flies are very good at discovery entry points into delicious elixirs. Cotton table napkins are a great option as the edges are hemmed which makes them suitable for washing.

☆ Always avoid contact with metal.

☆ When choosing a brewing vessel you may like to start with a two-litre glass jar. Once you get really into making your kombucha you may like to switch to a larger vessel made from ceramic, oak, or glass. Make sure the vessel is fairly even in shape. It's also a wonderful idea for it to have a spigot at the bottom so you can have your kombucha on tap!

If the jar is quite convex it can grow large sized scobys at the top which can be a little bit of a hassle as you drink your brew down, as the scobys are too big to be covered well with the kombucha liquid in the narrow base of the jar.

☆ It's normal for the scoby to float in different positions in the jar. Brown yeasty strings may form below or yeast may collect on the bottom of the brewing vessel. If your scoby develops a hole, bumps, dry patches, darker brown patches, or clear jelly-like patches, it is still fine to use. Usually these are all indicative of changes in the environment. Check where your kombucha brewing vessel is positioned. Is it getting too much sunlight?

☆ If you see mould on the scoby, (which is generally very obvious) discard the liquid and kombucha scoby and begin the process with new ingredients.

☆ Kombucha can be quite fussy when it comes to brewing with different sugars. If you'd like to experiment, wait until you have some backup scobys on hand and use the alternative sugar in a new vessel. This way if you have any mould issues, etc. you have some spare kombucha as back up.

☆ If you are extremely sensitive to sugar, you may like to make jun instead of kombucha. Jun looks identical to kombucha but is made with tea and honey. During experiments with jun I've always found it difficult to find a really healthy, active starter culture. In my experience it is much more susceptible to mould and weakening after subsequent brewing. Keep your eye out for a good supplier in your local area.

☆ Compost or discard your older scobys when your vessel gets too full or share with friends!

☆ When sharing spare kombucha scobys with friends make sure you give them some starter tea to go with it. The stronger the starter tea the healthier their brew will be. It's a good idea if you find yourself sharing kombucha often to keep a jar separate filled with strong starter tea - a minimum of a week old. Your starter tea can last for months. A new scoby will often form on top. The stronger the starter tea, the stronger the brew, which increases the likelihood of successful fermentation.

♥ Water Kefir ♥

Water kefir grains are also known as sugar kefir, tibicos, tibi and Japanese water crystals. The process of water kefir fermentation produces probiotics. Water and milk kefir 'grains' are self-propagating, so your first batch will likely last as long as you continue to make kefir. When fed correctly these babies rapidly grow and multiply.

Water Kefir Instructions

Ingredients
1 tablespoon water kefir
1 cup water (preferably filtered, no fluoride)
1 teaspoon blackstrap molasses
2 tablespoons of raw organic sugar, white sugar, jaggery, rapadura, coconut sugar or other sources of unrefined sugar

Utensils
plastic or bamboo strainer
glass jar
cotton cloth or paper towel to cover jar
wooden or plastic spoon
elastic band

Steps
1. Place water kefir granules into your glass jar. Add water, molasses, and sugar. Stir to combine with a plastic or wooden spoon.

2. Cover with a paper towel or cloth. Fasten cover with elastic band - this keeps out fruit flies.

3. Store away from direct sunlight for 24 to 48 hours and allow to brew. The longer the water kefir brews the less

sweet it will become. Leaving the brew for too long may starve the grains and place excess stress upon them or even destroy them.

4. When the water kefir is ready, pour the brew through the sieve to catch the grains. Store the fresh homemade water kefir in the refrigerator, or drink it straight away.

5. Start your next batch at once with the fresh kefir grains.

Bottling the finished Water Kefir (optional):

1. Pour the fermented water kefir into bottles (grains removed) along with any juice, herbs, sweeteners, or fruit you wish to use as flavouring. Leave about a half inch of air space in each bottle.

2. Until you get a feel for how quickly your water kefir carbonates, it's helpful to keep it in plastic brewing bottles. If you allow too much gas to build up glass bottles may shatter, so please be careful.

3. Store the bottled water kefir at room temperature out of direct sunlight and allow the water kefir to carbonate overnight or for a couple of days. Open the lid to release gas daily (to help prevent explosions).

4. Refrigerate to slow fermentation and carbonation. You don't have to worry about bottles breaking in the fridge, as this is much more unlikely.

Additional Notes:

☆ You can store water kefir grains in the fridge in a sugar, molasses, and water solution for up to a week (approximately). I have revitalised water kefir grains after about a month in the refrigerator stored in a strong sugar, molasses solution but the kefir becomes a lot less active and may need a lot of throw away batches brewed before it is fully active again. You can also freeze water kefir grains for up to 6 months. After freezing the grains, it may take several harvests to get the grains reproducing fully again.

☆ If you have too many water kefir grains, you can add them directly to a smoothie.

☆ During fermentation, you'll likely see the grains gently rising and sinking, as they produce gas when growing. This is a positive sign.

☆ Don't allow the water kefir to be exposed to metals. Stainless steel is safe to use.

☆ It's best not to purchase grains that have been dehydrated. I find they are never as strong or healthy.

☆ If you brew water kefir for too long, it tastes like vinegar. You can use it on salads or discard in the garden and start the process again.

☆ Water kefir on the bench in an unchanged sugar water solution, can lead to starvation of your grains and may kill them, or at least slow down their production. Pop them in the refrigerator if you don't have time to make your water kefir.

☆ Using natural sugars like jaggery and rapadura may change the flavour of the water kefir. The water kefir will generally taste less sweet and more like beer. I find the grains love these sugars and it helps them to grow very large and to multiply rapidly. If your grains aren't reproducing, it may be because you're not using enough sugar in the mixture or providing them with sufficient nutrients. A range of healthy nutrients is found in most unrefined sugars.

☆ Water kefir can be made with the liquid from fresh young coconuts. The kefir grains consume naturally occurring sugars from within the coconut water so it doesn't need any added sugar or molasses. Produced this way it won't be very sweet, but you can add a little sugar to taste if need be. It's a wonderful option for people who don't want to consume any sugar.

☆ Milk Kefir ☆

Milk kefir is a kind of runny yoghurt drink, similar to a lassi with an almost fizzy tang. It's made by adding special kefir 'grains' resembling cauliflower crumbs, to fresh milk. A combination of beneficial bacteria and yeast creates kefir grains. Over a couple of days, kefir grains ferment milk into a tangy, effervescent elixir

Milk kefir contains calcium, various amino acids, and vitamins A and D. Due to its high probiotic content kefir helps balance the flora and fauna in our bodies. Kefir contains 30-35 major strains of friendly probiotic bacteria, which are generally not present in store-bought kefir, acidophilus drinks, or yoghurt.

If you are lactose intolerant, you can produce milk kefir with coconut milk. If you are dairy sensitive, or conscious of consuming too much dairy, milk kefir as a health elixir used for a minimal time to sooth sensitive, delicate, wounded tummies is a highly valuable and effective elixir. Personally, I follow a largely plant based vegan diet but when my tummy has been in a tangle or if I'd taken a high dose of antibiotics, or encountered food poisoning, I've found milk kefir to be wonderfully soothing and regenerating. It is very high in good bacteria and probiotics and amazingly nourishing when used as a natural healing elixir, not simply as a daily food.

Milk Kefir Instructions

Ingredients
2 teaspoons kefir grains
1½ cups of full cream biodynamic organic milk

Utensils
plastic strainer (milk kefir shouldn't come into contact
with metal)
elastic band
cloth or paper towel
plastic or wooden spoon
glass jar

Steps
1. Place kefir grains into a clean glass jar and add milk.

2. Cover with cloth or paper towel. Fasten with an elastic
   band.

3. Send some love vibrations to your milk kefir. ♥

4. Leave the jar on the kitchen bench or in a pantry at
   room temperature for 24-48 hours. The longer you
   leave the milk kefir the sourer it tastes. Depending on
   the temperature, the necessary fermentation time
   increases or decreases. The ideal temperature for milk
   kefir is around 22°C or 71° F. It doesn't matter if you
   live in a hot or cold climate, with a little tweaking, and
   taste experimentation it's easy to get your kefir to taste
   just right.

5. When your milk kefir is ready, give it a stir with a plastic
   or wooden spoon. Use the plastic strainer to separate
   the grains from the kefir. Push the kefir through the
   strainer with your spoon, stirring gently.

6. You can now drink your kefir. You may wish to store it
   in the refrigerator, or add ice to drink it cool.

7. Optionally add some lavender or cardamom, and
   sweetener into the finished kefir milk and allow it to
   ferment for a day or night longer. Make sure it is
   covered. For the second ferment, all grains need to be

filtered out of the kefir. This can produce a very calming drink and is wonderful for restoring sensitive tummies.

8. Place the grains back into the kefir jar and add more fresh milk.

9. Enjoy your tangy kefir! Store milk kefir in the refrigerator.

Additional Notes:

☆ I like to use a plastic strainer with large holes as it makes the kefir easier to filter.

☆ Never allow the kefir grains to touch metal, as this will damage the grains.

☆ Share excess kefir grains with friends or blend into smoothies.

☆ If you need to take a break from making kefir, put your kefir grains into a jar with fresh milk, cover with a cloth and elastic band and store in the refrigerator. It's best not to store them for longer than a week, before providing the grains with fresh milk. But they can last for up to a month – rinse with filtered water before using again.

☆ You may culture milk kefir grains in coconut milk - canned coconut milk with no preservatives is best. Culture the milk kefir grains in cow or goats milk for twenty-four hours once every few batches to revitalise. You may wish to keep some grains spare to experiment with coconut milk. Kefir can also be made with whipping cream that has no additives. This produces a gorgeous ultra-creamy yoghurt, similar to Greek style yoghurt.

Living Well

For us to live healthy, happy, lives it's important we take time to nourish our inner sanctuary. Our wellbeing and diet often slips into unhealthy realms when we are feeling a little scared, unloved, or uncertain about life. Fear in our body can be a sign that we need to look at what we are putting into our bodies.

Many people are highly sensitive to a wide variety of foods. Even typically 'healthy' foods can cause reactions. Many people are sensitive to genetically modified foods, herbicides pesticides and fungicides, grains, corn, high histamine foods, gluten, rice, certain vegetables etc. so it's best we look at everything we are eating, when trying to align our body with new levels of health. When we choose foods with strong prana, or life force, we embrace a whole foods diet perspective.

If your diet or weight is an issue that concerns you try looking at it from a new perspective. If we worry about our weight, we project this negative thought consciousness into our body. Let's try a diet of positive thoughts and action. Inspired by a place of emotional self-care that encourages us to heal and live in love.

We attract foods into our lives that reflect our emotional state. Have you ever noticed that when you feel afraid, you eat foods that you know you react negatively too? When we become aware of how particular foods make us feel we can consciously choose to eat foods that make us feel stronger and more competent, especially when we are in need of support and nurturing. Also we can bring our presence and awareness to our dietary intake when we know we are consuming particular foods out of fear and anxiety.

Love is the greatest healer of all. When you acknowledge you are worthy of feeling safe, supported and loved you grasp that you're a naturally beautiful being and begin to consume beautiful, fulfilling foods. It becomes easier to digest life.

With love and care projected into our food, our ability to heal our emotions magnifies. We can create lives around enriching people who nourish our soul and share unity through food. The food we place in our bodies allows us to nurture our inner temple. It's not about regretting last night pizza; it's about embracing the wonderful opportunities before us.

Choose the diet that best suits you. That bests supports your wellbeing. Everyone has different opinions but what you consume is up to you. Food can empower your body, and nourish your soul when you eat whilst listening to your hearts guidance.

Liquid light of the sun warms our bare skin and sends healing rays of light through the earth. We glow from the suns radiance. We're enveloped in light as the sun caresses our skin. Trees absorb this nectar and produce fruitful bounty. The sun is our provider, it helps us unite and heal.

Water enfolded in our being, dew at dawn, rain clouds, rivers and oceans all simultaneously nurture our lands. The air we breathe is given to each and every one of us freely. It is the human race that's consumed with selling, buying, and judging. Nature does not judge, it gives unconditionally, and cares for us no matter what, no matter who we are.

We know in our hearts that machine created foods, create machine like human beings. We choose freedom, we choose raw, fresh, and wild. We release past temptations, knowing in the wilderness, we are free.

Free to explore. Free to discover. Free to be different.

Knowing the food we have is to share; we give to others and share with ourselves. Nature creates a warm, colourful, and inviting plate. We invite nature into our homes and our bodies.

We are wild and free and awakened to our inner radiance. Birds sing, frogs call, we share the knowledge that our soul's provider for this physical experience on Earth is Mother Nature.

In this we trust, from this grace thunderstorms form, rain patters, sunshine warms, and spring blossoms bloom. Nature governs our cycles. The moon's glow resting upon our food shines upon us. We are truly blessed.

Open your eyes
allowing the lashes to brush one another
top to bottom
Their soft embrace makes your body look half awake
and yet you see
what is yet unseen
the veil between the screen
When your eyes are tight shut
you see nothing much
But open them slight
to see a horizon of light
The darkness is there
but until pictures of the world fill the void
you are left devoid
of
scene
scenery
dreamily
you wake
Allow consciousness to burn
the embers of fire
your hearts desire
To discover the source of light
Silhouetted against the night

-    *Fire Horizon*

CHAPTER THIRTEEN

Accepting the Path

The journey of life is steeped in mystery and intrigue. Gradually the layers peel off and reveal to us the truth of our nature, divine bliss and love. We are all destined for miracles, for experiencing the wholeness of *being*.

When the journey feels stunted and the path to abundance, happiness, and joy looks bleak, look around you. What can you learn from the present moment? Where are you fighting for change? Where are you resisting it? Are you forgiving of yourself and others? Can you accept the moment? The more you step into the truth of who you are, the more you give yourself permission to unfold as flowers open towards the sun. You are always in the perfect place for your own inner healing.

Use your intuitive abilities and allow yourself to be divinely guided. When you sporadically bump into someone, see if they hold any clues as to the next direction in your life path. If you're unsure about an individual, see what happens in your life the moment you think about them, is it positive or negative? Look for signs and signals. This is how spirit talks to you, listen to the positive voices in your head, the way your body feels, and keep your eyes open.

Sometimes we go against our instincts, only to regret it later. Earth is a place to learn and grow. You're allowed to make mistakes, and you're also allowed to grow and expand your life experience. Be gentle on yourself. Treat yourself with the love and care you'd shine upon a newborn infant. Remember you're valuable because you exist. You are a holy being of light. Place this worth onto your own time, learn to associate with people who raise your consciousness, be it through health, wealth, or happiness. You are here to live abundantly and spiritually. You are worthy and divine. You are a gift to this world.

So many people feel cramped, living in dirty, stagnant environments both energetically and physically because we resist the truth of ourselves. We are resisting the truth of our nature. Love.

Love conquers all. Love removes limitations; it unwinds fear and clears judgement. It helps to remove the boulders that have formed on the way to our destination. We must remember the only recognisable and congruent destination for all in life is death. Death reinforces the cyclic nature of our being; that this too shall pass. For nothing living can continue in congruent harmony without death. We must allow a part of ourselves to die before we can confront the truth of our nature, the truth of our purpose on Earth.

When we let go, when we experience the lowest of the lows, something has died. A part of our soul feels as though it has broken and yet on Earth there's always birth. Seasons change, people change, they arrive on Earth for a time and then they go.

Babies embody joy. They show the power of the cataclysmic clash of birth, rebirth, and the distance we feel between separation of the spirit from the body and the journey into the unknown.

To find your path in life, stop forcing yourself to be someone or something. You already are enough. A light shines so bright in you that all those around can see your physical presence. The solidness of your body, your flesh, your blood, signifies the ripening of your soul and the journey you have dedicated yourself to for your life on Earth.

We cannot change others, and we cannot change ourselves. All you can do is to learn to release your perception of what makes you, you and become aware of the source of yourself. Stepping into compassion, joy and grace. Releasing the need to stay locked in limited perceptions of Self that make you feel worthless, small, and unloved. Until you learn that the truth of your nature is love, you miss the key link that can transform the fear in your heart into unaltered bliss.

You are wonderful. You are magnificent. You are bliss itself. When you learn to live from a state of love, the pain and suffering that's here to show the fragility of life on Earth; the ego as the boss of our soul, crumbles. The illusion starts to dissolve.

Suffering stems from your thoughts. From the illusion that you're worthless. From fears of your own insignificance. You deserve happiness. You deserve joy. You deserve freedom. No matter what you've done or where you come from, you deserve forgiveness. The truth is the only person that can give you this gift, is yourself.

When we learn to accept where we are and our egos perception of who we are, we learn forgiveness. Acceptance channels the pathway to divine prosperity, love, and infinite joy. We are all being guided towards the ultimate goal of merging with creation. Merging with the divine is the surrender of life into the hands of source energy.

If we're created from tiny filaments of dust, from fire and earth and if we can physically dissolve back into this abyss. There must be something more to this journey you're on than the fears and shadows of expectations projected towards you through the abyss of consciousness. Allowing your light to shine, with the knowing that you're one with universal consciousness gives you the creative freedom to step into your power as a conscious creator.

Life is about giving and receiving, birth and rebirth. Often we become jaded, and grind to a halt. Like dogs, we hold onto bones which seems to define our physical experience, money, children, families, people, homes, cars, careers, assets, pain, failures, suffering etc. However, these things do not truly define us; they're manifestations of the self-worth we abide by.

It's only when you deny the truth of your being that life becomes fearful. We've all been there, now it's time to claim your power. To release the past and surrender to the future.

Allow yourself to consciously wake up to the light within your heart, the burning truth that you are an infinite soul of creation, powerful beyond measure. You are magnificence. You are intuition. You are spiritual service.

Look into your heart and see the majesty of the gifts that allowed you to step onto this plane of consciousness. You chose to come to Earth for a reason. When you allow the freedom of expression of your soul, you align with source energy. Resentment, fears, and doubts merge with the divine, for in truth we are light beings.

The Earth needs you. When you give yourself permission to wake up to the essence of who you are, you allow life to express through you, not just happen to you.

Release the anger you hold towards others. When you're afraid, of what 'they' will say, allow the fears to come forth, be present with the fear. Look around your life and ask, am I truly happy? Where you feel you are not, feel your feelings of what is present, and witness how they hold you back and prevent your light from shining. Subtracting from the abundance of joy, prosperity, and happiness you wish to experience. When you extinguish fear with truth, it dissolves and loses the power with which it once manipulated your heart and mind.

When you realise you're one with the divine, your truth is enough to dissolve mountains. Many of us dream of the day we learn to release the veil that keeps us stuck in the confines of these material walls.

Allow light to flow down through your crown and to guide your being. You will be shown, through the gentle whispers of source energy the path that shall best allow you to share your gifts with the world and to prosper.

Remember to acknowledge the voice of fear. However, in the long run, when you die, what do you want to align with? Fear or love? Often our fears hold us back. Acceptance is everything. The mind is not your friend. When it realises you are awakening, it will do everything in its power to avoid destruction. Our mind imagines us into adored movie stars and then switches the film to a horror. Always ask, 'Who is it that is thinking these thoughts?' Once you discover your true nature, divine love, you will be eternally free.

When you live from the truth of your nature, from awareness of your 'beingness' you walk through life with grace, compassion, and love. The more we turn away from the truth of our nature; the more we step into fear, trauma, and tragedy.

If everyone could see the truth of their being, there would be no need for world peace. For we already are that, peace, bliss and compassion. Divine love is the truth of your nature. It is only when you seek outside for other things to fulfil you that your mind is led astray. Tame the mind. Free your spirit.

We all have a past and it's important to forgive yourself for where you think you've made mistakes. Fear of the future also can hold us back. For some it's a fear of making a mistake. For others the fear of life being 'too wonderful' can be crippling. When you cannot see the truth of your being, you remain trapped by your egos malicious programming. When we become tight in any area of our body, we invite illness and stagnation. You can accept this moment, right here, right now and honour your perceived flaws, this allows Spirit's grace to flow through your being.

We simply need to surrender to the process of life. Surrender to our wounds and heal our scars. It doesn't matter if this happens in an instant or over a lifetime. If we can simply be open to loving ourselves in the present moment, we give our soul permission to heal.

You're an extension of divinity. When you allow this knowledge to permeate your being the truth of your existence becomes an eraser and removes the darkness that hovers about your psyche. Be true to yourself, whatever it entails, and remember darling angel, *you are the light.*

You are filled with infinite potential. You have the power to create a life you love! All that is needed is to realise your power. When you are aware, you consciously create. Fear, be it subconscious or conscious leads to dark, and uncomfortable fates. When we release our fear, through the act of blessing it with love, acceptance and consciousness, we move forwards. Surrender all, and watch the illusion dissolve.

It doesn't matter how many seminars you attend, books you read, or inspirational movies you see. All it takes is for your consciousness to adapt to the belief that *everything* will be all right. That you're worthy and deserving in the now of all good, prosperity and joy.

When you love yourself, you make your own music. Seeds of the tunes your heart sings throughout the ether creating imperceptible shifts in those around you. If an individual is truly stubborn to change, when they hear your music they may avoid you, or try to tune you back into their preferred radio station. Or consciously try to block out the echoes of your new tune. Spirit will test to see you've truly mastered your mind and may place obstacles before you. How would you know how much you've grown if you don't flitter back and forth until grounded in your new reality?

When you experience consciousness shifts, it's best to associate with people who help to raise your platform of awareness. Connecting with those who see the light of source energy within you, makes it much easier to maintain a light consciousness frequency.

When you release you make way for renewal. The truth is we've sacrificed nothing. When you recognise source energy within your heart and the hearts of all beings, this light and love floods the universe and conscious awareness.

We are a society of do-gooders. Judging others, we perceive as bad and trying our hardest to be seen as positive lights. Judgement turns to rage, which turns to hatred, which allows demonic energies to control our reality. Forgive the darker aspects of your soul expression, your fears, and regrets. When you stop judging yourself and others, you illuminate the world. Releasing the shadows and embracing the light surrounding your existence.

Obsession overtakes when we worry about doing good or bad, it's often self-critical, self-deprecating, and negative. We are creations of the divine. Simply our existence on this physical plane means we are worthy and deserving of being on Earth. What if good and bad are only thought forms?

We are incarnate beings stemming from source. From divine light and this makes us intrinsically good. When you know you're an extension of source and stop judging yourself, you step into realms of light. The high vibration you emit has the power to dissolve hate, resentment, anger, and greed. Knowing you are being of love and truly feeling this light at the core of your being helps your daily life to unfold in a much more positive manner.

You are a vibrational being and thus your vibration can change. Your thoughts can change. Your life can change. Everything is made of tiny atoms vibrating. Our liquid crystalline bodies tune into that upon which we focus, be it conscious or subconscious. When we place the majority of our focus on love, this allows manifestation of light energy into our body helping us to embrace higher states of awareness.

You give your power away when you believe you are anything less than a miracle. Claim your sacred space. You don't have to stand aside as hatred and greed try to dominate this reality. Know you are a reflection of divine love.

Hate isn't the opposite of love. For love is all...

everything.

You're already perfect whole and complete. Remove the veil; loose the disguise you've used to hide your divinity.

Speak!!! Stand tall!!! Surrender to Love!!!

Discover the light hiding in your heart. Shine your light onto galaxies afar; you're a star spinning in the orbit of Earth.

You are Magical!!! Divine!!!

Illuminate the mind!!! Dissolve reality!!!

Set Yourself Free!!!

You are so beautiful, so magical, and so wonderful. I honour your soul through every fibre of my being. We are here to guide each other, to forgive, to learn together. Through pleasure and pain, we guide one another home. To the divine love that lives in all beings, that speaks through us, hears through us and sees through us. Love is everything. You are love.

My one wish for humanity as a whole, my wish for you. Is that through divine grace, you witness the truth of your being. If only for a moment. For you will discover that behind the fear, the shame, the past, the future, there is one great spark that lights your heart. You are a blessing to this world, a light of divine love.

Write your story your way
from your perspective
Let your heart soar
free evermore
You're a creator
Creative
The seed of the future lies in your hand
The past is a memory
You are heaven itself
Pure Magic
An angel
Now is your time to Shine
Light the World

-    *The Beginning*

Authors Note

I've found the more I allow myself to dwindle in directions others than my spiritual development I have increased the point of painful experiences in my life. In high school I had such a wish for universal peace I became distraught when talk of war, killing, and prejudice towards other cultures, races, religions and homosexuals arose. I also became angry, which was how I handled my distress.

I felt myself trying to escape the concept of who I was. At twenty, I left to travel through the ashrams of India. I found myself lost and overcome by the energies surrounding these spiritual abodes. My spiritual self was fighting to get free.

I wanted to deny this path. The more I denied my spiritual purpose on the planet. The more I fought against memories from past lives, and the deep spiritual truths I felt in my soul, the more disconnected I felt. I reached a point where I knew either death would take me, or I'd have to change. To be open to experiencing the power of spirit.

We can't fight that which we already know to be true and it wasn't until I allowed myself to surrender everything, that I gained so much.

May you walk in light, and know the heart of your being.
You are already divine, worthy and valuable.
The light of creation shines within you.
♥

About the Author

Nerissa Marie, loves sharing light and love throughout the universe. Nerissa Marie is an author, naturopath, and mystic. She sends blessings and smiles to all who surround her. She believes when we recognise the divinity within all beings, including ourselves we create a pathway to inner-peace and a harmonious planet.

Life is a journey and all emotions and experiences; are healing tools guiding us deeper within ourselves until we discover the source of our true being, bliss and love. She looks forward to meeting you on the journey to sacred union and to the awakening of humanity as all hearts unite in infinite peace.

Her goal is to serve universal spirit, and realise eternal love. She has an immense amount of gratitude, as she shares her heart through the written word.

Namaste.

NerissaMarie.com

Inspirational Books by Nerissa Marie

Available on Amazon and most other retailers in Hardcover, Paperback, Kindle and Epub format.

Abyss of Bliss, is an inspirational book containing a poetry collection exploring the purpose of life. Pain, guilt, regret, shame and lack often haunt our life. This spellbinding poetry book, goes beyond emotion, beyond form, beyond belief and explores the resounding truth of peace, love and wellbeing hidden in the heart. A beautiful collection of soul healing love poems that reach into the depths of the soul.

We are nothing more than beams of light floating through consciousness. Projecting desires in the abyss. All the while forgetting we are pure, simple, humble manifestations of bliss.

When fate hands you the perfect woman, it's easy to know what to do. For Hugo de La Laville, life's a little more complicated. He has three perfect, potential fiancées…

Paris Mafia Princess, explores the time we waste on trying to get even and finding the right partner at all costs. How our natural competitive instinct can be used constructively, and why we sometimes forget that the most important relationship we have in life is the one we develop within ourself.

Princess Kate, loves to meditate. One day deep in bliss, she levitates high into the sky, leaving behind her friends and family. Prince Ravi Yogi arrives at the kingdom, offering to help bring Princess Kate back down to Earth. Will they listen to his advice? Or will Princess Kate, forever float above the palace, just out of reach?

This books intention is to build your child's self-esteem through a story of mindfulness meditation.

CPSIA information can be obtained
at www.ICGtesting.com
Printed in the USA
BVHW040049111218
535315BV00008B/393/P

9 781925 647495